Heya!

my name is,
from Deal. This is my
first published book, I
hope you enjoy reading
it & would love your
feedback! please get
in touch ♥

Picture This

JADE PRENTICE

Instagram - authorjadePrentice.
Facebook - Jade Prentice Author.

Jade Prentice is a passionate lover of books, more specifically, romance. It's what keeps her going when she's off travelling the world. When she's not deep in reading, you'll find her writing another romance that you can escape to.

To those who said nothing when they could have said everything.

And to all the older siblings of the world, this one is for you.

This book does contain mentions of domestic and emotional abuse, death and alcoholism.

Be confident in your ability, not everyone will like it but loads will love it so who cares about the minority.
- My mother.

Playlist

Let It Happen - Gracie Abrams
Matilda - Harry Styles
Franklin House - Brenn!
Begin Again - Taylor Swift (Taylor's Version)
Light On - Maggie Rogers
The Good Ones - Gabby Barrett
You Make It Easy - Jason Aldean
Fearless - Taylor Swift (Taylor's Version)

1

Emberli

It's a good thing my mom raised me to be persistent.

My attempts at trying to stay somewhat calm and positive on the five hour journey to Shadow Peaks, on a scorching and aged coach, fail the minute I discover the aircon on here is also bust. After leaving me stranded without my car and two hundred dollars in a bug infested cheap-ass motel, my now ex boyfriend had forgotten to turn his location off, which means one thing and one thing only... I was going to track him down and make him swallow the toilet paper that he'd scribbled a pathetic leaving message on, because my mother didn't raise a quitter.

I think of how disappointed she'll be to hear of what Elijah had done and as much as I'd try to shield the truth from her, it would eventually come undone. There was something about admitting I needed help that I just couldn't do, hence why I wasn't returning to my family home in Haven Vale. I needed to do this for myself.

I'd often not tell my parents what Elijah was like, and I would even try to trick myself into believing the lies I told in the process.

I thought that if I only told them the rare good parts that happened with Elijah and me, they'd like him. Manipulation was a fine tactic when used on yourself. I also didn't want my parents to worry about me, and to be honest, I didn't want me to have to worry about me either. I was the eldest, and at twenty-three, should've somewhat had my life together. Yet self-discovery screams at me as I continue my journey down south, and I realize that I should have given up on Elijah a long time ago. I selfishly relied on him a lot more than I should have. It's my biggest regret now and as pathetic as the note he left is, I can't get over the ache it injects me with as I read it over once again.

Emberli,
I'm leaving you.
Don't take it personally babe. A pregnant woman just isn't who we want for the face of our band. If it's not clear enough, our relationship is over and I'm taking the car and some fuel money because of equal division.
Love Lij x

I didn't know if I should be more angry at him for scampering off with my car, or myself for trusting him. I guess this is what I get when I'm with someone who thought that equal division was relevant to our situation, someone who *clearly* didn't research what equal division meant. Elijah had another think coming if he assumed I'd let this go as the mother of his child. It appeared he lacked the capacity of holding responsibility for his *own* actions at twenty-five years old, so it was up to me to find him, contemplate murder and then remind him about the five month old baby I have growing inside of me.

Equal divide that, asshole.

I felt humiliated, knowing that the band I'd given my time and effort to, could take off and leave me as fast as they did. And Elijah. It was that easy for him to kick me out of his life. It was almost like

I was never there in the first place, and that terrified me. I gave him every piece of me and it still wasn't enough.

I've always been a *but why* girl, which is why I try to make excuses and find explanations. I need to know why something happened the way it did and I can't get over it until I have a satisfactory amount of evidence to know that it wasn't my fault. But again, I'm stuck in the whirlwind of not being able to understand how I'm so easy to leave when all I did was love Elijah unconditionally. He wanted more, and so I tore myself apart trying to find it, I even remodelled myself just how he wanted and it was barely adequate.

"How far along are you?" I turn my head to the older lady sitting in the seat on the other side of the bus. She leans over her husband who mutters her name with a subtle but firm message. "Sorry, it's just - I love seeing young moms!" Alice laughs and her husband looks at me as he mouths me an apology.

"Five months." It's the first time I've managed to open my mouth this entire coach ride without shoving my fist in my mouth in a feeble attempt to hold down the morning sickness, or the travel sickness, or the questionable and lukewarm breakfast burrito I had managed to get before boarding.

Note to self, don't trust vending machines.
Note to self 2.0, don't trust men who point you in the direction of vending machines.
Note to self 3.0, don't trust men.

"Five months! How magical! Do you know the gender yet?" The woman beams with excitement and I wish I could give the same back to her.

I glance down at my bump before shaking my head. Elijah and I were meant to find out the gender a week from now.

I should be as excited as this woman is, if not more. But instead I'm engulfed with disappointment. "No, not yet."

"And your husband? Where is he?"

"I'm going to see him now. He's busy working at the moment, so I thought I'd surprise him." A part of me feels guilty about lying to the complete strangers sitting next to me, but I have a feeling the truth would cause a very hostile and judgmental drive to Shadow Peaks. And besides, this version of the story, although false, made me feel a tad happier than I felt five minutes ago.

"Oh that's wonderful dear. Such stability!" *If only you knew Alice, if only you knew.*

I'm convinced a tumbleweed will roll past me anytime now - it's as if I've stumbled into a 20th century cowboy movie, or Rango.

Man, I love that film.

Shadow Peaks is not at all what I expected.

I had expected old gothic-style houses with darkened rain clouds over the town, but was instead met with a beaming sun shining down on me and smiles from every local I passed like we'd known each other for years. Call me the grinch, but it's infuriating when everyone around you is happier than you.

Despite this, I had no time to wallow. I was locked in with the job of tracking down my ex-boyfriend to get my car and my money back.

God. What was I doing?

What would I even say if I found him?

I really should have thought this through.

He was going to laugh in my face if I turned up as hopeless as I felt now.

I hesitantly walk into the first place I see, which is a bar called "Spooky Hoots" and I almost immediately regret my decision when the smell of liquor floods my nose.

My stomach practically churns at the smell and it's enough to stop me in my tracks as the double swing doors I've entered sway behind me. Personally I love the smell of alcohol, the baby however, does not and has not for the past five months.

"Morning, what can I get for you?" The brunette behind the counter

4

calls out with her head down as I walk in. It isn't until I walk closer that she looks up and her eyes flicker over me and my overnight bag that hangs on my shoulder, yet she says nothing.

Despite her staring, there's no judgement in her eyes.

"What's with the pathetic fallacy in this place? Spooky Hoots? Shadow Peaks?"

She lets out a laugh and she shrugs her shoulders. "I couldn't tell you, but I felt the same when I turned up a month ago."

"You did?" Somehow it makes me feel like less of an outsider knowing that someone is in the same boat as me, or maybe she's just jumped off with a life jacket. I should follow suit.

She nods again. "I'm Odessa. And you are?"

"Emberli." I tell her.

"So what are you doing down here?"

"I'm looking for someone."

Odessa's eyes meet mine with a curious glint to them, but again, she says nothing.

"Elijah Walters? Do you know him?"

Her expression remains unreadable but she thins her lips, "I don't know him personally but, I know someone who does."

The someone who does has got to be slightly above 6'4, stands with his arms crossed and his eyebrows closely knitted together. His cold demeanour alone has me feeling like I'm twelve years old again and getting told off for doing something I shouldn't have. His facial features are sharpened like the look he gives as he peers down at me, reaching his large hand out for me to shake. The man is gorgeous, there's no doubt about it. But he is also terrifying.

"Thayne Rawlins."

"Emberli Taylor."

"So you know Elijah?" Unlike the woman who stands polishing glasses next to him, his tone is laced with judgement. Or disbelief. Or maybe disgust.

God, I can't tell the difference. My brain functions to dissect others' brains, as if it's trying to gather information to conclude if they like me or not. I had an insane fear of not being liked and it often kept me up at night.

"I like to think so." I shift in my seat under his gaze. If this man was trying an intimidation tactic, it was working. Nevertheless, I thrived off people liking me and I was *not* getting those vibes from Mr. Broody over here. I was getting the opposite and that hurt my ego. "But at this point, I don't know."

"Do you happen to know where he is?"

I shake my head. "I followed his location until he turned it off two hours ago."

Mr. Broody lets out a noise that can only be described as a grunt. He actually grunts.

He doesn't say much else, but his critical gaze flickers over me again and his eyes rest on my growing bump. I place a hand on it protectively and his dark brown eyes shoot up to meet my own. His mouth opens yet he says nothing, not until the door swings open and then, and only then, does he murmur a 'for fuck's sake.'

"Thank goodness you're still here. I was worried my brother had scared you off." Thayne's brother appears in front of me, slightly breathless as he greets me with a wide smile. "Mack Rawlins."

It was hard to believe that the two men before me were brothers. And if it wasn't for their similar features and Mack's confirmation, I'd have a hard time believing that they were. They were somewhat of a similar height, although Thayne was slightly broader in size and dressed in dark blue Wranglers and a tight fitted top that was on the borderline of being white. Like his arms, his shirt had dark stains all over. He came across as hostile, uptight and grumpy.

Mack, on the other hand, is dressed in a spotless sheriff uniform, one that had a sheriff badge on the left side of his chest, and happiness radiated from him. His shoulders are relaxed and he continues to smile at me as he reaches his hand out. "It's a pleasure ma'am."

Elijah didn't tell me much about his hometown. He claimed that he was running away from what was expected of him because he wanted to be something else. And at the time I was so in love with the idea he presented to me, I found it mesmerising how he did what he wanted to do, not caring about what anyone else thought, because I could never dream of that.

My entire life had felt like a puzzle piece to me. And I often found myself asking for the advice of others before I carried out a big task, reassurance had me handcuffed for years and I couldn't do anything about it. It was the constant fear that I'd be wrong.

My mom was one of those from whom I'd ask advice regularly. That woman was my rock. I was never good at friendships growing up or relationships.

Shocker, I know.

Our relationship was strained a lot during those times, but we're closer than ever now. I missed her a lot when I was on the road.

I miss being back home and just being there in case I was needed by her or the rest of my family. It was hard being away as the eldest. I felt like I was abandoning them all to do what I wanted to do and I'd never felt more selfish. I couldn't bring myself to call her, to tell her that the man I boasted to her and lied about was in fact a lousy sleaze who stole my well-earnt car along with some money... Along with my dignity too. There were countless times in which I lied to my parents about what Elijah was truly like. He wasn't this hard-working and nice guy who I originally thought gave me everything I wanted. Instead, he was a professional in the art of gaslighting who I constantly worried about upsetting. And it was my fault, because I settled for that. I settled for him.

I settled for less when I deserved more. I didn't deserve a man who refused to communicate with me when that was all I ever asked of him, a man who was persistent in knocking me down and making sure I stayed that way, a man who walked away from our relationship scot-free whilst I was left to bear the consequences. I didn't deserve that. I didn't deserve this.

It appears I've been zoned out far too long and a glass of water clinks down in front of me.

Odessa's sympathetic smile cuts through me. "You look like you're on the verge of dehydration there hon."

Thinking back, I don't think I'd had anything to drink today. It was safe to say that I had been otherwise occupied and hence my reason for only picking up my first glass of water at three in the afternoon.

"Do those things help?" I nod to the huge bright pink insulated tumbler that sits on the bar.

The woman before me shrugs. "It's not mine. It belongs to Willow." Like I'm supposed to know who Willow is.

"Who's Willow?"

"The more bearable Rawlins' sibling."

"Heard that." The two brothers chorus.

"She has a new obsession every week, I guess this week it's - Stanley cups."

"We should have won that this year." An older gentleman who I hadn't noticed sitting next to me, grumbles into his beer. And the way Odessa rolls her eyes at him tells me he's somewhat of a regular here.

"Billy, we're not talking about hockey right now."

"No one ever wants to talk about hockey." Billy sulks and slides off the barstool and into a booth as far away from the bar as possible.

"He'll get over it." Odessa tells me once I turn back to her, trying to erase the image of the sad old man hunched over in the corner, alone.

My emotions can't handle that right now and they have been all over the show recently. So it was no surprise when I started to tear up.

I'd already cried once today due to an elderly couple sitting on a bench in the coach station sharing an ice cream.

But the funny thing was, I hadn't shed a tear about Elijah.

I think both the baby and I had agreed that crying over him would only be letting him win, and so we'd remain angry and *only*

8

angry at him. I also think a part of me shut off prior to Elijah leaving and maybe I can't blame him for leaving me if I was as heartless as he claimed. But I can blame him for leaving me knocked up, jobless and carless. Elijah and I were once attached at the hip and further than anyone around us in our own bubble.

Can bubbles suffocate you if you are in one?

Or was the said bubble already damaged?

I've got to write that down.

I grab a napkin and a pen out of my bag before scribbling down possible lyrics.

Bubble. Isolated?

Popped?

Slow deflation??

I wasn't one of these songwriters who could sit and stir up an entire song in two hours. Instead, I was the songwriter who often dissociated from real life and when certain things came to mind, I'd find myself scribbling them down for inspiration. Though I'd had none for a few years now. In fact, it was ever since Elijah and I began arguing a lot more frequently.

And for the first time in a long time, I'd finally gotten something.

"Forgot my beer." Billy mumbles as he reappears, grabbing the bottle from next to me. I watch as he drags his boots back over to his booth, slumping down in it with a grunt.

"Are you okay?" Concern laces Odessa's voice and I wave her off in an attempt to reassure her just as a tear slips away from me.

Damn you pregnancy hormones.

"I'm fine." My voice cracks. "Just hormones."

"Billy's fine. Thinks if you pity him you'll buy him a beer. He's harmless, like a spider."

"Some spiders are poisonous, you know." Mack reappears with his brother by his side. I'd been so zoned out that I hadn't noticed them huddled over by the jukebox, as far away from me as possible.

"Yes, but they wouldn't willingly attack you, not unless provoked." Odessa counters.

Provoked.

I scribble it down on my napkin just as she peers over inquisitively. "What are you doing?"

I look up to three curious pairs of eyes staring at me. "Inspiration. Us songwriters get it at the most random times."

"You write songs?" Mack asks and I don't miss the wide eyed grin he shoots at his brother, who doesn't share the same excitement. In fact, I'm beginning to think this man doesn't know how to smile.

"Yeah. I was the lead singer and I played guitar - Fuck." I slouch forward at the sudden realization. "That asshole took my guitar."

"You weren't the only one who he took from. Elijah has a habit of taking things that aren't his," Mack informs me, and suddenly the person I was so sure I'd spend my life with, I don't recognise.

That man knew practically everything about me, I was an open book for him. But I realized that I knew hardly anything about him and the cards he played so close to his chest.

"I'm so sorry." I felt an obligation to give an apology on behalf of Elijah. Quite frankly he'd never been good at them. I'd often find myself begging for him to apologize for things he did, though I would never get the full satisfaction knowing it was always half-assed and because I'd asked him to. It was never off his own accord.

"It isn't your fault."

My mouth is suddenly dry and I reach for the glass of water in front of me, taking a few sips. "What did he take from you guys?"

Mack shoots a glance at Thayne, who sighs heavily in annoyance. "Let's just keep on topic. Did… Elijah mention to you about where he was going?"

"No."

"Nothing at all?"

"Thayne. She doesn't know anything." Mack says.

"That's what she says. For all we know, he could have asked her to come here to distract us." Thayne was clearly the distrustful type and perhaps for good reason. However I hadn't done anything wrong towards him and was getting treated like I had.

Not to mention that his attitude towards me was agitating and all of my emotions were heightened to the hills.

"Distract you from what?"

"Oh I don't know. Stealing more money from the town?"

New information about Elijah kept surfacing and I didn't know how to respond to it. Perhaps it was a bad idea coming here. It was obvious that I wasn't ready to face the truth, nor was I welcome.

"I... I didn't know."

"So you've said."

Okay. Definitely has trust issues.

"None of that matters now." Mack says and this earns a grunt of disagreement from Thayne, who stands with his arms crossed tightly across his chest. "What matters is *now*." Mack shoots his brother a look before turning back to me. "What exactly did he take from you?"

"My car and a couple hundred dollars."

"Again, we don't know she's telling the truth." Thayne pipes up and I snap my head towards him.

"*She* is sitting right here."

"Yes. Unfortunately she is." He bites back.

"Here." I rummage through my handbag before unscrewing the note Elijah left, slapping it down on the bar.

The three of them crowd around it before Mack inhales sharply. "That's cold. I'm sorry."

"Again, this doesn't prove anything." Thayne grumbles.

Andddd snap!

The leash of restraint I had on myself snaps. "Look. I'm here for the exact same reason as you are. I want my car back and I want my money back. That's it. I've had a fucking long-ass journey and I'm tired and hungry and trying ridiculously hard not to break down about all this. So if you could quit acting like I'm the enemy, that would be great." I inhale and take another sip of water to quench my thirst just as Thayne turns, his boots thudding across the floor before he swings the main door open and disappears.

"I apologize for my brother. He's... not a people person." Mack grimaces.

"No. He's just an asshole." Odessa corrects. "I'd offer you food, but I've got out of date peanuts or an opened pack of Skittles that's been here since I started."

Appealing... If not for the fact that she'd mentioned how she'd turned up in town a month ago.

A yawn escapes me. I'm exhausted.

It turns out that my once greatest ability to sleep on long journeys had met its end and because of that, I was beat.

"Look, I'm tired. I saw a motel on the way in. I'm going to crash there for a night or two in case something comes up. Can I give you my number?" I look between Odessa and Mack just as I feel another body behind me.

"You can give *me* your number, sugar."

I look up to the ceiling. Someone in the sky was out for me, I was certain of it. Perhaps it was something I'd done in my past life. Regardless, I was being tested on the worst possible day to be tested.

"Beat it Joe." Odessa snaps.

"I'd beat something from this pretty lady right here if she let me." Joe whistles and I hear laughter behind him.

I turned to him. "Joe, was it?"

"That's right sugar." He winks down at me.

I had to hand it to him, he was attractive. But it was his overconfidence that deducted his points.

Yep. Someone up there was definitely out for me.

"Why don't I take you for a spin in my truck? I could take you for a ride... or two?" He winks again.

Fucking fucker.

"Joe. I would not touch you even if you were the last man on earth and we were the only ones left to procreate. Do you understand?"

More laughter behind him, though Joe doesn't find this very funny, and instead he resorts to trying to insult me.

"Alright lady, don't flatter yourself now. I only came over because you're easy."

"Easy?" I inch closer just before Mack pushes himself in between us.

"You heard Odessa, beat it."

"Yes, sheriff." The bitterness in Joe's voice is clear just as his eyes flick over me before he scoffs, leaving with his buddies trailing behind him. Mack turns to me with a relieved sigh.

"Why don't I drop you at that motel?"

"Thanks." I breathe out. "But I don't want to put you out of your way."

"Not at all. It's just down the road. I'll take you. Besides, it's dark out and my brother would kill me if I let you walk."

I raise a brow. "The brother who was here earlier? The one who looks as if he's skilled in the arts of being a hit-man?"

Odessa and Mack find this humorous. But even as Mack nods, I struggle to believe Thayne had a caring bone in his body, especially towards me - the woman he barely knows, yet seems to despise. It's rich coming from me. I've always been against judging a book by its cover, yet here I am doing exactly that.

"Thayne may appear prickly on the outside, but he's a softie on the inside."

"Like a... cactus?"

"Exactly like a cactus."

"Huh."

"Come on. I'll drop you home."

Home.

I'm aware it's a figure of speech, something casual that he didn't mean anything by, but something about this place was pulling me to it and I had nowhere else to be so I figured I'd stay for a few nights. Besides, apart from the off-putting grumpy bar owner, I finally had some inspiration for lyrics.

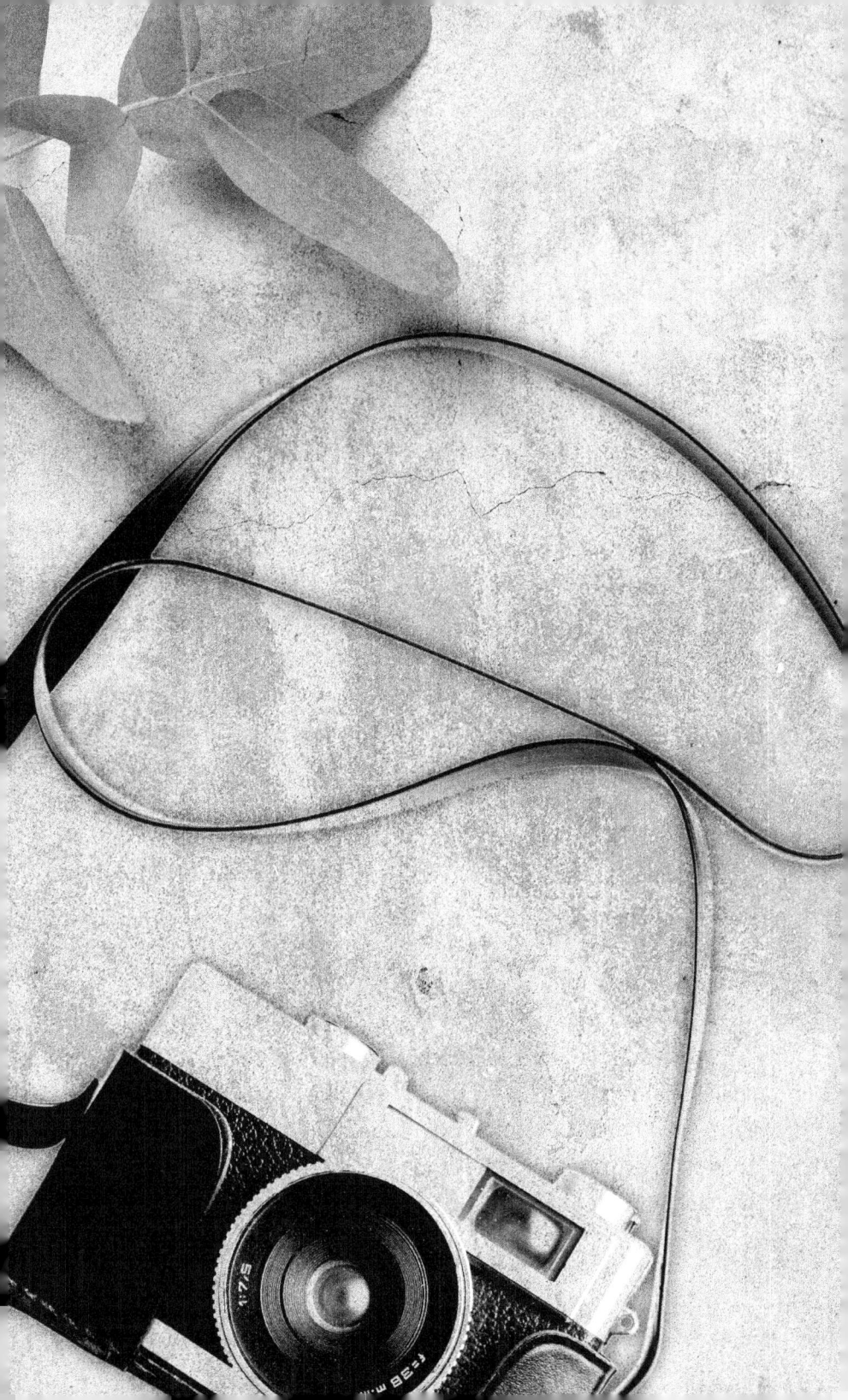

2

Thayne

"Do you remember the day I helped you escape from Lindsay Vattel?"

I turn to Mack, who I've seen more in two days than I have the last few weeks and he remains resilient. Hellbent on asking me to hire the woman who's been doing nothing but filling my head ever since she stepped foot into my town.

The town gossip most recently was that she was a runaway bride from London after she killed her rich fiancé with a cake knife.

Well I'd met the woman, and although feisty, I didn't think that she'd be quite capable of murder, despite her attitude.

And she was about as western as they come with her embroidered Ariat boots and a matching hat that was tied around her overnight bag, one that had stitched flags of countries and names of places I'd assumed she'd been to. There was no United Kingdom flag.

"I said no, Mack."

"Wrong. Your exact words were." He clears his throat and puts on his best impression of me. "I owe you one."

I dropped the hammer in the toolbox, knowing where he was going with this. "That was eleven years ago."

"Yup." He grins. "I'm cashing it in."

I raise an eyebrow. "Cashing it in?"

"Correct. After you do this, you will no longer owe me one."

"You want me to hire her." I confirm. For whatever reason, Mack wanted an excuse for Emberli to stay here in Shadow Peaks. I couldn't see the appeal. Aside from the fact that she was good looking, I couldn't understand why my brother would want her here, especially with no information on Elijah, which I didn't buy one bit.

Mack had been tearing his brain apart for the past two years on this investigation, I had no idea why he was blatantly distracting himself now.

Mack nods. "She needs the money, she's eager to work."

"No. I don't trust it. I don't trust her."

"You trust me right?"

I glance at him. "Of course I trust you."

"Then please, do this for me."

"Does she even have any experience?" I ask, running a hand over my beard.

"No but... "I sigh and Mack speaks again. "But, she can sing. I've seen videos and I think you should hire her as a singer."

"A singer? I don't do live music, Mack."

"Odessa's been telling you to find someone for weeks. The jukebox is fine and all but..."

"This is ridiculous." I mutter.

"She's good, Thayne. Real good. And I honestly believe she's not here because Elijah sent her, but because he hurt her just like he hurt you. Like he hurt us. I want to help her."

For fuck's sake.

"Why do you want her here longer anyway? It's best she and whatever trouble follows her leave this goddamn town and quick."

"What would be best, is if she stuck around. It would help the case against Elijah."

"What did you tell her?"

"Only what she needed to know."

"And she's what, she's happy to just be a sitting duck?"

Mack's grin only widens.

"What?"

"You. Concerned about others' feelings."

I roll my eyes. "I may be a lot of things. But I'm not an emotionless asshole."

"That's exactly what you are." I turn around to the sound of my little sister, who stands there with both hands on her hips.

A visual copy of our mom, only younger. Willow never got the chance to remember our mom. She died months after giving birth to Willow.

Heart attack. I was eight at the time.

Eight when I felt the heavy weight of looking after dad and clearing up the beer bottles he drowned his grief in before Flint or Mack saw, or Colton crawled upon the shards I'd hear shatter late at night. Eight when I was afraid to let my best friends' parents in to help because I was scared our family would be broken up by child protection services after dad hit me for the first time, that was when he realized I'd poured the beer out and replaced it with water.

If it wasn't for Aca seeing the bruises I'd developed, if it wasn't for Sally and Doug swooping in and determined to get dad better, I don't know what would have happened. I was powerless, unable to really help my family. It's why I was so driven to protect them now. That extended to Aca and his brother, Ryker and their parents, Sally and Doug, who became our primary caregivers when dad's liver finally gave up on him when I was fifteen. I was older then and I knew how to lie to the two of them about how great things were at home, how dad had stopped drinking. Truth is, I'd always found it hard to trust people. I think it came with the great responsibility of keeping my family safe. Which is why I took the beatings for Willow, who dad blamed for the loss of the love of his life, mom. It's why I'd saved up as much money as I could from doing odd jobs for the neighbors around the town so we'd always have an emergency fund in case we needed to run from dad. In case it ever got worse.

I'd always been the protector of this family, and they were always protected because of me. Because I protected them from harm. That wasn't about to stop now.

"Lovely." I grumble at the sight of my sister, whose unimpressed expression reminds me of the few times I was scolded by mom. "He's got you in on this has he?"

But I wasn't surprised in the slightest, the two of them often teamed up on the rest of us. It had always been the same. Even when we were younger.

"Yes because what has gotten into you? I thought we turned a new leaf with Odessa."

"Odessa isn't affiliated with Elijah." I mention as I stand, dusting my hands off on my jeans.

"Elijah hurt Emberli just as he did you. And I've met her and she's so sweet, Thayne."

If there was one thing about Willow, it was that she was too trusting.

I sigh. "I'm trying to keep us out of harm's way, and you intend to just dump us straight in the middle of it all?"

"She's a small pregnant woman who cries when old people sit on their own in diners, Thayne. There is no harm." Willow says. "And she's here and needs our help. Please?" I groan at this, could refuse Mack, or my other brothers. But I had a hard time refusing Willow. I had a soft spot for my sister and this wasn't a secret to anyone. Mack and Willow knew this which is why they were playing on my inability to say no to her.

The two of them look at me all hopeful and I decide that I can't be the one to ruin it. Not today. If hiring the town's most recent yet talked about newcomer to make my family happy, I'd do it.

"Fine. I'll do it. Tell her to meet me at the bar tomorrow at eleven."

Tomorrow comes around quicker than expected, and Emberli sits perched on the wall fifteen minutes early, engrossed in something Billy tells her. I watch as her brows knit together, concern flashing her face as Billy no doubt guides her through one of his famous emotionally manipulative stories about his childhood.

Billy was my first customer when I opened the bar ten years ago and he was a good friend. He was a raging alcoholic like my dad, and at times I thought that he was mocking me from the grave. Perhaps he even sent Billy.

But Billy was different. He was never loud nor violent but spent his days alongside Odessa, who I'd hired full time when she came into town last month.

It was nice to see her merging smoothly into the community. She was quiet at first yet dedicated to work. She'd made sure to tell me that she was only passing through, to build up some money and leave again. I remember asking if she was travelling, she said she wasn't. I joked about asking if she was on the run, and I don't think I'd ever forget the quick look of nervousness on her face. Regardless, I didn't hover. Odessa kept to herself when she could, despite Willow's numerous attempts to befriend her. She was more withdrawn, something Willow was not. In fact, I'm sure if you searched up sunshine in an image dictionary, Willow would appear.

I'd never understood how, no matter what life threw at her, she remained happy and always hopeful. I think that's why we were all so protective of her.

"Morning." The smell of vanilla fills my nose when Emberli glances away from Billy and towards me, her chestnut curls falling off of her shoulders as she smiles.

"Good morning!"

"You're early." I state.

"Yeah well, my neighbor isn't very accommodating."

That's right. Mack had mentioned she was staying at The Hollyhead.

I'd imagined it wasn't the quietest or cleanest for that matter. It was just on the outskirts of town. Those who occupied rooms were usually teen delinquents or married business men who passed through and picked up a local for the night. The people of the town rarely stayed there because of how unpleasant it was. We all knew the state of it, it was just that no one had ever thought to turn it around.

"You could always stay with me, you know. I have a spare room." Billy mentions and Emberli smiles again.

"Thanks Billy. But I'm... I'm okay." The look on her face gives off the impression that it pained her to say it and she reaches her hand forward, grabbing Billy's and squeezing it.

I unlock the door and turn to see Emberli behind me, her shoulders high and tense and a nervous look now replaced on her face.

"After you."

She swiftly moves past me and into the bar. I flick on the lights and focus on pouring Billy a beer as he takes his usual seat.

"I wanted to thank you for giving me the gig."

"Don't thank me yet." I mutter. "The locals might not like live music."

It's a dick move on my side, but she doesn't even quake. She just shrugs. "It's not for everyone."

"I personally love live music." Billy announces.

"Yeah, thanks Billy." I grumble. "Drink?" I ask Emberli, who runs her hands over her bump. She wears a similar sundress to the first time I saw her, only this one is a light colour of yellow with daisies swarming over it.

"Water, please."

I grab a bottle before handing it to her, leaning my hands on the bar as I study the woman in front of me.

She glances around the bar and her eyes sit on Billy before they gloss over slightly.

Fucking hell. Willow wasn't kidding.

Emberli blinks back the tears frantically and her hand shakes as she raises the bottle to her lips. They're a light pink colour, though glossed over with specks of glitter and an almost unrecognisable scent of mint.

A scent I should not be focusing on right now.

I should be focusing on attempting to scare Emberli out of town.

"When do you want me to work?"

"Huh?" I blink, bringing myself back to reality before clearing my throat.

"Uh, like what days?"

"Fridays and Saturdays are the busiest. Can you work tonight?"

I didn't trust this woman one bit. And as much as I should be keeping a close eye on her and what she's doing due to my siblings' naive tendencies. I also didn't want to risk her ruining the business I'd worked so hard for. And quite frankly, seeing her is just a reminder of Elijah and what he did.

"Okay." She nods. "I can do that. I can do anything."

"Why?"

She frowns. "What do you mean?"

"Why are you here? Elijah's not here. So why are you?"

Her mouth opens to speak but nothing comes out for a few seconds. "I just need some money."

"You can't go home?"

Her brows tighten once again. I'm aware I'm probably being too intrusive. There's probably a line that I'm crossing. But I can't help it. I need to know the real reason she's here.

"I can." Her jaw clenches and a small part of me enjoys seeing her so riled up. The way her cheeks flush a light pink color and her eyes fight me with determination. "But I don't want to go home."

"That's a bit selfish. Don't you think?"

"Excuse me?"

"You need the money. You could solve this all by going home. But you don't want to. Don't you think there's more at stake now that it's not only you you're deciding for?" I gesture my head down to her stomach and she stands abruptly.

"I didn't come here to be lectured." She flings her handbag over her shoulder and I'm quick to round the bar.

Okay. Definitely crossed a line.

"Hey. All I'm trying to do is work out the type of person you are." I try to tell her just as she spins around, another intoxicating whiff of vanilla flows past me. That scent had trapped me in a chokehold since her arrival yesterday.

"No. You've already decided that, Thayne. I know what you think of me. Okay? And I don't need your judgement. Forget it."

Except I told Willow and Mack that I'd help her.

Fuck's sake.

"I overstepped. I'm sorry." I call to her and she stops.

I watch her shoulders deflate before she turns around to me.

"Look. This just isn't a good idea. I'll find something else." She turns to walk again and I find myself reaching out, grabbing her wrist in my hand.

"I told my family I'd help. Please let me do that.

3
Emberli

"I just don't understand why you're so angry with me? I don't understand why you won't just talk to me..."

"Because you don't listen." Elijah snaps. His eyes roam up and down my body before he scoffs. "Why would you even wear something like that? It shouts that you're available. And the make-up? Seriously? Do you have that little respect for me? For yourself!"

"Make-up makes me feel good about myself, Lij. I want to feel good about myself."

"So I don't make you feel good about yourself? That's what you're saying. You're unbelievable, Emberli. After everything I've done for you and for us."

"Why does it offend you so much that I look like this?" I gesture down to my dress, which was apparently too tight and revealing for Elijah's liking.

The stupid part? I wore it in the hope that he'd compliment me.

"Because you look like you're not in a relationship. Is that what you want?"

"No. Of course it's not."

"You know what? I'm not talking about this now."

I sit at the bar after my first gig in Shadow Peaks. It went well.

Thayne had rostered for me to work when he wasn't. And to be honest, I didn't mind it because the less judgement the better.

Besides, he was keeping a close eye on me. Earlier today he'd made sure to point me in the direction of the flashing security cameras in the corner of the room, just in case I tried anything.

I wasn't entirely sure what his problem was, but I intended to stay as far away from him as possible, which I know sounds ironic due to me being sat in his bar. And if it wasn't for Mack and Willow cornering me in my motel room two nights ago, I may have considered otherwise. But the two of them had preyed on my inability to say no and here I was.

Damn. I really needed to work on that.

"You were amazing." Odessa compliments.

"You think?" I let out a sigh of relief and she nods.

"Hell yeah. Your voice is something else. Wish I could sing like that."

"It's true, she does. She sounds like a strangled cat." Billy whispers but Odessa still hears him, whacking the cloth in his direction.

"Asshole." She mutters out and he laughs.

"I'm only joking."

"You're only saying that so I serve you."

"Is it working?"

"Nope." She turns to me, handing me a plain envelope. "Thayne left this for you."

Billy peers over my shoulder and the stench of alcohol dripping from him fills my nostrils. Despite my attempts to grow accustomed to it over the past few hours, it still makes me want to hurl.

"Thanks." I tap the envelope in my hand just as there's a chuckle from behind me.

It sounds like Mack, but when I turn around it's not him. However

26

the resemblance between the two of them is uncanny.

"Billy, give the lady some space will you?"

"Sorry." Billy grumbles.

"Colton Rawlins. Nice to finally meet you." Colton Rawlins suddenly makes a lot more sense. He has to be a brother of the two Rawlins men I've met already. The resemblance is freakishly strong.

"Wow. The genes in your family are something else." I say as he swoops up my hand before kissing the back of it. "I'm Emberli."

"I know who you are." He chuckles. "Or I think I do anyway. There's a lot of excitement going around. So hard to tell which rumors are true." Colton grins before opening his arm up. "This is Ryker Lewis. He's a good friend of mine."

"Nice to meet you ma'am." Ryker dips his hat and offers his hand for me to shake. He's slightly shorter than Colton and seems a lot more close-mouthed whilst his friend screams the opposite - like an overly-excited golden retriever.

"Hope you don't mind us interrupting. I just had to meet the woman everyone's talking about."

I laugh. "I hardly think everyone is talking about me."

"They sure are." Colton assures me and this sends a swirl of doom down into my stomach.

People are talking about me.

What are they saying? Do they like me?

My heart rate picks up as I look around the bar and apart from the odd glances, no one really looks over at me. Maybe Colton is overreacting.

And as if he can read my mind, he laughs. "All good things ma'am. Don't you worry now."

Funnily enough, I'd always hated attention, which was weird considering my job as a singer- songwriter. I think it was more the fact that I didn't know what anyone was thinking about me, and being the obsessive overthinker I am, I absolutely despised it. Which was why this job was such a hit and miss for me. I loved writing songs just as much as I loved performing them. However, I had a constant feeling of uncertainty. I was frequently worried that people wouldn't like my songs, that they wouldn't like me.

When I was with Elijah, I felt as if I had to be the best. There was no room for mistakes because he'd know them, play them and bring me down because of them. He claimed it was constructive criticism, it's only now I'm out of the relationship that I see just how bad it really was.

I constantly wanted to be better for him so I lost myself in the process of it all, listening to him and being injected with his narrative and opinions.

Eventually I lost my true self. It appears pushing her away and subjecting her to nothing would do that. I'd do anything to be her again.

But it's true what they say, you don't know what you have until it's gone.

God. I miss her so much.

Now I was only the remains of what she used to be, and I wanted to apologize and tell her that it wasn't her fault what happened. She was just the younger version of me who thought that she was doing the right thing at the time.

I'm learning to be okay with trying to heal from what he did to me and the way I think or see things now because of him.

What's the saying? Love is blind and all that.

I don't know. I guess I figured Elijah would be different.

God. I never thought I'd be a part of the "I can fix him" club. Yet without even realizing it, I was fucking president.

And the number one award for biggest idiot of the year goes to… yours truly.

Yours truly.

I grab a napkin and pen off of the side of the bar before scribbling my thoughts down on it.

Short moments like these uplifted me for a split second. And for the first time in a long time, I actually felt productive.

"Gossip is just gossip, hon. Don't let it get to you." Odessa says. "It's not worth it."

And something tells me she actually believes that. I have a habit of continually aspiring to be that level headed. I like and repost inspirational quotes to change my mindset. But so far, nothing has changed. I worry that I won't change. As if I'll just be this broken forever. And how could I even know how to be a mom when I didn't even know myself?

I made a pact with myself as soon as I boarded the coach to Shadow Peaks that there would be no more excuses. And absolutely no more falling for cowboys with a cute smile who promise to give you the world whilst silently and sneakily crushing all of your hopes and personality.

Anddd breathe.

I was absolutely fine with staying as far away from men like that as much as I possibly could.

Famous last fucking words.

"Get in." The sound of tires screeching to a halt and an abrupt truck door opening stops me on the sidewalk.

It's Thayne.

"What?"

"Get in the truck. It's pitch black out here."

I recoil. "I know. The cold is refreshing."

"Get in."

"Has being this rude ever gotten you anywhere?"

"No."

"Didn't think so."

"Just get in the goddamn truck."

I do as he says because as appealing as it seems to annoy Thayne, I'm exhausted. So he's lucky tonight.

"Put your seatbelt on."

Before I even shut the passenger door fully, Thayne speeds off.

"Shut the door."

"I will if you give me a fucking minute. *Jeez.*" I mumble. "Has anyone ever told you that you're bossy?"

He glares at me, piercing brown eyes staring into my own as he says, "Plenty of times."

"Great. So I don't have to let you know that you're being exactly that right now."

He glares again before his eyes divert back onto the road. "Not being bossy." He shoots back. "You just seem completely oblivious to the dangers around you."

I scoff. "Since when did you care about what happens to me? And besides, what's the worst that can happen here? A bull escaping its pen and charging at me?"

"That can damn well happen." He snaps. " Or you could trip and fall and no one would see you. Not to mention the amount of drunks that are out tonight."

"I know what you're doing." I shake my head. "You're not going to scare me out of this town. I've met a lot more darker fates than a couple of drunks." Thayne just wouldn't quit it. It was clear to me from the moment we met that he didn't like me and so it was even more infuriating when he thought he could have a say in my decisions. I could make my own, and there was nothing more infuriating than someone thinking they could make them for you. I think that's why I started to despise Elijah.

"Right. But this time it's not only you who could get hurt."

My fists clench in my lap. "I'm aware of that. Funnily enough, I'm carrying the child and guess what?"

His eyebrows raise but he doesn't say a word, focusing on the road ahead of him. "I can protect them *myself.* Because that's what was sprung on me at the start of this week."

"All I'm saying is you shouldn't be walking in the dark. This town may be safer than others you've been to, but it's still a risk." Thayne says.

If I'd had more sleep and Thayne and I had gotten off on the right foot, I would have thought his concern for my safety was cute. But instead, I find it irritating.

I look out of my window, attempting to ignore Thayne when he speaks again. "Didn't Odessa call you a taxi?"

"There were none available and I wanted to walk anyway. The air is refreshing."

On cue, he winds down the window as far as it'll go, a smirk playing on his lips as the gust of strong wind springs my hair into madness.

"Nice." I nod. "Real nice."

"Still refreshing?"

"You're such an asshole."

Perhaps calling my new boss an asshole wasn't the cleverest of ideas, but I'd never been the smartest. And besides, judging by the amused laugh that leaves his mouth, Thayne doesn't seem to mind too much. Which, dare I say, is possibly character development.

He drops me at the motel five minutes later with a simple goodnight, and I hear his engine start up again when I lock my door.

Was he waiting for me to get inside? What a gentleman.

Nope. That's how they get you.

I get myself ready for bed and the excitement is next level. Only I spot my notebook in my bag and for a change, I'm suddenly more excited about writing lyrics.

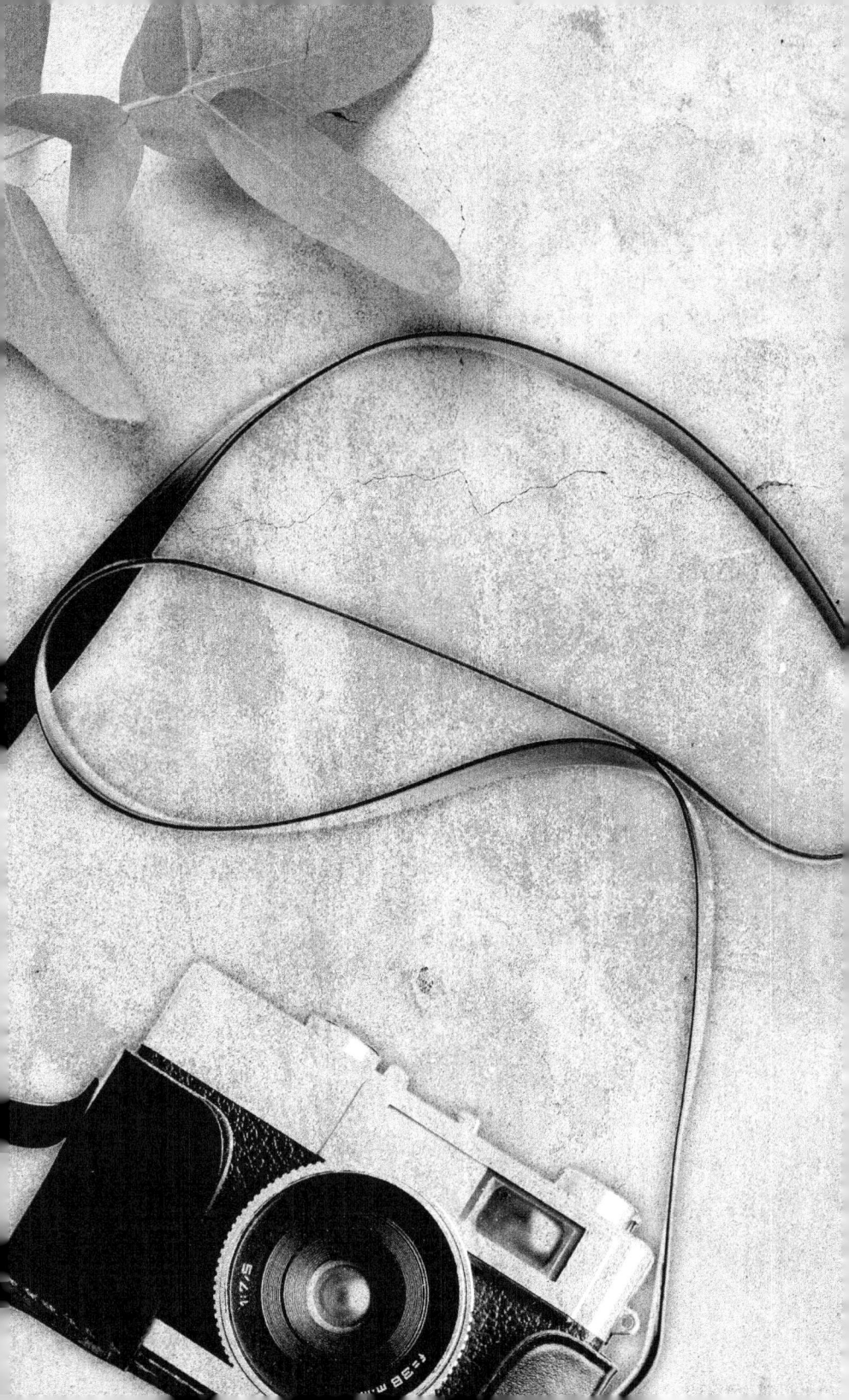

4

Thayne

"Been hearing nothing but good reviews on that singer you had last night." Flint speaks from across the table the next morning.

Flint was a few years younger than me and a brother that I relied on excessively.

At first, the ranch was supposed to fall under my name when dad died and then I'd own it. But I never wanted it, not like Flint.

To me, It was a constant reminder of my dad and I wanted no part of that. He was a lot harder on me than my other siblings, which is what I wanted. But unlike my siblings' relationship with my dad, mine was severed. Flint took good care of the ranch and its business and I took care of mine, occasionally helping out here when I could.

"Emberli." Willow's eyes dance with excitement as she sips her coffee. Despite being out until early hours of the morning, she somehow manages to pull herself together with no hangover. The same cannot be said for Lynnie, who sits next to her with her head in the palms of her hands. I'm pretty certain she's fallen asleep.

"She's great Flint. Such a good singer." Willow nods.

"She's a looker too, right? That's what I heard this morning at Big Al's," Sally says. Her eyes glanced around at us all for confirmation.

"She's pretty." Mack nods. "Don't you think, Thayne?" A smirk widens on his lips and I raise an eyebrow.

"I'm just saying." Mack raises his hands in defence. "She's a pretty lady."

Eyes around the table bounce back and forth at my brother and I.

I have no clue what he's playing at. But the less I entertain it, the better.

Granted, he was right. Emberli was an attractive woman and it was clear I wasn't the only one who noticed it.

I saw the looks she'd received last night through the security footage. Near enough all the men in my bar couldn't keep their eyes off of her. My brother included.

"Why don't you ask Colton? He seemed pretty friendly with her last night."

Before my brother can defend himself, Willow shoots her index finger out at him. "I swear to God, Colt. You stay away from her. Lyn? Don't you agree? Lyn?"

Yep. Lynnie was definitely asleep.

She'd been Willow's best and only friend since I could remember. Willow had a lot of trouble growing up making friends with the other girls of the town. We'd grown up with Lynnie as our next door neighbor for some time and the two of them were inseparable from the get go.

Her parents owned the ranch next door to us until they packed up and left one day without their daughter. No one knew where they went. No one knew why they left Lynnie behind either. Sally and Doug swooped in and took her under their wing the same way they did us.

Sally once told me that she and Doug had wished for a big family. Only when they tried for more after Ryker, it just didn't happen.

She called it fate, that we were all brought together, but honestly I never believed in that, or that everything happens for a reason like Willow always says. I couldn't understand how bad things happen to good people. If there was supposedly a reason for everything, why did those things happen?

Lynnie never spoke much of her parents when we were younger. Even now as an adult, she still doesn't. But I'm glad she sticks around. She's a part of the family, always has been and always will be.

"Listen. All I did was talk to her." Colton argues.

"Bullshit. I know your tricks, Colt. Please don't ruin this for me. That goes for all of you." she says, glancing around the room. "I really like her and I want to help her. I want her to stay."

"And what happens if she doesn't want to?"

"She will." Willow shoots at me. "If we show her what it means to be a family, she'll stay."

How did I feel about that?

Uncertainty looms over me, I didn't like how much hope Willow had for Emberli staying.

I didn't think she would. She was a musician, and they were always on the road. I was worried she'd leave once she got her fix and I knew it would tear Willow in two. I'd built her back up far too many times.

All she's ever known is people disappearing from her life, which is why it was so infuriating how purehearted she was. I'd be damned if I let another person take advantage of that, of her.

"Am I understood?" Willow asks. "No one scares her off."

Once she gets a satisfactory amount of nods, she turns to Lynnie, nudging her with her elbow.

"Lyn? What do you say? Should we binge *The Twilight Saga* today?"

Lynnie resurrects from her slumber at this, looking at my sister absolutely horrified. "I couldn't think of anything worse."

"I don't get it." Willow sighs, shaking her head. "You hate *Twilight* but you literally write romances like it!"

"I can't believe you've just insulted my books and I like that."

"What's wrong with *Twilight*? I like it." Flint says.

"Of course you do." Lynnie huffs. "Everything is wrong with that franchise. Team Bella."

"Who hurt you?" Willow looks beside her, concerned.

"How much time have you got?"

I slam the door to my truck as I pull up at the motel, scanning the doors in the hope of one of them revealing which one Emberli is in. After seeing the way Willow was regarding her earlier, I knew I couldn't not say anything any longer. I had to confront Emberli.

Bingo.

She appears in the doorway, closing the door behind her as she beelines for the vending machine. She reminds me of Willow when she was studying for her finals, she'd only ever come out of her room for lunch and dinner or the occasional carton of chocolate milk we had downstairs.

"Hey!" I call and she turns, eyes narrowing into a suspicious glance as she looks around, hugging herself.

"Hey?"

"I came to talk to you."

I had been thinking about what I'd say the entire ride here. And it's stupid because usually I wouldn't think too much into it. I'd just tell her how I feel, however I had this small voice in the back of my head telling me to be considerate of her own feelings. That voice belonged to Willow.

"Okay. Do you want to go inside or..."

"No."

"Right." Her eyes squint in confusion and I'm about to speak when a loud shatter of something that sounds like glass rings out.

Emberli stands, unfazed. "That's my next door neighbor. I call her Noisy Nadia. I don't actually know who she is, or if she has anything left to break." There's a thud right on cue before the person in there grunts loudly. "Obviously she does."

"I wanted to talk to you about my sister. She speaks highly of you and so I wanted to ask what your plans were."

"My plans?"

"Yeah. How long are you planning on staying here?"

"I don't... I can't even think about that right now."

"Look. She gets attached too easily and I'm worried that she's going to be disappointed when you eventually leave. Because let's face the facts here, Emberli. You're not the type of person to stay."

"You don't know the type of person I am, Thayne."

"I can sure guess."

She scoffs, looking out into the parking lot for a few beats until she turns back to me, a hardened look on her face.

"My life was literally uprooted not even a week ago. I... I haven't even wrapped my head around it all yet. All I know is that I'm really enjoying my time here and I'm grateful for your family's help."

"Yeah. Everyone is. Until they're done and then they just fuck off. Willow deserves better than that."

"And I get that, but I'm, I don't know."

"Look. I'm just going to come out and say it. Your boyfriend has hurt a lot of people. My family included. You being here is just a reminder of that."

"Are you speaking for yourself or for your family?"

"That doesn't matter."

"Of course." She laughs bitterly. "Because God forbid anyone else has an opinion around you."

"You're not very likeable." I tell her.

"Feelings mutual, shithead."

"I'm looking out for my family."

"Then let me look out for mine." Her hand darts down to her stomach before she brushes past me. I hear the door open before it slams shut and I let out a long breath.

Well, that went well.

5
Emberli

"Fuck me." Willow stares at me wide eyed when I open the door to her.

It's bright outside. When did it get bright outside?

The sun beams past her as she invites herself in, eyes scanning around the motel room.

She's horrified. That's for sure.

Admittedly not my finest moment. In the corner there's an overflowing stack of takeaway coffee cups with a collection of wrappers from the amount of energy bars I've divulged in. Apparently that stuff is addictive.

On the bed there's also a smaller collection of takeaway cups, more vending machine snack wrappers and ripped out pages from my notebook. After Thayne's visit yesterday, I found myself in the depths of writing. I'd written more than I had in a long time due to channeling my anger for inspiration. I should invite Thayne round more often, just have him sit in a corner as I write about how much he infuriates me.

"When was the last time you slept?" Willow asks, yanking at my closed blinds to let the light in.

"I don't need sleep. Sleep is for the weak," although I was severely deprived of it. It had been so long since I pulled an all nighter and no amount of canned lemonade can make me feel any less groggy. I'd tested that theory a few hours ago.

Instead, I settled with several cups of lukewarm coffee from the vending machine.

"Right. May I ask why you're hiding yourself away like a vampire?" she questions. "You're only letting Elijah win if you sit and mope around."

"This isn't about Elijah." She turns to me and raises her eyebrow like she doesn't believe me.

Okay. Maybe this is partially about Elijah. But I'm not moping around because of him.

With three new original songs written, I'd say I'm onto something better here. *A huge fuck you, to Elijah.*

"Come on. You have literal bags under your eyes, Em. Can I call you Em?" I nod.

"Em, You look like… a zombie," Willow states.

Ah. So we've reached that part of the friendship. I'd been here less than a week and already felt like I had a good friend in Willow. She'd turned up on my second day here and practically forced my hand in her friendship offer, promising me that she wouldn't let me wallow in my sorrows and Willow struck me as the type of woman who stayed true to her word. In the small time I'd known her, she'd put my needs ahead of hers, something I could only be grateful for. I figured her out almost immediately. She was strong-willed and appeared accepting of not only others, but herself. Obviously confident in everything she did, unlike me, who sought out reassurance from others before I did anything even remotely out of the ordinary. She was unlike anyone I'd ever met before, she never appeared unhappy and always showed up with a smile on her face.

I didn't have many friends back home and the ones I did have, I lost when I was with Elijah. I guess they weren't exactly the closest of friends because I never let anyone get close enough for that. I was always scared of disappointing them, or losing them. So I kept them at a distance, believing that I only needed myself. And then I met Elijah and suddenly all I needed was him. Another one of my not so fine moments was putting him first. It was a lesson I'd learnt when I woke up Thursday morning alone with a break up note and had no one to talk to about it. Not until Willow.

She took me to the local coffee shop and listened as I ranted about Elijah for two straight hours and she never interrupted me, she just listened. She *really* listened.

There were times when I'd open up to my friends back home about Elijah, and they'd tell me to leave him. Stupidly, this only pushed me away from them further. I'd claimed I wanted their advice but never took it. There were phone calls I made to the same people and asked them if I was crazy, if what was happening was always my fault like Elijah had tattooed into my brain and even when the answer was no, I still went back.

Now that I'm out of it, I can't understand why I did end up going back so many times or why I let him treat me the way he did, I only feel sorry for the girl who was so infatuated with him that she didn't care that he was hurting her. The same girl whose inner child only wanted to be loved by a man who claimed he could do so yet proved otherwise with his actions. The older sister who just needed someone to take care of her the way she took care of everybody else.

That was all I ever asked for.

That was all I never got.

"When was the last time you ate?"

I gesture to the wrappers on my bed and she raises an eyebrow. "No. Properly."

"I had a ham and cheese wrap from the vending machine?"

"My God." Willow mutters just as a blonde appears in the doorway. "How the fuck is the vending machine empty?"

"Lynnie, Emberli. Emberli, this is Lynnie."

"Pleasure to meet you." Lynnie smiles.

Nadia next door smashes something else and I jump. One of these days, something is going to come through the wall. That I'm certain of.

I wince. "Maybe not. I'm afraid I'm the culprit of being the vending machine snack thief."

Lynnie's eyes widened. "All of them?"

"All of them." I confirm.

"Damn, girl. That's got to be a world record or something."

"See? I knew you two would get along." Willow calls just as she opens the window. "The two of you can compete for world records."

"What's your world record?" I ask.

Lynnie rolls her eyes. "Apparently I drink too much."

"Apparently?" Willow snorts in disbelief at this. "I'm pretty sure you can outdrink the entire town, Lyn."

"So I enjoy the occasional cocktail. Sue me."

Lynnie sighs dramatically before she sinks next to me on the edge of the bed, watching Willow frantically pick up the rubbish sprawled around my room.

"I was going to tidy later." I say.

Willow only shakes her head, waving me off with her hand.

Lynnie leans in as she tells me, "Wills is a clean freak. You just gotta let her do her thing."

"Good thing I thought to come by to check on you." Willow mumbles. "Where were you yesterday by the way?"

"Yesterday? I had the gig at Spooky Hoots."

Willow and Lynnie share a glance between them. "Em, that was two days ago."

My eyes widen as realization hits me. I hadn't pulled just one all nighter, but two.

How did that happen? How could I just casually let two days pass?

"Oh my God! Have you not slept for two days?"

Willow's hands reach out for my arms as she worriedly checks me over. But all I can think about is how great this is.

Before I stepped foot in Shadow Peaks, I hadn't opened my notebook in two years. Now I have at least three songs written. It goes without saying that I'm not at all ready to leave yet.

I *can't* leave yet.

This was the most work I had done for myself, for my career in a long time. And not only would it be the biggest *fuck you* to Elijah, but it would be something I'd finally done for myself.

I felt on top of the world, which could possibly be exhaustion or the numerous energy bars I ate earlier on. Or the amount of caffeine I'd drunk. Either way, I didn't feel tired like I should be. Only excitement.

"I may as well start practising for when the baby arrives." I joke, though the low blow I suffocate myself with reminds me of how I'm doing this alone.

"Pfft." Willow scoffs. "You're still getting your beauty sleep, girl." She points her finger at me and then at herself. "You won't be doing the whole baby thing alone. Not if we have a say in it. Right Lyn?"

Lynnie nods beside me.

"I don't get it." I shake my head. "I don't get why you're helping me."

Thayne's words stay on a loop in my head and I can't help but feel guilty for allowing her to help me so much when I haven't done anything to deserve it.

"It's what we do here, Emberli. We look after our own here." Willow says and she grins. "And I've just officially claimed you as my own."

After Willow demanded she clean the entirety of my motel room, the three of us went out for a late lunch, which consisted of mostly dissing the other Rawlins siblings and trying each other's food.

I'd never done something like this before and felt as comfortable as I did, which is another small stepping stone I've reached. I try to push back the thought of how time will eventually consume me, and how I won't be just me anymore, but a mom. And the truth was, I don't know the first thing about how to be one. The thought alone stirs the nausea I feel brewing, and I'm unsure if it's the anxious thoughts I'm having or the unhealthy amount of junk food I've consumed recently.

"I just, I don't get it. He's so invasive. They all are." Willow leans back in the booth and she shakes her head. "It's as if they forget I'm a twenty-three year old woman now. I can take care of myself."

"They just think they're protecting you, Wills. That's all any of them want to do." Lynnie replies.

"Yeah well, it's fucking annoying." Willow grumbles before she turns to me. "Do you have any older brothers, Emberli?"

I shake my head. "I'm the eldest."

"Great. Can I pick your brain?" Her beady green eyes stare back at me and I nod, because after all she's done for me this is the least I can do.

"You care about your family, right?"

More than anything.

I nod again, unsure of if I should interrupt because Willow seems to be on a roll, sitting upright and passionate about the topic of the table.

"And you respect them, right?"

"Of course."

"Would you say that you'd get involved in your siblings' business?"

"Depends what the business is." I shrug. "I don't usually hover. But they know I'm there if they need me." At least I hope they do, I'd told them more than enough times. I was constantly caught up with the idea of them needing me. The constant what if.

If my parents hadn't ushered me to go on the road to pursue my music, I don't think I would have ever gone. I was fine being on standby for my siblings or my parents in case they ever needed me in their life, completely forgetting about my own because that was just who I was.

And it was why being away from them was so hard. I felt so out of touch and helpless.

"But you wouldn't like… get involved with their dating life, would you?"

"God no. I wouldn't want to know."

"See!" Willow stabs a chip with her fork. "It's just basic, common human decency. I don't get why none of my brothers have any."

"They're all men. That's why." Lynnie says. "Men don't think before they do things. It's like a rite of passage."

"So what did your brothers do?" I ask.

"Flint and Mack took it upon themselves to scare off my date before we even had the chance to order dinner last night."

"Seriously?"

Willow hums. "Yep. Rudy told me he was going to the bathroom and that was it. The asshole stood me up *and* I had to pay for the bottle of wine too. I ended up drinking it all but that's not the point. The point is my brothers are overbearing and intrusive and…"

"Love you so much that they want to protect you?"

Our waitress asks as she places another bottle of tap water in the middle of our table. I'd noticed that she'd been eavesdropping on our conversation.

She'd even wiped down the table next to us twice, though I don't think she'd realized it.

"Mavis, this is a private conversation."

"Then don't have it in a public setting. Your brothers care about you and you should appreciate that. If they think a man is wrong for you, then the man is wrong for you." The older woman scolds.

Willow sinks back in her chair just as Lynnie sits forward.

"Willow isn't a teenager anymore, Mavis. She's a grown woman and can see who the hell she wants because of it."

"She should be grateful that she has people who care about her. You of all people know what it's like to not have that."

Lynnie doesn't flinch, she just raises an eyebrow at the imposing lady who stands hovering at our now uncomfortable table. "You want a tip or not?"

Mavis doesn't say another word, she only grunts before sauntering away in silence, occasionally shooting looks over at us.

"I'm sorry for rambling. I just... It feels like they still treat me like a little kid, you know?"

I nod because I can understand how hard it must be on Willow. To be a grown woman treated like less.

Just because someone cares about you doesn't give them the right to diminish that.

Lynnie's hand reaches over for Willow's and she squeezes it before her gaze flies past her.

"Uh oh."

"What?" Willow and I turn around just as Thayne enters, his gaze scans the room before he makes his way over to us.

"You're still here." He points out as he nods at me.

"Where else would I be?"

"Beats me. Word of the town was that you'd left."

He slides in beside Lynnie, sitting opposite me with an unreadable expression on his face.

"Don't sound too excited."

I watch as a smile cracks at his lips, but it's gone as quick as it appears. "Can't help it. Was hoping you'd be long gone by now."

Lynnie jabs his side but he doesn't budge, just as I don't.

As much as the man before me attempts to irritate me, probably in the hope that I'd lash out so I'd quit or he could fire me, I need this job. So I have to be on my best behaviour. No matter how much I want to smash the coke bottle in front of me over his head.

But with my luck, Thayne Rawlins wouldn't even flinch. He was a broad man who was practically all muscle. I could see how those in his shoulders define the rest of his upper body under the black skin-tight shirt he wore, and when he moved around, I'd catch glimpses of a possible six pack that I most definitely should not be looking for.

It was clear that he looked after himself and I concluded that he would probably break the coke bottle before the coke bottle broke him. Therefore I voided my experiment that definitely would cost me my job.

"Careful. You and Colt are the only two brothers I like right now." Willow warns him and amusement strikes his face.

"What happened?"

"Flint and Mack happened." She grumbles.

"I tried telling her to be respectful and grateful, Thayne. But she wouldn't listen." Mavis reappears, pouring Thayne a cup of coffee before jumping at Willow's sudden outburst that draws looks from other tables nearby.

"Oh suck it, Mavis."

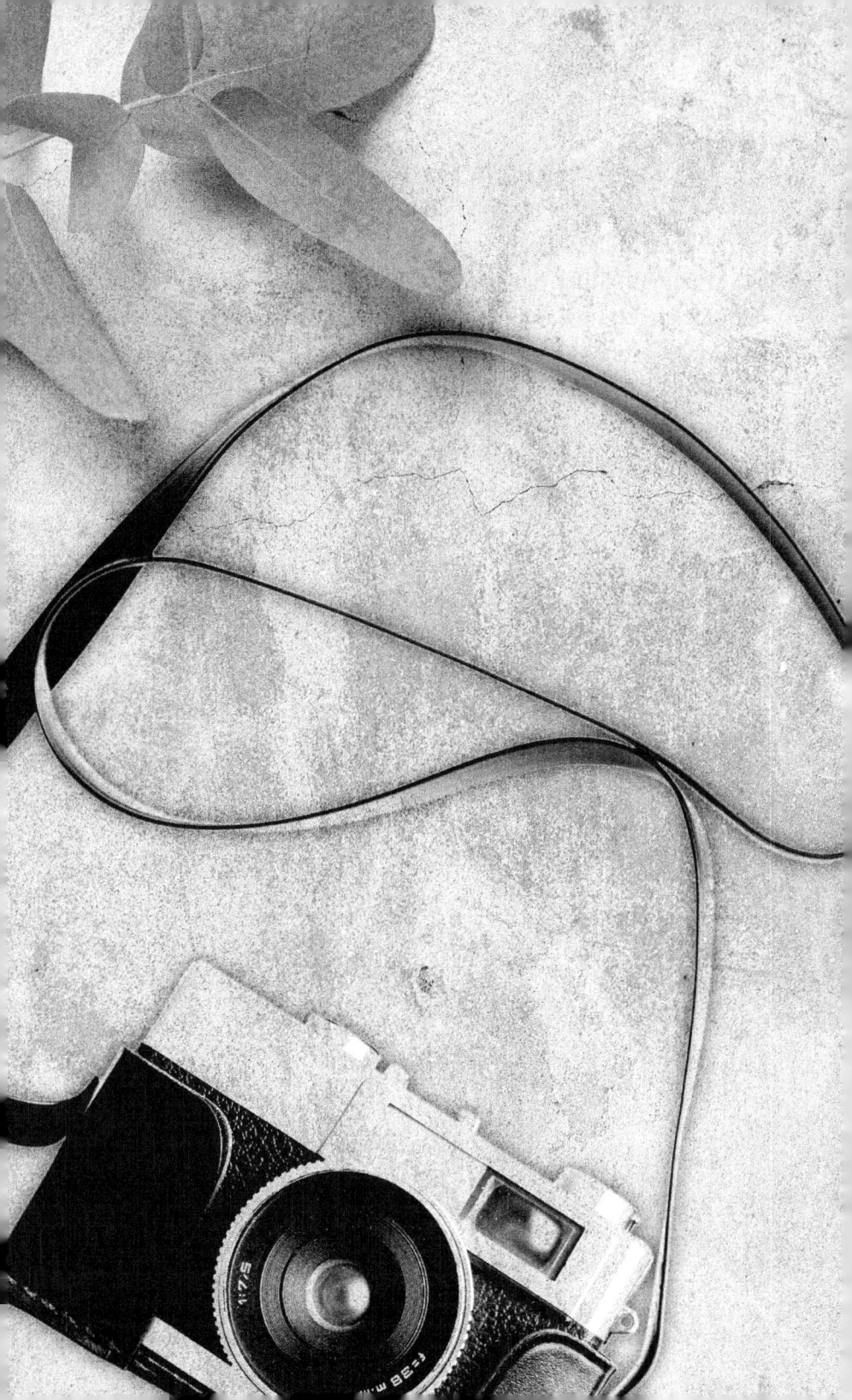

6

Thayne

I was sure my mother was punishing me from the grave for not being more trusting towards people. Before Odessa, it was only me who ran the bar and that was how I liked it. Only I was severely paying the price tonight.

She'd called me up this morning with a fever and I told her to stay home and rest. She often happily overworked despite me attempting to split the shifts evenly between us so I knew this day would eventually come. Her first sick day.

Not only was the bar ridiculously busy, but I had the task of watching over the woman captivating everyone's attention.

Emberli.

She stands with Colton's guitar looped around her neck, strumming the chords effortlessly to Carrie Underwoods' *'Undo it'* per the request of Willow who is hellbent on showing up for her and who is in the middle of the dancefloor with Lynnie belting out the lyrics Emberli is singing. Her voice was raspy and annoyingly good. And as if I couldn't see for myself, the locals just had to rub it in. I couldn't feel more like an asshole than I already did when I turned up at the motel a few nights ago. She hasn't spoken much to me since, but I guess it's a good thing we both keep a distance.

It's clear that she doesn't like me very much and the feeling is mutual. I don't trust her intentions with this town and the people in it one bit, regardless of if she's a good singer or not. She wears a thin strapped, long dress of silky black material with small roses dotted around it. Her hair falls to her shoulders in bouncy waves, more tightened than usual and she wears a full face of make-up. As much as it pains me to say it, she's stunning. And the men of the town all crowd her, looking more lively than I've ever seen them look as she leaves the stage, squeezing her way towards me for her drink that sits at the end of the bar. I hear her apologize profusely and decide I can't keep watching her struggle.

"Move out the way!" I snap, rounding the bar and shoving them to the side, left and right as I grab her wrist and pull her out of the swarm of masculinity she suffocates in.

"Thanks." She breathes out before reaching for her drink.

"That was good, chick." Billy says.

"Yeah?"

"Real good. Your mom a good singer?"

"The best. But she doesn't sing professionally. Just around the house."

I find myself wanting to know more about Emberli's background and her parents but due to the cold shoulder she gives me, I don't think I'm going to know more about her anytime soon.

Her focus is solely on Billy as the two of them chat away, it's as if she's doing everything in her power to not look my way and this, for some reason, irritates me.

"Bet your dad's proud of you." Billy speaks from beside her and she turns to him. A look of shock on her face before she gulps down a few sips, nodding.

"I hope so."

"He is. I know it." Billy confirms.

This obviously means something to Emberli. I can see it in her

52

eyes as they soften. "Thanks Billy."

Billy nods, taking another sip of his beer just as her gaze loiters on him slightly longer.

It becomes apparent to me at that moment that perhaps she isn't as callous as I'd assumed.

Maybe I'd got her all wrong.

"How do I look?" Flint asks as he poses in front of his ranch, his question is directed at me, but Lynnie cuts in.

Flint had asked me to get some photos of him and the ranch, claiming that he wanted to put us more on the market and eventually open up the ranch to the outside world.

"As stiff as the fence behind you. Wouldn't kill you to smile more either!" Lynnie yells from beside me.

I can't help but laugh as he glares at her. "I don't smile."

She snorts. "Captain obvious over here."

"Why are you even here?" Flint bites. "Don't you have anything better to do?"

"Nope. This is brilliant."

I chuckle, taking a few more photos of him with the main house behind him. It's in desperate need of a repaint, but no one is ever willing to do it.

The sound of a truck pulling up on the gravel pulls me from my thoughts as Colton and Ryker step out of it.

"Finally. Where have you been?" Flint grumbles.

"Downtown. There was a sale at Lacey's."

"Get in there." I gesture next to Flint. Colton and Ryker both groan before taking a side each next to Flint.

"What are you even doing?" Colt looks from me to Flint, who continues to look as displeased as ever.

"Can't you see? Flint's changing his career to modelling." Lynnie laughs.

"Still don't get why you're here." Flint sighs.

"I wouldn't miss this for the world. Now chin up, look more approachable. Nobody's going to want to visit this place if you look the way you do. We need a full reset."

"And who the hell put you in charge?"

"Shut up and smile." Flint puts on his biggest smile yet, looking at Lynnie as if to say *'This good enough?'*

Despite what he may say, I know Flint cares about what Lynnie thinks. She's always been good at artistic visions and she was exactly what Flint needed for the upcoming revamp on the ranch.

"You should take your tops off!" I whip my head round to the familiar voice of Emberli, who is walking towards us with a huge grin on her face, dragging along our mare, Becky, next to her.

To her right is Willow, who makes a gagging sound at the unexpected yet surprising suggestion from Emberli.

"If you wanted to see me topless, you only had to ask." Colton winks at her. He was definitely the most flirty out of all of us, with Mack closing in at a tight second place. But whilst Colton flirted with everything that walked and talked, Mack's fixation was Odessa and it had been that way since she strolled into town a month ago.

"Em's got a point. It may attract more clients." Lynnie shrugs.

Em?

For fuck's sake. They're even on a nickname basis now.

"I am not taking my top off for this." Flint grumbles.

"Then get out of the shot."

Lynnie and Flint compete in a small stare off before my brother slides his shirt over his head. "Happy?"

Lynnie rolls her eyes and I hear Willow gag again. Emberli, however, claps her hands together and squeals excitedly. "Hope you three don't mind being objectified for a minute or two." She blurts out. "Hormones are high at the moment."

"Am I supposed to feel offended?" Ryker questions.

"Right? Because I don't feel offended." Colton flexes his biceps with a grin on his face, earning a jab to the ribs from Flint.

"Alright. Let's just get on with it." Flint grumbles and I raise my camera, attempting to ignore the small giggles from Emberli behind me, who seems to be lapping this up.

"The world is going to luurrve this!" She exclaims.

"Where have you two been anyway?" I murmur, attempting to distract myself from how good Emberli manages to look in a simple pair of gray pants and a black vest top.

I couldn't understand how Elijah managed to score with the woman behind me. It was evident her standards were low.

"I was just giving Emberli a tour of the meadows in Shadow Peaks. We took the horses." Willow explains and I turn to them both.

"You rode?"

The two of them nod.

"And that's a good idea?" I gesture to Emberli's growing bump.

"Becky's a good girl aren't you mama?" Willow pats down the horse who is only after the treats hanging out of Willow's pocket. "Besides, Emberli has horses back home. It's not like she doesn't know how to ride."

"She faster than you, spark?" Aca appears with a toolbox in hand, a huge grin on his face when he sees the boys propped up against the fence. He was never going to let his brother live this down, that was for sure.

"Not yet." Willow winks at Emberli. "But she's fast."

"And what the fuck is going on here?" Aca tips his head to his younger brother, who just mumbles a "Don't ask."

"Speaking of things to ask..." My little sister wraps her arm around my own and smiles at me with a smile I know all too well.

She wants something.

Willow always used to smile the same signature smile even when she was younger. Beaming up at me with a pleading look on her face. "Can you give Odessa Wednesday night off?"

I raise an eyebrow.

"Please? I need her for Woo Woo Wednesday."

"Woo Woo Wednesday? What's that?" Emberli asks.

"You know the cocktail? Spooky Hoots does an entire night dedicated to them, courtesy of Odessa of course. No chance this guy would come up with such brilliance on his own." Lynnie gestures her thumb behind her at me.

"Thanks Lyn. It's not like I'm right here or anything." I grumble, setting my camera down as the guys get dressed.

"So what do you say? Please? I want the four of us to have our first girls night." She nods over at Emberli before turning back to me, mouthing please over and over again until I eventually nod.

"Fine. I'll take her off Wednesday."

"Great. And can you pay her too?"

She sees the unimpressed look on my face and smiles sheepishly. "Please? I'll even work a few shifts if you need me to make up for it. I want her to come but I know she won't take the day off willingly." Willow was right and I hate the idea of letting her down when all she seems to want to do is have a girls' night. I'd be a dick to turn her down when I can afford it. And like the pushover older brother I am, I give in.

"Fine. Wednesday only. And you help me out Friday and Saturday."

"Done. Love you." She hugs me tightly before high fiving the girls, thinking I don't hear her when she says, "Works every time."

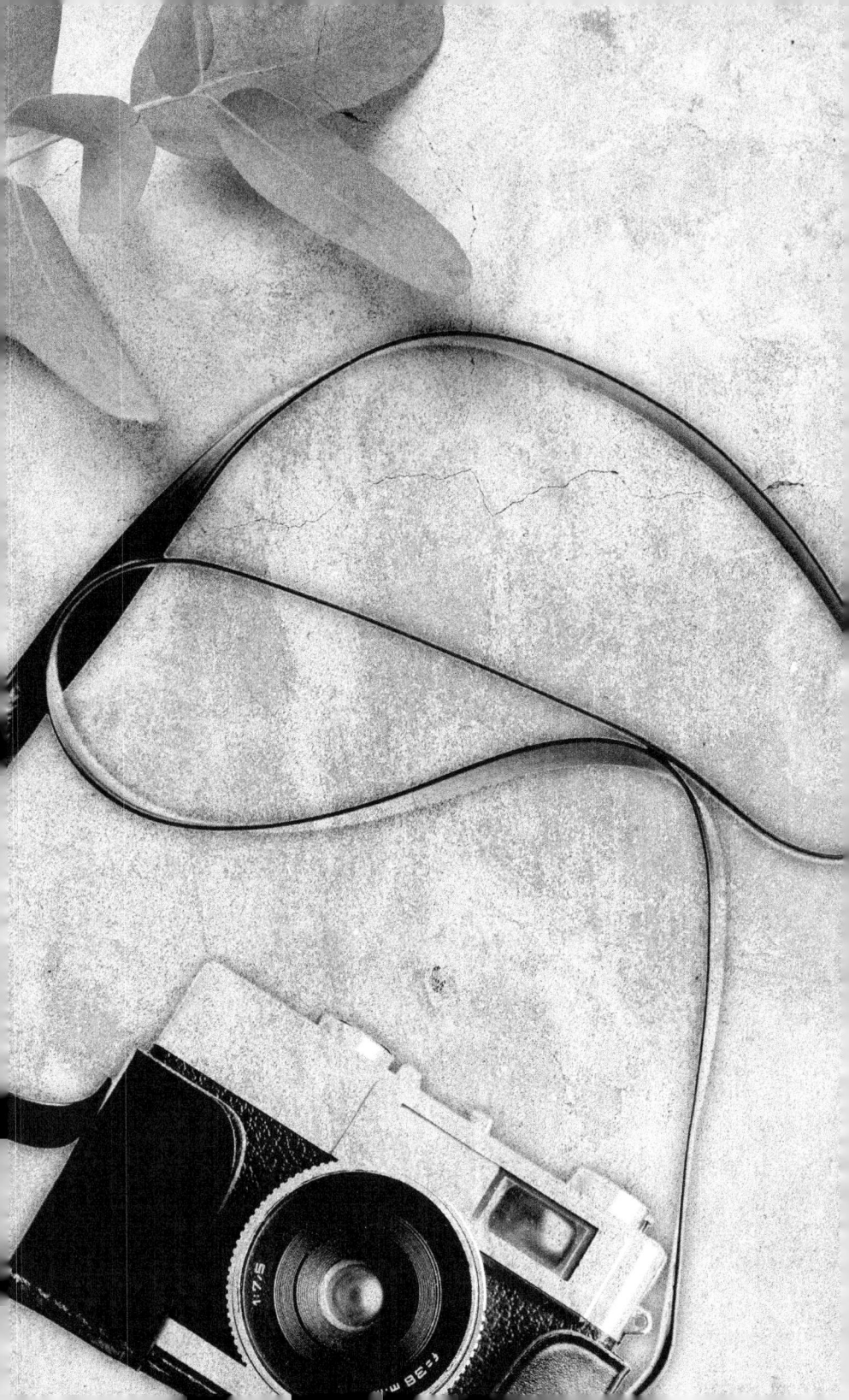

7
Thayne

The thing about small towns is that you're always seeing those you're determined to avoid.

I've seen more of Emberli than I'd anticipated these past few days and now, as if I'm not already late enough, she holds up the queue in Laceys' general store as she rummages through her handbag.

"I know I had it! I swear I... I swear I just had it," I hear.

I can get eggs another time. I could just walk away. But what I should and could do are two very different things.

"I'm so sorry. I think I've lost my purse."

I sigh, leaving my place in the queue and snatch the eggs off of the conveyor belt before jumping ahead a few spaces, standing over Emberli, who is so deep in her bag she doesn't even notice those around her who are starting to get annoyed with the prolonged wait, or me as I reach the eggs over her shoulder.

"These too please, Doris." I show her my card and feel Emberli's gaze peering up at me from under her eyelashes. "You don't have to."

"Just take the help, trouble."

She stands silently, pursing her lips together as I pack her shopping away for her. And then she follows me out and to my truck as I toss the bags into the back.

"Get in. I'll take you wherever you want. Just hurry up. I'm late."

It seems she doesn't get the memo, because she just stands there with a thumb over her shoulder, gesturing to my sister's bicycle.

"I rode here."

I move past her, grabbing it before tossing it onto the truck bed. "Christ. Is there anything else you want to borrow?" I freeze as soon as the words leave my mouth. That was a low blow, a lot different to our usual fleeting comments.

"Wow." She laughs and before I know it, she's next to me, dragging out the heavy two wheeler.

"What are you doing?" I clamp my hands down on it and she too holds a firm grip, but I don't budge.

We stand there for a few seconds like we're engaging in a tug of war.

"What are you doing?" I ask again.

"I'm not getting in the truck with you." She says.

"I said I'll drive you back."

"No."

My jaw clenches. "Why do you have to make things so hard? Just get in the fucking truck."

"What? So you can shame me some more? This may be a joke to you, Thayne. But this is my life right now and I don't need you to humiliate me when I already feel humiliated enough."

I swallow down the guilt that attempts to drown me as she stands in front of me, her chest heaving with the same anger that presents itself on her face.

"It wasn't my intention to."

"Bullshit." She yanks again at the bicycle. Only this time she pulls harder and leaves my hands empty. "I don't need your help, Thayne. Especially if it comes with a price."

Her breathing is shallow yet quick paced as she straightens the

60

bicycle, it's only then that I see the chain has snapped. "You can't ride that."

"I'm getting really sick of you telling me what I should, shouldn't and can't do." She snaps, rage flashing in those green eyes of hers, her cheeks are reddened into a crimson color and it's clear as day that I've upset her.

Instead of the usual kick of satisfaction I'd get out of annoying her, it's replaced with regret.

I didn't mean to upset her. And I sure as fuck didn't like seeing her upset either.

"No I mean, you really can't ride that home. The chains snapped." Her eyes divert to where mine are and she sighs.

"I can fix it."

"You can't fix it. It'll need replacing."

"I can do it. Just go." Her cold tone slices through me as she lowers herself to get a better look of the chain. And as a sigh leaves her, I know she's seen what I have.

"I'll drop you." I stop speaking immediately when I watch a tear run down her cheek, darting my thumb out but she dodges it, wiping it away herself as she holds her flat palm out at me, stopping me from getting any closer to her.

"I'm fine." She tells me. But her icy demeanor doesn't push me away like it's supposed to. It does the opposite. "It's the hormones."

And even if it was, one thing is clear. I hated seeing Emberli cry.

"I'm sorry." Her eyes dart up to mine and she shakes her head before she inhales a long breath, letting it leave her lips a few moments later.

"Don't. I'm not even crying because of you. It's the hormones. Know that if this was me, I would have punched you in the face."

I try to hide the smile that attempts to make an appearance on my face.

There she is.

"And look, I get it okay? I get you're mad at Elijah. But that is no reason to be mad at me. And I'm sorry. I'm sorry for whatever he did to you or took from you that makes you hate me so much. But he took a lot of things from me too, you don't see me being an asshole about it."

The sternness in her voice shakes as she wipes at her eyes, the make-up she wears is smudged all across her face but yet she somehow manages to pull it off.

"I'll drop you back."

"No. I'll walk."

"Emberli, will you let me drop you back? Please."

She hesitates. "Fine. But you don't talk to me and I don't talk to you. Got it? We can't even have a normal conversation." I open the passenger door for her in response, biting down the small objection that tells me she's wrong.

That perhaps in another reality, where she wasn't the ex-girlfriend of the only man who managed to hurt me on par with my dad and where she wasn't my employee, or my little sister's new friend… maybe things could be different with Emberli and me.

8

Emberli

Thayne listens to my request and doesn't speak to me for the entire ride until we're back to the motel. He tells me he'll fix the bicycle and bring it around when it's ready. I thank him and take my bags, telling him to dock my paycheck this week when I don't find my purse in my bag. Instead, I find it inside, where I lean against the front door for some stability. Some peace.

Thump. Smash.

Never mind. Just some stability.

Smash.

"Oh my God." I mutter as another smash vibrates the wall separating Noisy Nadia and me before it's replaced with complete silence.

Thank God.

I'm exhausted after the minimal chores I've carried out today, and can only blame the little baby that's growing inside of me.

I know at some point, I should book myself in for a check-up, but it's as if I can't quite bring myself to do it. So I've been pushing it off as long as I can. Seconds after I close my eyes, my phone rings. I scramble to the bottom of my bag to find it before answering.

"Hello?"

"Hey you, it's Willow. Are we still on for tonight?" It's Wednesday and I completely forgot I'd been invited to join the girls at Spooky Hoots for what Willow explained was their weekly meet-up. I know I should go, especially after everything Willow and her family have done for me, and a hint of fear of missing out pricks at my brain. Willow must hear the hesitation in my voice because concern fills hers. "What's wrong?"

"I'm just tired. What time are we meeting?"

"Em, if you're tired. Rest. You don't need to feel like you *have* to come." She sympathises and I sigh out in relief that she understands.

"Are you sure?"

"Of course I am. Is everything okay though?"

"Yeah, why wouldn't it be?"

"I heard about your run in with Thayne. Want me to talk to him?"

"No." I breathe out. "I think in his own fucked up way, he's trying to help. I don't know. Either way, it'll be nice to have a break from him tonight. I've been seeing far too much of him recently."

Willow laughs. "I know that feeling. But you're right, I think he is trying to help you. He's just not sure how, and... as you would have figured out by now, he doesn't trust easily. Elijah really hurt him, you know. I think he just struggles with that."

"What happened? With him and Elijah?"

"It's not my story to tell. But I think you two could be friends, if you tried."

It seems impossible to be friends with someone like Thayne, especially when he's already made his mind up about me in the same way I've made mine up about him.

"Yeah. Maybe. Are you okay though?"

"Me? Yeah. I'm fine."

"Good."

"Emberli?"

"Yeah?"

"Thank you…for asking."

Willow turns up at my door within the next hour with Lynnie and Odessa both behind her.

"We brought Woo Woo Wednesday to you!" Willow exclaims as she shakes the bag she's holding. She slides past me eagerly and grins as the girls follow her in with boxes.

"Are you prepared to lose your virginity?" She says, in the most serious tone ever.

"I hate to be the one to break it to you, but that ship has long sailed." I look down to my stomach and hear the laughs of the girls around me.

I smile, rubbing at my bump in comfort. I can't wait to bring them into this world, to meet the girls who've made my time here so enjoyable.

"I should have specified. Your Woo Woo Wednesday Virginity." Willow wiggles her eyebrows.

"I'm ready." I breathe out.

"Odessa makes the *best*. You've never had anything like it." Lynnie tells me. "Personally, I like the ones *with* alcohol. But Odessa tends to cut me off when I get to eight so I know just how good her mocktails are. And they're delicious."

"Hang on, did you say you can drink eight cocktails?"

Fucking hell. The girl can drink.

My limit was three, max. I was the definition of a lightweight and would not stand a chance in a drinking competition here.

They're more advanced than those back home. I've seen a few after my gigs at the bar, and each one Lynnie manages to win, annoying the misogynistic men who claimed they would outdrink her prior, they even bet on it too.

"On a bad day." Lynnie winks.

"Yeah. When Flint pisses you off, your threshold seems to disappear. She can drink for days, I'm sure of it." Odessa shakes her head as she and Willow unbox cocktail shakers and glasses.

"Thank you guys for doing this."

"You kidding?" Odessa turns to me. "If I've got to be involved in this, so do you."

Willow bumps her shoulder. "Don't act like you don't love us deep down, you're a softie at heart."

"It's not love, it's more tolerance."

More laughter fills the room, almost drowning out the noise that Nadia makes next door. It's clear that, like myself, she has a huge fear of missing out and is making herself heard.

"What was that?" Willow asks.

"That's Noisy Nadia. I've never met her but I always hear her."

"Are you joking? Report her." Odessa says.

"I feel bad, what if she gets upset that I reported her? Plus, it's like white noise - helps me sleep."

"It has to absolutely suck being an empath."

"Yep." I nod. "It does. It's also impossible to stay mad at someone. I just feel bad for them. It's why I'm not angry at Elijah. I just - I don't really know." Lynnie's hand rubs at my back soothingly.

"Has Mack heard anything at all recently?" Odessa asks and Willow shakes her head at this.

"Nope. That man is running." Her emphasis on running leaves me thinking about if he'll ever come back. I sure as hell didn't want him to anymore and I think I was holding him to a higher standard when I thought a part of him would want to be involved in our child's life.

"He was an asshole, Emberli. It's not your fault."

I sigh. "Sometimes I think it is. I think I fell out of love with Elijah when I realized nothing was changing, and so even though I stayed, I wasn't... there. If that makes sense."

"It makes perfect sense." Odessa nods, her eyes soft with understanding.

From the time I've spent here and my numerous talks with her at the bar after both of our shifts, I've learnt that Odessa often wants to know things about everyone else but is closed off herself. I feel deep down she relates to what I'm saying, like she's been through something similar.

She observes but she doesn't hover either.

And because I'm someone who's never felt understood, speaking to someone who only likes to listen heals something in me.

I feel at peace here, which is weird considering that this was my ex-boyfriend's hometown and his people. I feel accepted by the group of girls that swooped in to help me from the moment I arrived. Friendship. It's something I've been almost alien to and often kept at arm's length in order to protect myself from hurt, but now? I almost can't imagine my life without the three girls who sit in my old, definitely in need of a health check, loud motel room.

"But seriously, if you need a place to stay, we'll find somewhere for you." Willow tells me. "I mean, Lyn and I share a cabin on the ranch and that's small enough but I'm sure we could make some room and Flint's building some more cabins on the ranch, you could even have one when the baby comes. If you were planning on staying that long." The girls all look to me for an answer after Willow stops talking.

"I don't want to intrude on you guys, besides I highly doubt Thayne would be happy if your brother gave me a place on the ranch."

"Thayne's never happy. Try not to take it personally."

I laugh. "It's a bit hard to not when he's out to get me."

"My brother is just an asshole. But, he has a good reason."

"Good reason for being an asshole?"

"You two got off on the wrong foot."

"Both of my feet are wrong in Thayne's eyes." I say.

"You just have to give him time." Odessa replies.

"He'll come around and like you just as much as we do."

Highly doubtful, but I nod anyway because the girls all seem hopeful.

"What the fuck are you doing?" Odessa blinks at Willow, who is opening various bags of candy and tipping them into a bowl.

"It's called a candy salad. I saw it online a few days ago."

"A candy salad?" Lynnie asks. "That amount of sugar does not seem very salad-like to me."

Willow shrugs. "It makes me feel better knowing it's some form of salad."

"It's not a salad, Wills."

"I'm sorry my bike broke on you earlier, it's been rusting away in the stables but I honestly thought it would be okay." Willow tells me.

"It's not your fault. You couldn't have known."

"I know, but I'm sorry you got stuck with Thayne." She grimaces.

"You got stuck with Thayne?" Lynnie turns her head to me. "Ouch."

"It's fine. I told him not to talk to me and surprisingly, he didn't. It was silent the entire ride back."

The girls all look at each other, seeming somewhat shocked by this.

"Really?"

"Yeah. But I did unleash my tears on him and threatened to punch him. So..."

The girls again crack up at this, laughter filling the room as Willow shakes her head.

"I've never known someone to put Thayne in his place the way you do."

"I'd call it more him being terrified of me crying than me putting him in his place."

"That's true. He's never liked it when you cry, Wills." Lynnie says.

"He doesn't like it when any woman cries, that's just Thayne."

That's... actually kind of sweet.

And if we weren't talking about the asshole of a boss I have, I would have let it be known that I thought so.

"But I am sorry, Em. Today is always a hard day for him."

I'm about to ask why when Odessa cuts in. "I'm sorry. Did you say you threatened to punch him?" she asks as she sips her drink, a highly amused look on her face as she tries not to laugh.

"Yeah. Not my finest moment." I wince.

"That's hilarious."

"I'm waiting for my termination of employment letter."

"You won't be getting one anytime soon. Thayne's laptop is broken and besides, you've been giving him more business than he's had in years." Willow's revelation is a shock to me. The gigs I'd been doing had always been busy, but I'd just assumed that they were always that way with Spooky Hoots being the only bar in town. I'd found this out through Billy, who I'd grown fond of. We'd talk a lot, like Odessa and I did, in between my sets.

Billy would always threaten any creeps that tried to ask for my number. I learnt that he never had children and his wife died four years ago. He'd told me that he hated feeling as lonely as he was, so he'd come to the bar and spend his time there. He was a genuinely nice person, one that turned to alcohol in the hope that it would drown the reality of his life.

It was a cruel thing, life. It could be everything you ever wanted, but it could be gone in an instant. And thinking like that makes me want to appreciate what I have, and guilty about yearning for things that I can't.

I'd often find myself thinking about the meaning of life or more so, what it meant to feel alive. I felt like my life as Emberli was over, and my new life as a mom was just starting. And selfishly, I was scared about what that meant for me.

The past years as of late, I've been surviving more than living, desperately clinging onto Elijah as if he was my source of life. I didn't realize at the time but he was the opposite, he was pulling me down with him and every part of my body and soul was rejecting him because it knew something I didn't. But still, I refused to see it because I was so blindsided by the idea of being loved.

I was never unloved as a child, I was brought up with loving parents and a caring family, which is why I couldn't understand how I was so flawed in the art of needing more love. It was selfish really.

I had been self-critiquing for so long that I thought I needed someone else to save me from myself in the way that Billy relies on alcohol to save him. I was in love with the idea of Elijah more than I was in love with Elijah himself.

We shared common interests and at times, deep conversations. I felt like he understood me and I grew fascinated with him. But was that even love? Or was it just… fascination.

I was so infatuated with other parts of Elijah that I ignored the red flags that had been in the air waving at me since the beginning, and that terrified me. I'd always thought myself a smart girl but it appeared otherwise.

Even if I was clothed with the incapability to find love with another, I'd make sure that the little person growing inside of me would know so much of it just from me alone.

I dive to my desk and grab my notebook.

Fascination. The idea of love.

"I'm just saying, no one would blame you if you did." Lynnie's voice brings me back and Willow scoffs, throwing herself back on the couch. "I do not fancy my brother's closest friend."

I curse myself for zoning out again at the wrong time. It appears I've missed some important information that makes Willow's aura reek of denial.

"You seem pretty annoyed about him going on a date, Wills." Lynnie raises an eyebrow.

I pick up my glass, taking a few sips from it and attempting to be as quiet as I can when Willow decides to speak. "It's not that. I've just, I've seen the amount of girls over the years that only want him because of the popularity and press he gets. They only want him because of his job."

"What's his job?" I whisper to Lynnie.

"He's a bronc rider."

I nod.

"I don't like Aca like that." Willow says and a huge bang makes us all jump. The plaster within the walls crumbles and Lynnie jumps to her feet. "That's it. This needs to stop."

Lynnie's line of patience is a lot shorter than mine, she's been here less than an hour and storms out of my room, knocking loudly on the perpetrator's door.

The girls and I remain in the safety of the room as we peer our heads round.

Lynnie's fist thuds on the wooden door in front of her.

"Open up!" She yells.

Silence.

Nadia has seemingly shut up, but Lynnie doesn't take this. Her hand darts to the doorknob and she swings it open despite the whispers from the three of us.

Her face is stripped of its colour and shock dominates what's left.

"What is it, Lyn?" Willow whispers below me.

"It's a…" Lynnie's words are cut off with an ear-deafening growl mixed with a roar. She reaches in, slamming the front door shut before rushing back into my room and locking the door breathlessly.

Panic girdles her as she paces back and forth.

"Noisy Nadia is a grizzly."

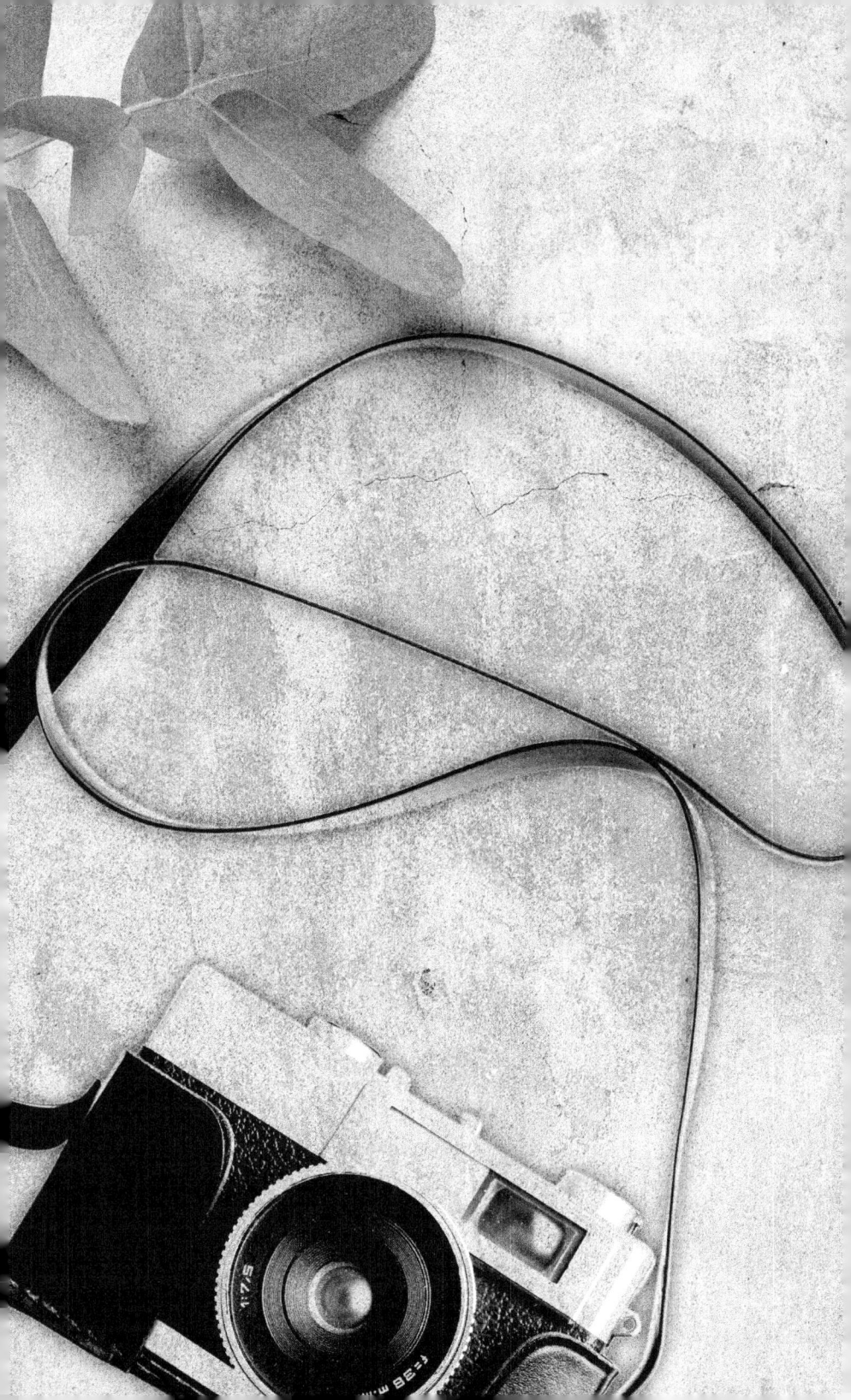

9

Thayne

This evening has consisted of numerous customers coming up to the bar and asking me where "the beautiful singer" was this evening. They were disappointed when I told them that she wasn't performing tonight and asked when she'd be in next.

The bar is a lot less busier and I can only guess that it's the non-existent sound of Emberli's voice that keeps them away. A small part of me hoped that I'd be seeing my sister and her friends so I could keep a close eye on them. It was known that Woo Woo Wedsnedays had a habit of getting out of hand, especially if my sister was the ringleader.

But they're a no show.

"I was wondering if you wanted to grab a bite to eat sometime soon?" Annie Clemments sits in front of me as I dry off the glasses that have just come out of the dishwasher.

"I'm not interested, Annie. I'm sorry."

"Come on, just two friends having dinner?"

"Annie." I shake my head. "No. "

Annie wasn't just a girl who'd been persistent over the years in asking me to go on a date with her, but she'd also broken Colton's heart a while back when she cheated on him. It was the first time I'd ever seen him as heartbroken as he was and I think that's why even now, all these years later, he often put on a mask, presenting himself as the shameless flirt around town who "doesn't do relationships."

"I don't get why you won't just go on this one date with me, Thayne!"

"So it is a date?" Billy speaks from beside her and she groans in frustration.

"Shut up. Billy."

"Hey. Don't talk to him like that." I say. "No means no, Annie. Okay?"

"One date."

"You wanna pop down to the library, Annie?" Aca appears, leaning on the bar as he peers down at her in a flirtatious manner.

She's at a loss for words but manages a nod. This woman would do anything for a grasp of male attention, it didn't matter who it was from.

"Yeah?" Aca chuckles.

"Yeah. Let's...let's go"

"Go and get yourself a dictionary. Search the meaning of no, and study it." I grin, and Annie glances between us before balling her hands into fists and squealing in annoyance, storming away from the bar.

"When will she quit?" he asks me as he turns to the bar. I grab a beer for him and place it down in front of him.

"I don't think she ever will."

He laughs. "You gotta stop being such an irresistible man. Soon I'm not going to be here to save your ass."

For as long as I can remember, Aca had always been behind me to do so, I was grateful to have a friend like him. And no matter what, he'd always been there for my family and I.

Even growing up, if I was getting in a fight with another boy from the neighborhood, Aca was right behind me, ready to jump in. And he'd done that throughout my teenage years in which I faced a lot of anger and resentment for my dad. But Aca stood by me throughout it all. The same way he stood by my brothers when the same feelings overtook them. He took good care of Willow too.

Aca was a competitive bronc rider and his rodeo season was starting up again which meant that we wouldn't see him as frequently as we do now. He'd put rodeos on hold when Elijah left us all in shit. And yeah, it benefited us all that he was home, but I knew he missed it. I knew he was excited to get back into the arena.

"When do you go back?"

"Two weeks."

I nod, two weeks left and then he'd be gone for ten months.

Man, was I going to miss him.

I take a sip of my beer.

"Aren't you working?" Billy asks. That man had a habit of judging me for my poor life choices when he'd practically taken residency in my bar.

He grumbles something that sounds like 'never mind' when he sees the look on my face and slides off of the stool, traipsing over to his booth in the corner of the bar.

"Can I ask a favour?" Aca asks.

"Anything man."

"Will you look after Ryker for me?"

"Of course man. You don't even have to ask." Ryker had come back into town early last season. Like his brother, he was a professional bronc rider, but during the semi-final of his competition, he was thrown off his horse and onto his shoulder moments before the horse stumbled over him.

I remember watching it like it was yesterday. Sally's screams, the live TV cutting out to an overly long and torturing advert break and the image of Ryker lying on the floor unconscious before the cameras went black.

Two severely broken ribs and a dislocated collarbone later, Ryker made his way back into Shadow Peaks. He recovered physically in under three months, but you could see that it was more the mental side of it all that brought him down. Two years later and Ryker still hadn't gone back, nor had he rode a horse since. Sally and Doug tried everything to help him and even sought therapy but Ryker wasn't ready to help himself yet. He often resided in his own company or spent most of his time down at the ranch with Flint unless Colton dragged him out to a pub crawl.

Ryker never brings up what happened that day, so we never do either. I know all too well the feeling of wanting a memory to be long gone and buried. And although Ryker is one of Aca's biggest supporters, I know it has to hurt watching him get on a horse and bring home championship titles. Even if he never says it.

"Thanks. I'm just worried about him, you know?"

I nod. It's one thing Aca and I understand about each other. Worrying about others.

"Don't worry. I won't let him go under."

"I know I can rely on you man." Aca dips his head and shakes it. "Do you think I should stay?"

"Absolutely not. You've got a championship to bring back."

"What if I'm leaving at the wrong time?"

"There's never a right time, Aca. You have to go. I won't let you be held back here any longer than you have been already."

He nods, sliding onto the bar stool whilst I serve a few customers.

"How was yesterday?"

I swallow down the emotion that begins to clog my throat. Talking about my feelings had never been my strong suit, but my therapist had told me that it was important that I did after what happened.

"Yeah it was... fine," is what I settle with.

"Fine?" Aca raises an eyebrow at me. "That's all I get?"

"It was good. I dropped the flowers off at the grave after I dropped Emberli off."

"What's going on with that, man?"

"With what?"

"You and Emberli? The little feud you've got going on between you."

"There is no feud." I told him. "She doesn't like me and I don't like her."

"Thayne, you're lying."

"Yeah. Maybe I am," I grumble.

The recurring image of Emberli's face and the tears that ran down her cheeks as she cried kept making an appearance in my brain, causing me to get next to no hours of work done. Even though I deserved it after what I said.

The very image tortures me even now as I speak to Aca, even when she's not in this room. Emberli is in my fucking head and she won't leave, which is not good for me and is certainly not good for either of us, seeing as I find myself wondering when I'll next see the woman who manages to irritate me beyond belief.

"I don't know. I went too far and said some things I shouldn't have said."

Aca snorts. "Sounds like you."

My phone buzzes in my pocket and I see Aca check his at the same time. It's the family group chat.

WILLOW: SOS

MACK: What's wrong?

I hit play on the voice note of chaos Willow sends through. "MACK! When someone says SOS that means…" There's a chorus of screams in the background. "GET HERE AS FAST AS YOU CAN!"

The next message that shows up is her live location. She's at the motel that Emberli is staying in.

Emberli.

I grab my jacket and slide it on.

"Where are you going? You can't leave the bar unattended."

Shit. Aca is right. But there are not many times when he's wrong. Used to piss me off growing up, how smart he was. Still does occasionally now but I like to think I deal with it a lot better, like not punching him in the face.

"Shit." I grumble. I trusted no one but Odessa and my family to help me with the bar, and given the amount of replies to Willow's message, there was about to be a family gathering at The Hollyhead Motel.

"Everybody out!" I yell.

"You serious?" Aca asks.

"Fuck yes, now help me get everyone out."

Despite all the groans and protests from the locals, I'm finally able to lock up in under ten minutes. I jump in Aca's truck as he speeds through the town.

The girls are fine. That's the first thing I take note of as Aca pulls into the parking lot. There's a huge crowd already, members of the public, staff of the motel and a mixture of cops and wildlife officers. People were already on their phones, documenting the argument my brother was having with our park ranger from upstate.

"There was a grizzly bear here, Amos. Find it."

Amos looks around in response, flinging his arms around. "I don't see a bear, Mack. Okay? Maybe these girls have had one too many drinks." Amos points his finger to the collection of empty jugs on the motel floor before nodding over at the four girls who sit on the grass whispering amongst themselves.

"A grizzly?" I ask. Mack nods in response.

I take a quick look inside where more of Amos' men look around the room. There's a huge indent in the wall between room fifty-one and fifty-two and regardless of the shards of glass and plaster that cover the floor, the room is disgusting. And I can't believe Emberli's been staying here.

There's mold in every corner of the room and a damp smell to match it. The shower curtain in the bathroom is loose and is easily a slip hazard for Emberli.

"Are you suggesting my sister is lying?" Mack snaps.

"I'm saying, she's probably drunk and maybe smashed a few things and didn't want to take responsibility."

"You're a real piece of work, Amos." I stop Mack, putting a hand on his chest before he reaches Amos. He'd been losing his cool more frequently than usual. I had guessed that it was because of the Elijah situation. I think he hoped Emberli staying in town would give him more information and he was just realizing that I was right about the whole thing.

It hurts to be right all the time.

"Maybe we should all calm down?" Flint suggests, his eyes flickering between our brother and Amos. "There's no need for hostility."

"Your brother is right, Mack. Look, let's all just go home. There's no point scaring the public over a lie."

Willow straightens at this. "I'm not lying."

The crowd murmurs at her response and she frowns, looking at me for help. "Explain all of the things that got broken. You really think I can pull a TV out of the wall? Really?" She raises an eyebrow. "And the indent of a literal size grizzly bear!"

"Maybe your friend here thought it would be funny to run through the wall." I'd hoped he wasn't saying what I thought he was, until his head nodded directly at Emberli.

What a fucking asshole.

I waste no time in delivering a satisfying punch to Amos' nose, hearing it crack beneath my fist as he goes flying back onto the pavement and knocks himself unconscious.

***

"You could not have picked a worse time to punch that guy in the face" Mack tells me as we leave the station. "I mean there were fucking groups of cops, man. Dumbass."

I never thought I'd see the day that Mack lectured me. Usually it was the other way around.

But this time he was right.

It was stupid of me to rush to Emberli's aid, but I couldn't help it, nor could I do anything to stop it. It was becoming a habit as of late, and I didn't know if I liked it or not.

Mack sighs. "Regardless, I got a call saying they found the bear. Or more, the bear found them. Rocked up to claim its room back. Emberli said she's been hearing the noises since her first night here."

That long? I try not to think about the long list of possibilities that could have happened during Emberli's stay at the motel but it's near enough impossible.

No matter what I do, I can't seem to get Emberli out of my head.

"Where is she now?"

"Staying in a different room."

"You let her go back?"

"Where else was I supposed to send her, Thayne?"

"Not fucking there. Did you see the state of that place?"

Mack smiles, and it's the kind of smile that's teasing and highly irritating.

"What?"

"Didn't realize you care so much about our new arrival, big brother."

"I don't." It's a lie. I realize it as soon as the defensive tone leaves my mouth, but this only makes Mack smile wider.

"I knew it."

"You don't know shit. We may not get along but that doesn't mean I don't care about her wellbeing."

"Are you trying to convince yourself or me?"

"Fuck you," is all I can muster and his laughter circles the truck as he drives me back to the bar, where I take my own truck home and hope to get a better amount of sleep than last night.

10
Emberli

"I need you to talk to me about these things. If I've upset you, I want to know."

"You haven't."

"Then why are you acting as if I have?"

The silence was the worst part. It held me captive as I begged for Elijah to respond, to give me anything.

"Elijah, please."

"Nothing is wrong, but you keep pestering me and it's making something wrong."

"But you're treating me like something is." I feel as if I'm going crazy. As if my mind is playing tricks on me and perhaps I am the problem here. That Elijah is right.

"How am I treating you, Emberli?"

"Like you're angry at me."

"Well now you're just being stupid." He scoffs.

My heart is pulled from my chest as I try to reason with him, but as always, it's hopeless. I can never reason with him.

"This is how I feel, Elijah." Pleading, I take his hand in mine *but he yanks it away.*

"Then let me ask you something, if I'm so bad. Why are you still here?"

"Because I want us to work!"

"I'm not going to sit here whilst you yell at me. I'm not talking about this now."

I'm having one of those more frequent moments where I can't stop writing down possible lyrics in my notebook and it's gotten to the point where I'm soon going to need a new one, which excites me beyond words because buying new stationery has to be one of my favourite things to do.

My inspiration for the sudden bundle of ideas? Thayne.

My heart feels tender as it skips a beat, remembering Thayne's entire body as it went rigid before he swung for the guy who sought to offend me.

He defended me.

I push the resurfacing thought to the back of my head as I try to focus, but it's deemed harder than I thought it would be.

Despite my loathing for the man, it's also clear he's become my muse, and a damn good one at that.

My phone buzzes with a message from my mom and I'm swarmed with regret for not messaging her sooner. I checked in a few days ago but left out the part where Elijah had left me and I've temporarily moved to his hometown. I didn't want her to worry, and knowing my mom, she always did. I wanted to make sure that I at least had a plan that I could tell her so she wouldn't freak out so much.

I hover over the send button before pressing it.

ME: Can you call?

It's a matter of seconds before her name flashes on my screen.

"Is everything okay honey?"

"Hey mom, Everything's fine. How's everyone back home?"

"We're all good."

I'd sent messages to my younger sister to check in, but the distance between us felt emotional just as much as it was physical. And I took full blame for it because I was the one who moved.

No one ever talks about how hard it is to be the eldest sister. Whilst I'm trying to hold together the entire family, I'm also trying to hold together myself.

"I need to talk to you about something, mom. Do you have time?"

"Yeah. Of course. What's up?"

I take a breath before telling her everything, not missing out a single detail from the past few weeks.

In truth, my best friend was my mom. But it hadn't always been that way, we'd argue a lot when I was growing up.

I thought, like any teenager, that I knew better and if I could go back knowing what I know now, I would have never treated her the way I did.

She wasn't just an older sister herself or a mom, she was also her own person and yet took on the responsibility of so much more.

"Honey… I wish you told me sooner."

"I didn't want to worry you, mom and I knew you'd tell me to come back."

We both laugh at this. "Of course I would."

"And how many times have I come back?"

"A lot."

"Exactly. I need to do this for myself."

Hesitance fills the silent line between us. "Are you sure that you're okay there?"

"More than okay, mom. I've met some really cool people and I've got myself a job. To be honest, I was staying here in case Elijah had come back, to hold him responsible. But I was just scared. I don't need him."

I don't need him.

Wow.

A huge weight feels like it's been lifted from my shoulders, like the chains around me have rusted too much and now they've broken off.

I don't need Elijah. As a matter of fact, I never did.

"I'm proud of you." I don't think my mom knows just how much I appreciate those few words, how they make me feel like I'm doing the right thing.

I wasn't used to doing things on my own and this temporary move to Shadow Peaks was completely out of the ballpark. It couldn't have been more far from my comfort zone, yet I felt at peace here. I felt like I could stay.

"But if you need any help, honey. Please let us know. Coming back isn't failing."

But how do I tell her that it felt exactly that?

"Thanks mom. I better go to sleep. It's been a long night." I failed to tell her that my previous neighbor had in fact been a grizzly bear and had smashed its way through the wall between us. Because she'd definitely worry and that was one thing I did not want her to do.

She had enough to worry about.

I wake up the next morning to the loud sound of knocking on my door and when I peek out the curtains. It's the last person I expect to be standing there with a bouquet of flowers in his hand.

It's Thayne.

There's no way I can answer the door to him looking like I've just been dragged through a hedge backwards.

I contemplate just pretending I'm in the deepest sleep of my life or just pretending not to be in, but those plans both fail the minute his eyes lock with mine through the window.

Great.

I quickly shut the curtains and pace around the room in an attempt to find a different shirt to the coffee stained one I've definitely overworn. I give it a sniff and almost gag at the smell, pulling it over my head.

There's another knock at the door.

"Be right there!" I call and make a quick change into some shorts and a plain black shirt, catching a glance at myself in the mirror.

"Oh God." I groan before putting my hand to my mouth and do a smell test on my breath.

Absolutely not.

Thayne is going to have to wait.

"Just coming!" I lie, dodging into the bathroom to brush my hair and teeth, ignoring the harder knocks that take place on my door.

"Fucking hell, Emberli. How long does it take to get to the damn door?"

"Com-OW! FUCK!" I groan, holding my big toe that throbs from the whack it's just taken on the side of the bathroom door frame.

"What happened? Are you okay?" The doorknob rattles just as I get to it, swinging the door open. Thayne glances at me, giving me a quick once-over.

"What happened?"

"I stubbed my toe trying to get to the door." I explain, the pain in my big toe begins to subside and Thayne glances to my feet.

"Can you not stare at my feet?" I ask. "It's weirding me out."

"Sorry." he grumbles.

"What are you doing here anyway?"

"Can I come in?"

I move out of the way to allow him in, noticing how his well-built frame fills the door, and how he's too tall for it. He dips his head before his eyes lock with mine again. It's a glance that stops my heart from its regular pace, setting it on an uneven track as he clicks his tongue. "I brought you these." He holds out the bouquet of tulips. "They're blue."

"I see that. Thank you. What's the occasion?"

"I owe you an apology for the day at Lacey's."

"Lacey's?"

"The store next to the library."

Oh. That day.

"I told you, I wasn't crying because of you."

Okay. Maybe a small part of me was crying because of him. The hormones continue to wreak havoc around my body but I was also tired and not in the mood for Thayne's judgement which he continues to share where it isn't needed.

But this gesture? Turning up at my motel room with an apology was heartwarming.

Funnily enough I never got an apology without asking for it with Elijah. I guess that's the difference between a man and a gentleman.

God. I'm never going to tell Thayne I just considered him a gentleman because he'd never let me live it down.

"Since you've come here I've tried figuring you out, and one thing I have realized is that you're not a liar, Emberli."

I take the flowers from his hand. "Thank you. They're perfect."

"Yeah well, I was an asshole. I figured you deserved them."

My eyes meet his once again and they linger for a few more seconds than usual, desperation sinks its teeth into me as I wonder what he's thinking.

I can never tell what he's thinking. And I don't know when I began to care about what he thought either.

Thayne was remarkably good at frustrating me, I'm pretty sure that he even took pride in doing so. It was a dynamic between us that I'd grown to accept after realizing his views on me wouldn't change, and yet seeing him standing here in front of me. I can't help but feel like those views of me have faltered the same way mine have for him.

"How did you know what room I was in?" Thayne had been escorted off the premises last night in handcuffs, so there was no way that he would have known what room I'd been transferred into.

"I bribed Rebecca at the front desk."

"Oh great." I say sarcastically. "The level of confidentiality this place has is concerning."

"It's a small town. What do you expect?" He takes it upon himself to examine the room, his attention fixating on my notebook until I slam it shut, peering up at him.

"Nosy much?"

His lips twitch in amusement. "I never said I was done figuring you out yet, trouble."

"What's with the nickname?"

"You're trouble."

I shake my head. "Yeah well, you're annoying but you don't see me going around and calling you…"

I stop when Thayne raises his eyebrow.

"Okay. My point doesn't stand." Grabbing my notebook, I shove it in my luggage. "But I'm not trouble nor am I here for any, despite what you may think of me, Thayne… I'm here for peace."

Thayne strides towards me, feet heavy yet somewhat slow as his boots collide with the floor. Every step he makes takes us both into unfamiliar territory until he stands towering over me, closer than ever before. I hold my breath, as if I'm scared to miss what he has to say over the rapid thumping sound of my heart in my chest.

Can he hear it? Surely he can.

I'm almost angry at my body for betraying me. We were meant to be collectively against Thayne and at this point, I feel the complete opposite.

"Thing is, I think I'm starting to believe you." He moves, glancing around the bathroom before turning back to me with an unimpressed look on his face.

"There's no way you're staying here."

"What?"

"You're not staying here. Over my fucking dead body are you staying here."

I'm that imprisoned by shock that I can't move, I only watch as he begins to throw my clothes and various possessions into my bag.

"What are you doing?"

"This place has to violate numerous health codes and I've been restraining myself as much as I can but I can't let you stay here. Aca's leaving next week. You can stay with me until he does."

If that wasn't a recipe for disaster, it was certainly one for murder. Up until yesterday, Thayne and I could barely be within the presence of one another for more than an hour. An hour and living together were two very different things despite my newfound tolerance for him. What he was proposing we do, was the literal definition of playing with fire, just adding smaller pieces of wood.

"What? Do you hear yourself?"

"Look, I'm your last resort. So just take the help, okay?"

I shut up, but not because I'm letting him win, but because I have no clue what to say to the man that I thought I'd already made up my mind about.

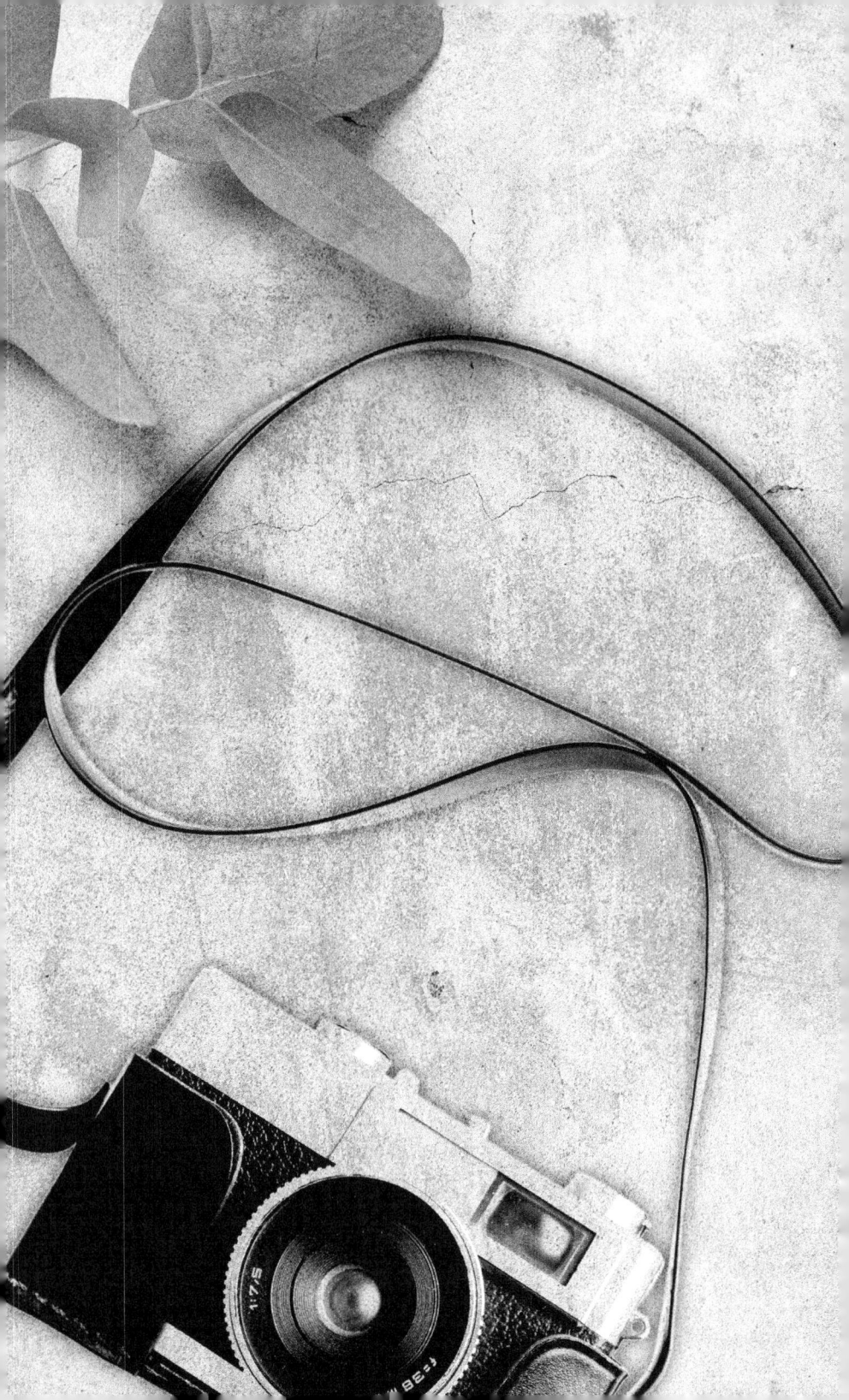

11
Thayne

MACK: Found the bear. Just wanted to let everyone know.

WILLOW: Yay!

COLTON: I found him too. So weird to see him working for once.

LYNNIE: Perhaps a certain singer is the cause of his newly found motivation to work?

ME: Fuck you all.

"So what? You just casually invited her to stay at your place?" Odessa looks at me with a hand on her hip, her eyebrow raised and the classic look of disbelief before she shakes her head.

It's clear that she's been hanging around with my sister and Lynnie too much and, as happy as I am that she's settled here with some good friends, she now fills half of her shifts interrogating me about Emberli, who stands on the makeshift stage smiling as the crowd cheers for her as she ends her set for the night.

Not only has she got a great voice, but her emerald green orbs are enough to draw in any man, myself included. Her hair was slicked back into a ponytail tonight, but her chestnut curls stayed bouncing behind her with hints of a caramel color flooding through the strands.

She wore a flowery light blue sundress that had daisies decorated around the bottom of it.

This woman really loved her sundresses.

"Yes. I just invited her to stay with me. Have you seen Mack?" My attempt to change the subject doesn't go unnoticed by Odessa, who shoots Billy a look that only the pair of them are in on.

She shrugs. "Why are you asking me? I don't know."

"Because wherever you are, Mack's usually two steps behind you." Odessa rolls her eyes at this. But she knows I'm right, because despite his rough and tough appearance, Mack tends to follow my most trusted employee around like a lost puppy and has done ever since she stepped into town. And the amount of dates she's declined didn't push my brother back, it only inspired him more.

He wasn't one to give up, it's why he was so good at his job.

"Stop changing the subject." she snaps.

"You first."

Her eyes narrow at me. "I'm just curious what's going on here."

"There is nothing going on here. She's staying with me until Aca moves out. I've already asked him if it's okay."

Her suggestive eyebrow raise indicates she doesn't believe me. "Thayne, you literally punched a guy for her."

"How many times have I punched a guy for you?" Countless.

I hated disrespectful men. My dad wasn't the best example, but when mom was alive, he worshipped the ground she walked on.

96

And I was lucky to be raised by Doug, whose intentions were the same and made sure to teach my brothers and me the importance of women. It's why I hated seeing women being belittled by my own gender. Most men of Shadow Peaks were big on respecting those who birthed us and raised us but we did have the odd few that didn't align to the same morals.

"Not the point. Besides, you've been giving evils to every man who's looked her way tonight. Right, Billy?"

Billy nods at this. Of course he fucking does.

That man agrees with everything Odessa says, not only because she gives him alcohol, but he often says how Odessa is like the daughter he never had. I'm sure if she murdered someone, he'd cover it up or blame himself.

"Don't bring Billy into this. Besides, he'll always defend you because you're his favourite."

Odessa scoffs but Billy shrugs. "It's true."

"Not fair Billy. I've known you a lot longer." I say.

Billy laughs at this. "Yeah well, this one is more likeable than you are."

"I can be likeable." I argue.

"Tell that to Emberli." Odessa smirks at me. "Besides, Billy is a witness to my case."

"By all means, present your case."

"I think you like her." She nods her head over at Emberli, who packs up her borrowed guitar from Colton, still chatting away to the locals that have grown to love her.

It's no secret that she's a favorite. I hear the talk around the town, which is why it makes it so much harder to keep my distance.

"Your case is invalid." I finally speak.

"Hell, if I was new in town, I'd assume you two were siblings with the way you bicker." Billy shakes his head, taking another swig of his beer. "If you two are done. Can I have another?"

"That's your limit, Billy." Odessa tells him, discarding the empty bottles on the bar into the bin.

"Oh come on. One more?"

"No. No more." Billy doesn't ask again. Deep down he knows that she's doing it to help him and when she places down a cup of hot chocolate in front of him, he smiles at her.

Lord knows my dad wouldn't have had that reaction. Hell, I tried multiple times to cut him off from drinking or replaced it with water or lemonade.

Whatever I could find really. It never worked.

I often wondered why my dad wasn't more like Billy as an alcoholic.

I wondered how much different our life could have been if he chose his family over alcohol. I wondered if he'd still be here.

Would he be proud of me?

Sounds stupid, wanting the reassurance of someone who fucked you up so bad. But I can't help it.

It's as if he's constantly looking over me, waiting for me to mess up, almost like he's waiting for me to turn into him. It was my biggest fear. But despite sharing the same blood as him and the same family name, I sure as hell would never be anything like him.

"Look, you don't have to try to convince me. If you say you don't like her like that, I believe you." Odessa shrugs.

"I have a duty of care to my employees."

She turns to me before pointing to the top shelf. "If you cared so much about your employees, you wouldn't put the pint glasses on the highest goddamn shelf."

I grab her a glass, holding it out to her. "You know I'd fire you if you weren't the most reliable member of staff I had here."

"I'm the only member of staff you have here, Thayne."

I try to make myself look busy as Emberli arrives at the bar and pour a few customers their drinks, trying to listen in on her and Odessa's conversation.

"You okay? You look pale."

I can't help but glance at Emberli. Odessa is right, she does look pale. Maybe she was sick.

98

It wouldn't surprise me if it had something to do with that motel room she was staying in.

I should have helped her sooner.

"I'm fine." Emberli shakes her head. "I don't know if you're busy on Wednesday but... I was wondering if you'd come with me tomorrow morning. I booked a check-up and I... I really don't want to go alone."

Odessa's hand reaches over to Emberli's, squeezing it soothingly. "Of course I'll come."

12

Emberli

"I'm not ready to be a dad, Emberli." Elijah's hand covers his mouth as we both stare at the positive pregnancy test.

"I know. I'm not exactly ready to be a mom either." I rest my hand over his moments before he pulls it away, running it through his hair.

"Why do you have to do that?"

I pale. "Do what?"

"Make this all about you. It's always about how you feel."

"Where is this coming from?" I ask. "I'm sorry."

"Sorry isn't good enough. Everytime I tell you how I feel, you make it about you." He snaps, eyes narrowing at me. The eyes that once looked at me with love and now seem only to be replaced with annoyance.

"I didn't mean to, Lij."

"I don't want to do this right now. I don't want to talk to you about this."

"Except you never do." He turns to me, shocked.

"Because this is how you act. You make it all about you."

"I said I was sorry, Elijah."

"And I said I'm not talking about this."

"Everything looks good." Stacey, my newly appointed midwife nods as she wheels herself away from the sonogram machine. "Have you got any concerns that you wanted to discuss? I noticed you haven't had a check-up appointment in a few months."

"I've been travelling around a lot." I'm sure it makes me sound like a terrible mom-to-be and judging by the short gaze Stacey holds before she taps at something on her computer, she definitely agrees.

"Okay, well it would be good for you to come back every month until you're at 28 weeks, then we can assess you every two weeks. How does that sound?"

Staying here throughout my pregnancy sounds as inescapable as it seems, but I nod regardless, because my midwife is scarily intimidating and I can't say no.

"Okay, sure."

"Great. I'll book you in for next month. Is the twenty-eighth okay with you?"

It sounds permanent. Terrifyingly so.

Maybe I should just go back home. No matter how disappointing, I could always make my family proud some other way. Maybe I should just accept defeat.

"Em? You okay?" Odessa asks from beside me and I nod.

"Yeah. That seems fine." I say.

"Great." Stacey taps away at her computer and Odessa glances at me.

"You sure you're okay?"

"Yeah. It's just starting to feel a lot more real now." I feel pressured, like I'm losing time and there's nothing I can do to get it back.

My shoulders weigh heavy with the reminder that I have to figure my shit out before I bring this baby into the world, because it's my mess, *not theirs.*

"It's normal to feel pressure." Stacey speaks behind her desk, like she's heard this a dozen times. Only her reassurance is said in a dull tone, like she's bored. And suddenly I couldn't feel any more like an inconvenience than I do right now. "But you're very supported. I hear Thayne is helping you out by giving you a few shifts at the bar. You should feel relieved."

"I do."

"I'd be grateful if I were you. There are a lot of mothers that are worse off."

"Correct me if I'm wrong, but I thought you were supposed to give clinical advice, not personal." Stacey's eyes dart to Odessa, who stands with her arms over her chest. "I guess I could always ask your superior, couldn't I?"

"There's no need for that. Do you have any other questions, Emberli?"

So, so many.

How do I be a mom?

How do I wake up when they cry at night?

How do I bathe them?

How do I know what they want?

How do I do all of that, alone?

"Emberli, are you sure you're okay?"

My throat tightens as I speak. "Yeah, I'm okay. No questions." I'm worried that Stacey will perceive them as stupid and deem me an unfit mom. And worst of all, I'm scared that she might be right.

"Did you want to know the gender, Emberli?" Stacey asks.

"What? Oh. Yeah, sure."

"Wait! We could throw you a baby shower." Odessa smiles excitedly. "We could do the gender reveal then. Everyone will be so excited to know what you're having, Em."

I nod, gulping down the persistent lump in my throat that keeps appearing.

I feel like I want to be sick, and it's not the morning sickness I'm so used to.

"Okay. Yeah, let's do that."

"I'm sorry about Stacey. She's just nosy like the rest of the town." Odessa tells me as she takes her eyes off of the road.

"It's fine. I'm used to others' opinions."

"It doesn't mean that they're acceptable. How you feel is how you feel and nobody should tell you otherwise. You know what I'm fucking tired of?"

"Mack?"

She bursts out laughing at this. "Close. But no."

It was no secret that Odessa and Mack seemed to annoy each other to higher extents than Thayne and me. I'd discovered their rivalry was in fact filled with chemistry neither of them wanted to admit.

"I'm tired of people thinking that they have a say in our lives and what we do and what we should feel." She looks at me. "Aren't you?"

I nod because I know exactly how she feels.

I felt Odessa understood me as much as I understood her, which is why we instantly clicked when I first came into town. She made me feel not so different, and even when I claimed to her that I was, she said being different was a good thing. Odessa was one of those who obviously had her own troubles, yet thrived off helping others, whether that was just to distract her from her own thoughts, or to change mine on my outlook of myself.

"I am." I sigh.

"We really shouldn't care as much as we do." She chuckles.

"Thank you. And thank you for coming along today."

"I'm here for you, Em. I hope you know that. If you need anything or need me to come with you to more appointments, I'll come." She says softly.

"I really appreciate it. I don't know how I could ever repay the help

I've received."

"I know exactly how you feel. But the townsfolk? They don't help you in order to get something back. They help you because each and every member of this town has been through something that they didn't think they could get through. They all help others for nothing in return".

"Then why do I feel so guilty?" I chuckle.

"Because you're a good person who doesn't think that they deserve it." Odessa couldn't have been more inside my brain. She looks over at me again.

"You do deserve this, Emberli. And if you decide to stay or you decide to leave, I hope you do know that you're worth so much more than what happened to you."

"I just feel... empty and ungrateful. I've got this life when there are women out there who can't have that."

"Stop comparing yourself to others," she tells me. "This is *your* life. You don't have to feel guilty for feeling how you feel about it." I try to listen to what she says, but it's hard when I've convinced myself I'm the most disappointing daughter, sister and soon to be mom on earth.

I'd always managed to bring myself down, counting achievements as pure luck, and something that could possibly disappear whenever. I think that's why I had such a huge fear of time. I wanted to be someone. Not just someone's daughter or mom, I wanted to be me. And I didn't know who that was anymore. "You're worth a lot more than you give yourself credit for."

A familiar beat plays on the radio, one that I can't quite put my finger on until the guitar comes in and the vocals of a woman. She's singing *my* song.

How is she singing my song? The song that's tucked away in my notebook - *Oh my God.*

"Are you okay? You look like you've seen a ghost."

"This is my song." My voice cracks and my throat tightens until I have to open my mouth for air. "This is my song."

"It's not here. Why is it not here?" I throw my notebook to the side as I rummage through my overnight bag.

It has to be here. It's two A4 pieces of paper and it's not here.

"Why is it not here?" My hands dig through my bag.

I can't believe that asshole stole my music.

I can't believe him.

"If it was on Starville County radio, then he's still somewhere in the county." Odessa speaks.

"And do you know just how big this county is? He could be anywhere." Thayne replies and I feel his gaze lingering on me.

"Then we call all the radio stations in the county and ask if they have a number we can contact. Mack can track the number from there and get a rough location."

I remember spending hours writing the lyrics I heard on the radio today, for him, for our band. I remember it because I knew how hard he'd been on me to come up with something. I'd been under so much pressure that when I finally produced something that wasn't three lines, I felt relief, a huge weight lift off my shoulders.

I don't think I'd ever seen Elijah as happy as I made him that day, which was something that I held onto even as he was pushing me away from him.

I held onto the small, happy moments in the hope that they'd bundle together to defeat the recurring moments that weren't so great.

A phone rings but I continue my search, digging through the smaller compartments as my heart continues to ache.

It was precious and it was mine and Elijah took that from me.

"It's Mack. I've got to take this."

I glance up at Thayne, who looks deep in thought as he stares at me. "Can you help, please?"

"Emberli..."

"It has to be here."

"Emberli..."

"I know it's here."

"Emberli…"

"What, Thayne? What!?" I snap, my chest heaving as I dig further through my bag until two rough hands lock around my wrists, restricting them.

"What are you doing?"

"You need to breathe." Thayne grumbles. His hard yet concerned stare slices through me.

"What I need is to find these lyrics."

"They're not here. You know that."

He's right. I do know that they're not here, Elijah has them.

I sink back against the wall when Thayne lets go of my hands, and I cover my face with them.

This cannot be happening.

I push my ego aside and let myself go for a second, not caring that this is, in fact, the second time I've cried in front of Thayne.

Only this time, I don't try to hide it, and say goodbye to any remaining dignity I have left, sobbing into the palm of my hands.

"Hey, hey, hey." I feel the warmth of Thayne's hands again as they place themselves on my knees.

"There's something wrong with me." I tell him.

"Emberli, look at me."

"Not right now." I mumble. "Let me cry for five minutes and then I will."

I hear him chuckle. "Emberli, please look at me."

I sigh, removing my hands from my face just as Thayne reaches for my eyes, wiping them gently with his thumbs. "There is nothing wrong with you."

"There is. I know there is. I'm not… normal."

"Who is?"

"Normal people. Like you."

He laughs at this. "Emberli. I'm not normal either... and that's okay."

It's silent for a few seconds before he speaks again. "You know, you're a pretty crier."

I snort. "You're just saying that to cheer me up."

I hadn't seen much of this side of Thayne, it was unfamiliar to me. He was crouched in front of me, wiping away at my tears when usually he couldn't stand to be within three meters of me, and I, him. The prominent scent of his cologne told me both of us were way too close for comfort. But it was... nice. Different.

"No. I just don't like seeing you upset."

Knowing where I stand with Thayne was the only thing I thought I knew for certain, but now I wasn't so sure. It was as if we'd somehow crossed the line both of us were so clear on establishing.

"Don't waste your tears on someone like him."

"He always wins, Thayne." I bite the inside of my lip as I try to pull myself together. "I mean he's living his life like everything is fine. He gets to have that." I sob.

To say I was having a bad day today was the understatement of the year. "It's unfair."

I'm a blubbering mess at this point, wiping away at the mascara I'd applied earlier this morning in an attempt to make myself feel better.

It didn't work, I still felt like crap.

"I'm not saying I'm not excited for this baby because I am. I'm just scared. There's so much I haven't done, so much of my life I put on hold for Elijah and - and now I've got nothing to show for it whilst he gets off scot-free like his child isn't about to be raised single-handedly. I don't understand. I don't understand why this is happening to me. Do I even care about the music? I don't even know if I want to do that as a career. I love it but... Oh God."

"Emberli, listen to me. You don't have to figure anything out right now. You're not going to be raising this baby alone." Easy for Thayne to say. He and his family had no obligation to help me with my unborn child, and it terrified me knowing that they could just decide one day that they didn't want anything to do with them, with us.

If it wasn't clear enough, my issues with trust had overpowered my ability to think straight. For that, I thank Elijah.

"If you do decide to stay here, I'll help you."

"Help me?" I snort. "Thayne you don't even like me."

Thayne's narrowed stare held my own, it was something he'd been doing more frequently as of late. Usually, our stare count was two seconds max. But lately, Thayne has been doubling that.

We were at four seconds of intense staring before he turned, sinking against the wall next to me with his arms resting on his knees as he mirrored my position.

"What are you doing?" I ask.

"Sitting with you. I thought that was obvious."

"But why?"

"Well, I don't know if you're aware, but there is this woman who is sitting in my cabin having a breakdown."

I shove at his shoulder, which I realize at that moment is severely muscled and hard.

God fucking damn.

"Do I have to remind you of the repulsive looks you used to give me before this moment whenever I spoke?"

"Yeah well, maybe you're not too bad." He grunts. "Hold on. Is the Thayne Rawlins admitting he was wrong about me?"

"Don't get ahead of yourself, trouble." His shoulder bumps with my own and I laugh, instantly feeling better than I did a few minutes ago. "I just don't like hearing you so defeated. I'm used to seeing the tough girl act."

"She's in here somewhere." I sigh. "I'm just being dramatic right now."

"Can you give me a warning before she returns? Don't tell her, but she kind of scares me." He whispers and the corners of my mouth betray me as they rise once again into a smile.

"Why are you doing this? Be honest."

He sighs and silence consumes us for a few seconds before he speaks. "I meant what I said. Don't waste your tears on someone like him."

"I worked so hard on that song, Thayne." Of course my voice decides to crack at this point and I suddenly feel like I'm oversharing. "I'm sorry."

"Can you do me a favour?"

"What is it?"

"Don't ever apologize for crying."

My lips are parted and I'm about to speak when Odessa walks back in.

"Okay…" She stops in her tracks like there's a layer of glass in front of her, and she spins on her heels before leaving, entering a few seconds later.

"What was that?" Thayne asks.

"Sorry. I thought I stumbled into an alternate reality where you two actually got along."

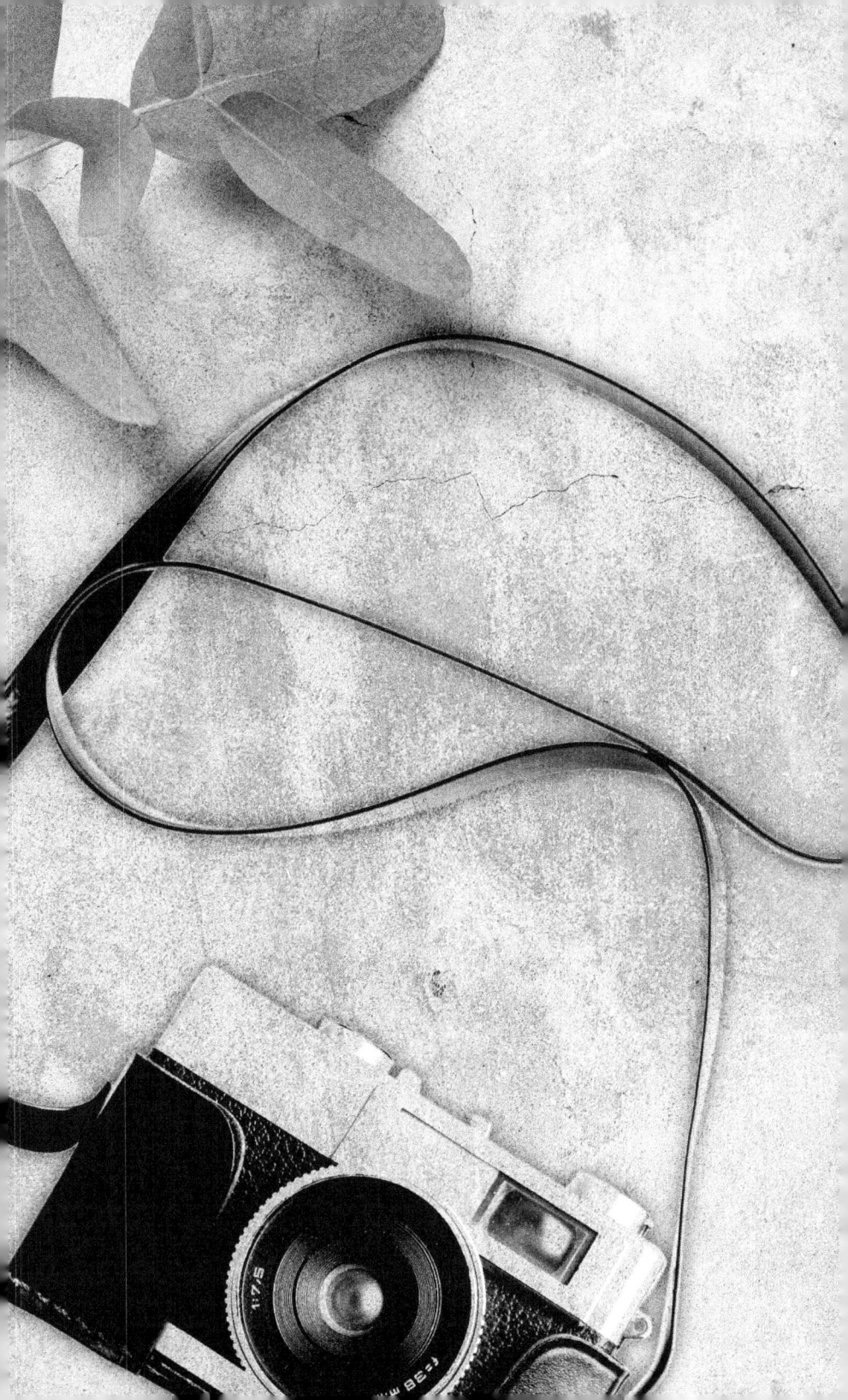

13

Thayne

"I haven't seen you with a piece of paper and a pen since high school." Sally laughs as she places down a hot plate of bacon and eggs in front of me.

I'd come over to the main house to give Emberli some breathing space. I demanded that if anyone had any news about Elijah or his whereabouts, they consult me first before talking to Emberli, who I heard up in the early hours of this morning. When I came downstairs, she'd fallen asleep on the couch with her face under that notebook of hers that she always carried around.

"That's partly why I came over, I didn't have any at my place and besides, it's not for me."

Sally takes a seat in front of me, a serious expression on her face. "Who is it for?"

"Emberli."

"The singer you hired? Aca told me you two didn't get along."

"We don't. But it's best I keep her close to monitor what she's doing." The lie rolls off of my tongue before I can take it back and Sally gives me her famous look of disappointment.

She was always great at keeping my siblings and me in line, even at school, and if any of us messed up, we'd be greeted by the exact look she was giving me now.

Despite her pushiness, I was grateful to have someone like her. She was a mother figure to us all after losing our own and that meant being hard on us at the times we needed it. I don't think I could ever thank her enough.

"I know you don't mean that."

Did I mention this woman sees straight through me?

For some unknown reason, Sally has always held me to a higher standard than what I'm worth and I never understood why.

"Fine. I'm trying to do my part around here. Everyone else is." I grumble, stabbing through the yolk of the egg in front of me.

I didn't tell her that my perspective of Emberli had suddenly shifted, that maybe she isn't as stuck-up as I'd originally thought, that maybe I was wrong. "Don't smile like that."

I've seen this smile one too many times from all the women in my life when I so much as mention the name of another female, because God forbid a man speaks a few words to the opposite sex.

Despite me telling her on numerous occasions that I didn't need a life partner to determine my happiness in life, Sally was always hopeful that I'd find someone.

"Like what?"

"Like that."

"Okay." She breathes out a long sigh, calming herself down from the over-excitement that's written all over her face. "May I ask why you're doing this?" She gestures to the paper in front of me.

"Because I want her to write a list."

"And she didn't have any paper herself?"

As I said, she sees straight through me.

I glance up at the woman who knows me all too well as she sips from her mug.

"Fine. Maybe I do need a bit of advice."

She grins and rests her chin in the palm of her hand.

"She mentioned to me yesterday that she was worried about what it meant for her when the baby arrived, that she had nothing to show for her life prior."

"It makes sense she feels that way." Sally nods. "It's a huge responsibility for a partnership, let alone doing it all on your own like Emberli is doing. Especially whilst healing from Elijah leaving her on her own like that, and let's face it, we know Elijah. So does Emberli. We don't know what she's been through."

I take all of Sally's words in, suddenly feeling guilty for the hard times I've given Emberli. She was only healing, just as I am.

"Should I ask her?"

"You can try. She might not want to talk about it just as you don't."

"So what else can I do?" I ask.

"You can only be there for her, Thayne. Like you already are." She sighs. "I couldn't imagine raising you guys without Doug."

"I don't want to overstep but I thought I'd get her to write a list of all things she hasn't done yet but wanted to do before the baby arrives. I'd help her complete them."

I suddenly regret telling Sally any of this and look for possible escape routes as my flight or fight kicks in.

Flight. Flight. Fucking Flight.

"Don't look at me like that," I groan.

"I can't speak for Emberli, but I think that's really sweet of you to do."

"Okay." I nod slowly, hoping Emberli would feel the same way.

"Can you just make sure that you're also looking after yourself as well, please?"

"I'm fine, Sally. Always have been."

"You may be fooling everyone else, but you're not fooling me, kid." Sally's hand reaches for mine as she gives it a reassuring squeeze. And even with my best efforts to disguise the hurt I've faced, Sally knows the truth, as well as her eldest son who plonks himself down next to me and snags a piece of bacon off of my plate.

"What are we talking about?"

Aca glances between Sally and I as he chews loudly and reaches for another piece of bacon.

Sally slaps his hands away. "None of your business. You best have taken your shoes off, boy."

Aca stops chewing and he slides out of his chair, cautiously walking over to the door in the hope that he and his very dirty boots won't be seen. His mom sure could be scary when she wanted to be.

Sally turns back to me as soon as Aca's out of the room. "So what's going on between you and Emberli?"

"Nothing."

"You and your lack of communication is worrying. Can't you give me a little bit of an insight? I heard she's even staying with you now."

"She is."

"Thayne. I need more than one or two word answers."

"She's only staying with me until Aca moves out."

"What?" Aca blurts out as he re-enters.

"We had this conversation, remember?"

Aca blinks and it's clear that he doesn't.

"And have you seen The Hollyhead? Someone ought to check that out. It's got to violate like ten different health codes."

"I heard that you two were talking yesterday, next to each other and everything." Aca grins, feeding his mom's delusions even more.

Fuck me, news travels fast in this goddamn town.

"Look. Emberli isn't who I thought she was. Is that what you want to hear?" Seeing Emberli as vulnerable and unguarded as she was yesterday woke something in me. I wanted to make sure she never felt like that again.

I dig into the breakfast Sally had made for me and ignore the stares from the mother-son duo who, judging by the way they're looking at me, seem to think they know something I don't.

"You have to invite her for breakfast. Please?" Sally asks with a glint of hope in her eyes.

116

I groan, because Sally is one of the few women in my life who I try to steer away from disappointing like I have done in the past.

Call it human growth or just a pushover, but I just couldn't say no to this woman.

"Fine. I'll invite her for breakfast tomorrow but I can't promise she'll come."

That night, I hear the engine of a truck pull away from the drive just as the spare set of keys I gave to Emberli jangle against the front door. I told her to take a few nights off work if she needed it but she claimed she didn't and I knew exactly what she was doing. I knew better than anyone how to distract your mind when everything around you was plummeting into the ground.

She sighs at first, not realizing I'm sitting in the living room. "Oh, hey."

She drops her bag off her shoulder and places the guitar down next to her.

"Mack drop you off?" I made sure he would.

She nods. "Yeah. He did. I didn't think you'd still be up."

It's one in the morning and usually I'm not, especially on my day off. But my mind couldn't shut off tonight, so here I am.

"I couldn't sleep."

"I know the feeling."

Right. She does.

It seemed Emberli and I were more alike than I thought.

"You've been invited to breakfast at the main house tomorrow."

"I have?" She asks, surprised.

"Aca's mom won't give me a break until you come, so please consider it."

Her laugh fills the living room. "Okay. I'll come."

"And after, if you're not doing anything. I was wondering if you wanted to go for a walk."

She points between us. "You and me? Walk? Together?"

I roll my eyes at her dramatics. "I want to talk."

She pauses before nodding and turns, walking into the kitchen before she begins to open numerous cupboards in search of something.

"What are you looking for?"

"Decaf?" Emberli turns to me hopefully and groans in disappointment when I shake my head.

"I've got no decaf. When you're up early every morning like I am, you need the real thing."

Her head thumps against the cupboard in defeat.

"Are you okay?"

She shakes her head and turns to me. "Not really, no."

Did something happen at the bar?

"What's wrong?"

"Just thinking about the whole Elijah thing." She waves me off with her hand before reaching for a glass in the cupboard.

I made a mental note to rearrange the cupboards so that things were more accessible for Emberli, who stood at around 5'6 and was evidently struggling.

Her defeated sigh haunts me and I find myself stepping closer.

"Here. Let me help."

14

Emberli

I turn, just as Thayne's body closes in on my own, and forget how to breathe properly. I press myself up against the counter, clinging on to it for dear life as he corners me.

His cinnamon and leathery scent surrounds me as he closes in, so close I can hear his breathing that turns irregular once he realizes just how intimate we stand. His arm darts past me, reaching above my head, letting me snag a look at his well sculpted biceps before the moment ends and Thayne looks down at me.

I pray he didn't catch me practically objectifying him but God, he's even more attractive up close. Thayne holds the glass in front of me, creating a distance between us that makes me wonder what would happen if I happened to close it again.

"Thanks."

"It's only a glass, trouble."

I quickly dive under his arm that rests on the counter where my hands grip and run the tap.

Thirsty. So fucking thirsty.

"So listen, I was thinking about what you said."

I listen as I gulp down a glass full of water, eagerly filling up the next before I turn, resting against the counter once again, but this time Thayne stays at the opposite end, like it's some line of prevention.

Oh God. He definitely caught me staring.

Great. Now he must think I'm a creep.

"Write a list."

I frown, unaware of what he's talking about.

Did I hear him correctly? "Write a list?"

He nods. "Write a list of things you haven't done yet. Things you want to do before the baby arrives."

My heart slams against its ribcage as the words leave his mouth and I fear, with the hormones skyrocketing around my body right now, I could burst out crying at his thoughtfulness. I try to ignore the voices in my head that ask about a thousand and one questions as to why.

"I want to help you."

I'm met by the more frequent side of Thayne that's been showing recently and I nod slowly.

"Really?"

"Anything. Just write it down and I'll do my best to help you complete it."

"But why? Why help me?"

"Because I was wrong about you, trouble. And I want to spend some time making that up to you. If you'd let me."

It occurred to me that family meals back home were nothing compared to the Rawlins' breakfast table. At home there were five of us, and occasionally we'd have all of us sit down together when we weren't working. Here, every seat at the table was full.

122

The smell of coffee filled my nose and I couldn't wait to get my hands on it. I followed Thayne towards the laughter and chatter that reminded me of my own family.

I missed them.

The older sister's guilt was real, and often kept me up some nights, knowing that my younger sister might be struggling and feeling like she can't speak to anyone about it. And I'm… I'm not there to tell her that everything will be okay and figure itself out. We message now and then, but it's not the same. And Buck, I'm not there to play his games with him nor am I there to hug him, even though he swears he hates it. I realize how much I miss him when I find myself engrossed in Colton and Ryker's video game.

"Damn it! I keep getting killed!" Ryker groans, flinging himself back on the couch.

"That's because you're shit."

"Language!" I hear a woman yell from the kitchen.

"Hey Em, nice to see you." Colton grins over his shoulder. "Wanna play a match?"

I shrug. "Sure."

The both of them shuffle up on the couch and Ryker hands me a controller. "Win this for me, please."

Ryker and I hadn't exchanged many words and I had put it down to him not being much of a talker. Whilst the other guys seemed to not stop, Ryker was a lot more withdrawn.

"I hate to break it to you, but I'm undefeatable." Colton smirks.

"Kick his ass, Em." Lynnie says from behind me.

I have to thank my brother for forcing me to play these games with him religiously, because the shock on Colton's face when I beat him twice in a row is priceless.

"I can't believe you finally got your ass handed to you." Mack laughs.

It appears our match has become center of attention and Colton demands a rematch for the second time.

He remains just as shocked when I beat him a third time and I high five Ryker who I've spoken more to today than I have the past few weeks.

"You're fucking amazing," he states.

"Marry me." Colton rasps from my other side and earns a whack around the head from his sister, who mouths an apology to me.

"Breakfast is ready!"

Everyone seems to swarm to the table, diving into the trays of food before they even sit down.

"You must be Emberli." Standing before me is an older woman with oven gloves covering her hands. She takes them off before opening her arms. "I'm Sally, Aca and Ryker's mom."

"Hi. It's so nice to meet you." I swallow, taking in the sweet scent of what smells like strawberries, as she hugs me.

"You're even prettier than Willow said."

I'm certain by the familiar warm feeling rising to my cheeks, that I'm about as red as a tomato.

Oh. I'd kill for a tomato… or an entire bowl of them. Cravings had only gotten weirder throughout this trimester, I'd found myself dipping celery into a jar of peanut butter just last week, and this week I'd had the undying urge to demolish every salt and vinegar packet of crisps there ever was in a sour cream dip.

"This is Doug, my husband." Sally gestures to the man who nods his head at me with a smile, digging into the pancakes on the table that everyone seems to swarm for.

"Come and sit down, Em." I take a seat beside Willow who grins at me reassuringly.

"Dig in sweetie. These boys are like gnats at a barbecue when it comes to food." Sally says.

"Coffee?" Opposite me, Mack holds up a jug of coffee just as Thayne appears next to him, holding a mug before he reaches over the table and places it down in front of me, along with a jar of sugar and a jug of milk.

"Decaf," is all he says.

I blink and before I can thank him, he turns to Aca and laughs at

124

something he said.

"How far along are you sweetie?" Breaking me from my thoughts is Sally, who leans forward intrigued, her face in the palm of her hand. "Five months."

The reality hits me like a slap in the face, and I gulp down a lump in my throat.

I was five months pregnant.

Five months.

"Do you know what you're having yet?" I shake my head. "Do you have a preference?"

"Honestly I'm freaked out either way." I chuckle. "But, as long as they're healthy."

Willow's hand reaches mine and she squeezes it. "You're going to be an amazing mom."

I'm glad someone thinks so.

Being an amazing mom was all I wanted for this baby.

Fuck Elijah. In fact, fuck all the men who decide they don't want anything to do with the baby, ditching the minute it's a double lined pregnancy test. A part of me wondered what he was doing now, and whose life he was ruining next.

The weirdest part? I felt for him.

He would never truly be happy with himself and that was better than any revenge.

"I hear you're staying with Thayne until Aca leaves." Sally comments as she stands up.

"Where are you going now, mother? Sit down and eat." Ryker scolds and she waves him off, returning a few moments later with another tray of bacon.

"About that, there's a leak in my cabin."

"Why didn't you say something sooner?" Flint turns to Aca.

"Because I wanted to sort it myself." Aca grumbles. "Evidently I couldn't." He turns to me. "I'm sorry, Emberli."

"It's fine. You can stay with me until it's fixed. There's no issue." Thayne says as he battles Mack for the last pancake on the tray.

Once he claims victory, he smacks Mack's cheek with it before biting into it.

"I can get it fixed within a few weeks. I just need to order in some more pipes."

"What about baby names?"

Sally's interest was great, heart-warming almost. But it reminded me just how much that I hadn't planned. I felt like I was doing this entire baby thing wrong. Like I was neglecting my child and I hadn't even held them in my arms yet.

"I haven't…" I gulp down the growing lump in my throat as I shake my head. "I haven't thought of any yet."

God, did that make me sound like a terrible mother? It definitely did.

"There's a lot of time for you to decide sweetie." Sally grins widely.

"Yeah, names like Mack can be for either a boy or a girl. Mackenzie or… Mackenzie."

"She's not going to want to name her baby after you, dumbass." Willow scoffs and looks at me, rolling her eyes. "Here's a tip for you, ignore everything Mack says."

"Oh yeah. You're especially good at that Wills." He shoots back and her head whips over to him, eyes flashing with annoyance.

"What's that supposed to mean?"

"This weekend I literally had to practically drag you home. You wouldn't fucking budge without a burger and fries from Big Al's."

"That's my girl." Doug chuckles, Willow beams at this before she turns to Mack.

I look down, seeing her hand still overlapping mine. I wasn't used to friends, let alone those who showed affection through touch.

It was nice, different. Like she was telling me that she was there for me without actually saying it.

"Blame it on Lynnie. I had to venture out all by myself because she was sick."

Lynnie reels back at this. "Hang on. It's not my fault I was sick."

126

"And you absolutely should not be going out by yourself." Flint pipes up and Willow rolls her eyes.

"Have we forgotten that I am indeed twenty-three years old?"

"We know, Wills. We just want you to be safe." Colton says.

"I'm always safe." Willow counters. "I'm not a little kid anymore."

"No, but you'll always be our little sister." Flint brushes past her, planting a kiss on her head before finding his seat.

"Don't I know it." She grumbles.

"Do you have any siblings, Emberli?" Doug asks.

"Yeah, I have a younger sister and brother. Ebony and Buck."

"Do you argue like this lot?"

"Not much." I chuckle. "But they're a lot younger than me, so."

"That must be hard." Sally sympathises and I nod.

"I miss them a lot."

I may have been born with the urge to travel, but I was also born family-orientated, which is why it was so hard to leave originally.

Two years later and here I was. My battery for travel had run out and I was ready to settle down. I just didn't know where.

I'd always loved home, but I felt like a failure going back there and apart from my family, there was nothing for me there. I had to do what's best for me, what's best for the baby.

"Well, we can be your family whilst you're here. Do you know how long you plan on staying?"

It's as if a horse has just claimed my chest as a seat and I shake my head with the feeling of heaviness.

"I don't know. I never thought I belonged anywhere until I came here."

"Well we love having you here." Lynnie smiles across at me.

"We really do." Willow nods.

The rest of breakfast went smoothly and despite my attempts to help clean up, I was shot down immediately and sent back to Thayne's cabin with an extra plate of eggs that either the baby or me seemed to take an interest in. Sally also disappeared into the garden for ten minutes before returning with a punnet of tomatoes. I'd let slip about tomatoes when she asked me about my cravings. Her questions surrounding my pregnancy made me somewhat more comfortable throughout breakfast, especially when she told me stories of her own.

I didn't know much about Thayne's parents, but from what Willow had told me, the family had grown up with Sally and Doug instead. Sally was clearly a natural at being a mom. I couldn't speak for myself however.

***

"Dancing in the rain?" Thayne's eyebrow raises suggestively as he looks over my list that I created last night.

"I've never done it." I shrug. "I've seen it in movies and I just want to do it. It looks so freeing."

He nods, his eyes scanning over the rest. "Okay. This all seems relatively easy to do. A helicopter ride? Anywhere specific?"

I shake my head. "I just want to ride in a helicopter."

"Swim in a rooftop infinity pool?"

I nod and he glances down once again.

"A rage room?"

I shrug. "I've never done one."

"Okay. Tattoo?" He raises an eyebrow at me.

I shrug. "I haven't got any."

"They're permanent, you know."

"A child is also permanent, although I did read in one of my books that it's advised to not get tattoos when pregnant."

He must hear the worry in my voice because he looks up. "It's your decision, trouble."

I nod. "I want to do it. Does that make me a terrible mom?"

"No. Not at all. We'll take precautions. Willow used to go to school with the woman who runs the tattoo studio in the town, she's professional and great at what she does. We can talk to her about any worries you may have."

I nod and he drops his head, eyes scanning over the sheet of paper before they widen. "Skinny dipping in a lake?"

"Also seems freeing."

"Is that a euphemism?"

I crack a smile and he looks down at the list. "Learn how to salsa and go camping." He murmurs before placing the piece of paper down with a nod. "Okay. It all sounds do-able."

"Really? We don't have to worry about the helicopter ride or infinity pool too much."

"Emberli. Do you want to do it?"

"I mean, yeah. I'd love to."

"Then we're doing it."

15

Emberli

The boardwalk on the nature reserve is filled with numerous people who walk past us with friendly smiles and greetings. Twigs snap beneath my boots and leaves rustle to the side. The occasional group of women pass us and whisper amongst each other when they see Thayne, their excitement drops the minute their eyes switch to me, disgust is a better word for the looks I get after.

"You're pretty popular around here." I state as I sip the coffee that warms up my hands.

The weather had dropped recently as we came out of summer and into a more colder season. The sun still shone and there were often fleeting spells of warmness that took part in keeping me mellow.

I hug my cardigan closer to my chest as Thayne glances down at me, clueless. "What?"

"Do you not see all the women who look at you when you pass them?"

"Not really, no. I'm not interested in them."

Typical man. So unknowing and naive.

"Interesting." It seemed most of the females in this town would jump at the opportunity to date Thayne, but he showed no interest in doing so.

"Are you homosexual?"

Thayne looks at me once again. "No."

"Interesting."

"You've said that twice now."

"Right."

Silence consumes us as we walk in sync, listening to the chirping of the nearby birds and clicking of my boots. I had no clue why Thayne asked me to go on this walk with him this morning because it was as if the man didn't know how to converse properly. Instead, we walked in the quiet.

I understood why Thayne and his family loved it here so much. This town was special. I wasn't sure the reason for Thayne's recent kindness, or for showing me around his family's reserve, but I didn't speak much of it and instead, admired the moments that came.

"What do you think?"

Pulling me from my thoughts, I realize we've stopped at the end of the boardwalk, overlooking the land that Thayne's ranch is on.

It seems as if it's miles away and I didn't realize we had walked so far, but the view is worth every second.

Seeing the dumbfounded look on my face, Thayne's lips curl with humor. "What do you think of the view?"

"It's beautiful." I nod and he agrees, looking out onto the spread out meadows before us. "Why did you bring me here?"

"You've seen Shadow Peaks but you haven't seen the hidden gems of it."

"And this is a hidden gem?"

"Do you see anyone else around?" I take a look around us and see not a body in sight.

Turning back to Thayne, I raise an eyebrow. "Are you going to kill me out here and dump my body?"

He laughs. "Not my style, trouble. I actually brought you here to talk."

"To… talk?" I say slowly.

"That's what I said." He sits on a bench, before gesturing to the seat beside him.

"Christ, Emberli. You look so uncomfortable." He comments as I sit down on the hardened bench. I feel just as uncomfortable as Thayne paints me out to be. My back has suddenly straightened to a firm piece of wood and everytime I move, it's as if I'm Pinocchio.

"Sorry. You don't seem like the type to talk."

He shifts and tilts his head. "Well, you're right. But I figured we'd better start, considering we're living together now."

"Okay. What do you want to talk about?"

The bonus of this is that it could not get any more awkward than it already is. I sit in forced elegance with my legs crossed, which is unbelievably hard to do when pregnant and in a dress, may I add.

"Elijah."

"I don't know where he is."

"Emberli." His hand shoots out to my leg, resting his hand on it as his eyes lock with mine. "That's not what I was going to ask."

He pauses for a moment, neither of us talk about the palm of his hand that rests on my kneecap. "What happened between you two?"

I suck in a breath. The only people who knew mostly everything about Elijah and what he did to me were my mom and Willow. And even then, I didn't tell them everything. Some of what Elijah did would definitely be warranted prison time.

"If you don't want to talk about it, we don't have to."

"It's fine. You should know." I nod. "It wasn't the healthiest of relationships and at the time, I didn't think it was as bad as it was."

"What was he like?"

God. How do I even answer that question?

"He was… nice. Until he wasn't," I say, staring down at my hands. I'd never been one for sharing information, especially the type that had hurt me, but here I was, lowering my walls for a man who I'd only recently started to get along with. "He never hit me. Not, not aggressively. He never hurt me like that," I specify after seeing Thayne's hardened glare of indignation shoot through me. He doesn't say a word, he only listens.

"But it was his words that did and his… I don't know. It sounds stupid but his lack of care, I guess. I think he loved me more as something he could control rather than me as a person. And I was just stupid enough to do anything he said because I was scared to lose him. I prioritised him over everything, myself included. I didn't even know who I was anymore when I woke up and he was gone. That sounds pathetic doesn't it?"

"No." Thayne's voice is so quiet that I almost can't hear him.

"We argued all the time. And most of it was my fault because I'd spring how I felt onto him. It would always end in an argument and I'd always be the one apologizing. He… he would say that nothing was wrong and then treat me like there was. I'd feel as if I was going crazy and I'd become a major bitch. I mean major. I would yell and cry and scream wondering why he wasn't listening to me, but I was just feeding everything he was saying. That was when I knew I didn't love him. I'm not sure I ever did. I think I was more in love with the idea of love and everything Elijah promised me. Everything he never gave me. He simply kept me by stringing me along and promising things that never happened. I was just stupid enough to think he'd change like he promised. The saddest part is, when I woke up and he was gone, I felt relieved. I felt like I could finally breathe."

I don't even realize I'm crying until the tears drop onto my hands below me.

"Oh my God." I mumble, reaching up to wipe my face when Thayne's hand gets there before me. His expression is almost unreadable but his eyes remain soft, unguarded.

"Hey… hey, hey." He pulls me into his arms and holds me there. And for the first time in a long time, I feel safe. "It is not your fault. You hear me?"

I nod and try my best to put aside my pride once I realize how ridiculous I look.

134

"I'm sorry for what he did to you."

"He didn't hit me." I shake my head. "He didn't."

"No. He may have not hit you, trouble. But he did just as much damage."

"Thayne?"

"Yeah?"

"I'm sorry for what he did to you too."

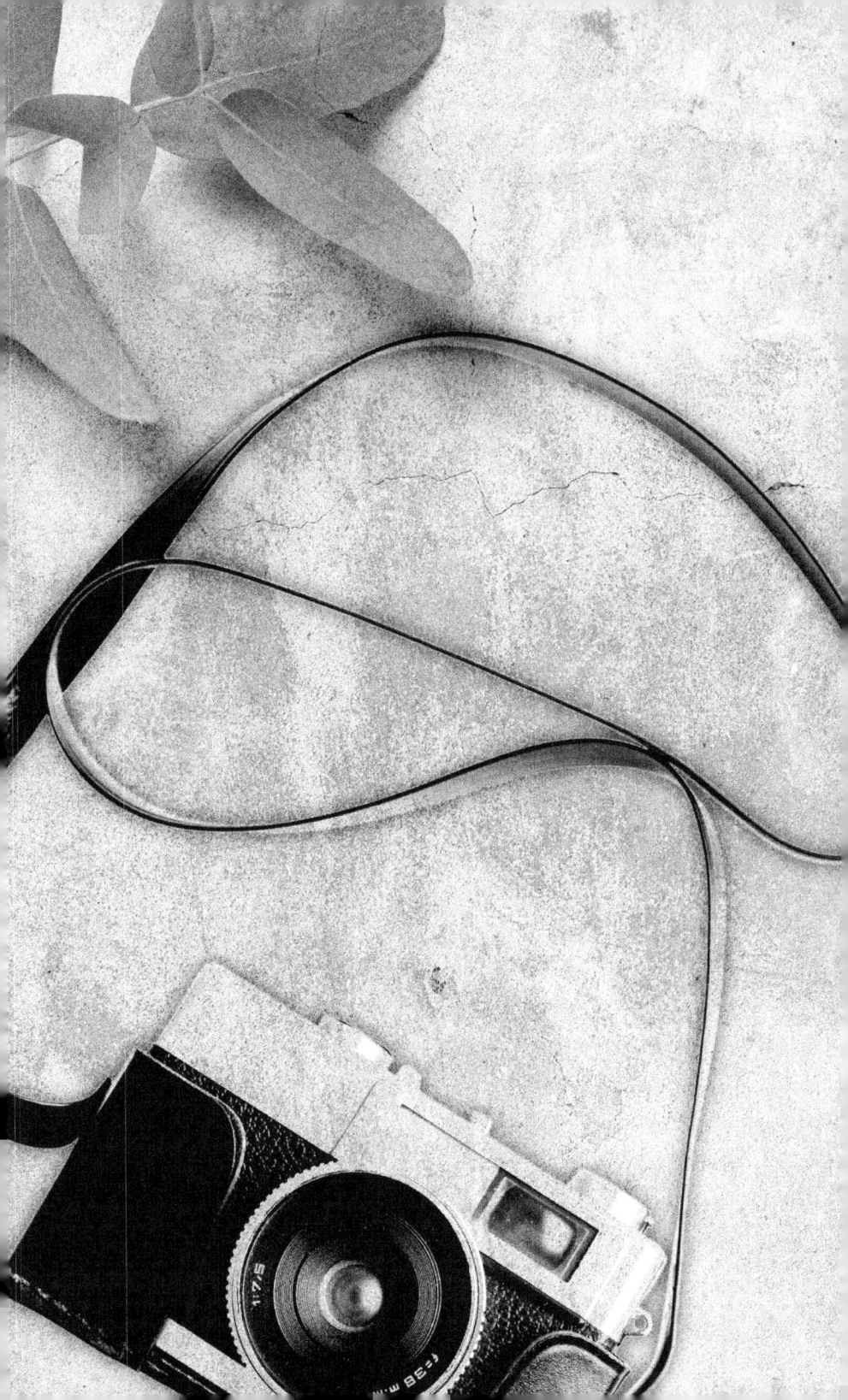

16

Thayne

"I need to talk to you about something." Aca turns to me stiffly, like he isn't sure he heard me correctly.

"Talk?"

Talking wasn't a big thing in the Rawlins family, and Aca wasn't one to hover, which is why our friendship was so great.

"Yeah." I slam the hammer against the bolt in the gate that broke at three in the morning due to our bull, Blaze, charging his way through it.

He then found his way to Lynnie and stuck his head through her bedroom window. I'm pretty sure that Australia heard her screams.

Blaze's recent antics had put my brother in the foulest of moods. A mood that was only worsening as Lynnie unleashed hell on him for what had happened earlier.

"I said I'm sorry, Lyn! What else do you want me to say?"

It seemed there were bigger things at play here that I shouldn't stick my nose into. It was unlike Lynnie to lose her shit over something like this, but regardless, I didn't step in. I learnt quickly to not engage with Lynnie when she was in a rage.

"I want you and that fucking bull to stay away from me!" Lynnie yells.

"I'll gladly drive you to someplace else, if you aren't happy here. You could always get a place of your own!"

"Fuck you!" Lynnie storms away from him and he watches her leave before turning away himself and marches into the main house, slamming the door behind him.

"Is it just me or are they more intense than usual?" I ask, glancing over at Lynnie, who's annoyed squeals can be heard even as she disappears down the hill.

"They've been like it all week." Ryker pipes up, tossing a rope over his shoulder as he shakes his head. "I'm yet to figure out why."

Blaze huffs beside us, his horns smacking against my hand as I try to keep the gate stable.

"You've created problems, Blazey boy." Though there had always been problems with Lynnie and Flint. Problems that no one really knew much about except the two of them, and they all seemed to suddenly be surfacing.

"So, what did you need to talk to me about?" Aca asks.

"The fuck do you look so nervous for, dude?" I frown.

"You're weirding me out."

"I just said I needed to talk to you."

Aca looks at me stupefied. "Exactly. You never need to talk to me."

"Stop being weird."

"You stop being weird."

"Uh, how about you both stop being weird," Ryker suggests, snatching the hammer out of my hand. "Since you're doing fuck all with this, I'll fix the gate. You guys go… talk or whatever."

I push the empty beer bottle to the side and glance at Aca, who sits opposite me with a suspicious look of his own.

"I hate to ask this of you man, but do you happen to know someone with a rooftop infinity pool?"

What looks like relief seems to flood over his face and he leans back in the booth.

"That's what this is about?"

"Yeah. What else would it be about?"

In the years I'd known Aca, this was one of those times where he was being more awkward than he usually was. And he was always awkward.

Aca was right, we didn't usually talk about emotions or ourselves.

Instead, we usually spoke with our fists. A few punches either side and we'd be even, that's how we dealt with things when we were younger. "Nothing." He says quickly. "I don't personally know one, but I can ask around. Why?"

"It's a part of Emberli's list before the baby arrives."

"Seems cool. Nice of you to help her, man."

"Yeah. Well, I figured I best stop giving her a hard time before Willow has my head."

"Or maybe you've just realized what a dick you were to Emberli?" Aca laughs and I shrug.

"That too."

"Have you seen her lately?" I ask.

"Who? Emberli?"

"No. My sister. When I went round to escort Blaze back to his pen, she wasn't there. Think she slept somewhere else last night."

"Oh yeah? You know where?'

"If I did, dispshit. I wouldn't be asking you. I just want to know where she's staying and who she's staying with."

"She's a grown woman you know." Aca sips on his beer and I narrow my eyes at him.

"I worry about her, just as you worry about Ryker."

"I get that. But the more you suffocate her, the more she's going to want to go against you."

"Since when did you turn into Dr Phil?"

Aca cracks up at this. "Shut the fuck up."

"Whilst we're on topic, you don't happen to know anyone with a helicopter, do you?"

By the time I get back to the ranch after my chat with Aca and calling into Lacey's on the way home, it's five thirty. Emberli's shift at the bar starts in an hour and it felt weird not seeing her all day.

I'd been out of the cabin ever since Flint called me early hours this morning and, when I got back, Emberli was standing outside on the porch excitedly.

Now this, I can get used to.

The wind whistles past us, hitting the chimes above the porch door and Emberli combs her hair back behind her ears as she waits, jumping up and down until she can't help herself, running down to meet me and closing the distance between us, shoving her notebook in my hands.

"What's this?" I know what it is. I've been eager to get my hands on it ever since I first saw it.

The notebook, of course.

"Six songs." She grins widely.

"Yeah?" The look of happiness on her face is contagious and brings a smile to my own.

"Six songs, Thayne!"

"That's amazing, trouble." I shake my head in disbelief. "This what you've been doing all day?"

"It's the only thing I've been doing all day. What's this?" Her attention turns to the jar of decaf coffee I'm holding before her eyes widen, holding mine for a longer period of seconds than usual. And I don't find myself hating it.

"I got this for you."

"Thank you." Her voice is laced with surprise. "How much was it? I'll send you the money."

140

"I don't want your money."

"But…"

"Nope. Have you eaten today?" I ask as I brush past her.

"I ate the entire punnet of tomatoes that Sally gave me and about three omelets."

"New craving?"

"No. Just hungry. However, I have been really into the idea of avocado on toast."

Huh. Sounds nice.

"With melted chocolate."

Never mind.

"That does not sound like it would go well."

"Don't knock it until you try it."

"Have you?"

"No. I was waiting for you."

When I reach the kitchen, there's a tray of bread, avocado and chocolate with a toaster next to it. Emberli grins next to me, happily.

"Colton went and got this for me. It's amazing what people will do for a pregnant woman."

I bet. Especially my brother.

I'm not exactly thrilled at the idea of leaving Emberli around him no matter how much I love Colt. He's unpredictable and only cares about himself. I don't try to change that as much as it infuriates me, because it's just who he is and I've learnt to accept that.

Besides, he's my brother. So I'm kind of obliged to love the little shit.

"Do you want to try it with me?" I grunt in response and she claps her hands.

"We have to be quick because I have to work in an hour," she explains.

I admire the way she moves around the kitchen like it's her own, like she belongs there.

She hums what I only imagine to be the tune of one of her songs before she places down a plate of avocado on toast in front of me and a bowl of melted chocolate between us.

The idea of it is repulsive, but I don't want to upset her and so I hesitantly pour the melted chocolate over the food. Her eyes look at me all hopeful, eagerly waiting for my response as I take a mouthful.

Yep. Just as I figured. Repulsive.

"Mmm." I nod. "It's… it's nice. It's something."

It's definitely something.

She looks at me suspiciously. "Your face says otherwise."

"I'm just… taking in the flavours."

She grabs a piece of toast before adding avocado and chocolate to it and, taking a few bites, her mouthfuls begin to get slower and her face paints a sour look.

"That's disgusting," is what she settles on.

"Yeah. I was trying to sugar coat it."

"I don't think this can be sugar coated." A look of realization crosses her face just as the color seems to drain from it.

She's out of her seat as soon as I blink and I hear a door slam open before I hear the sound of her hurling up her most recent meal.

I'm following her now, pushing any form of self-control away as I open the bathroom door.

"Don't come in here!" She coughs but I ignore her.

"I said don't come in here!"

"If you think I'm going to stand by whilst you're struggling, then you're wrong." It was about time she let me take care of her.

"I'm not struggling. I'm perfectly fine." I roll my eyes. The independent tough girl act could only go so far and I was shutting it down.

I grab a handful of her hair in my hands as she clutches the toilet seat with a groan. "This is so embarrassing."

"Don't be embarrassed. It's natural. Besides, if it makes you feel any better, I've done this for Willow countless times."

Once she's finished, her hand lazily reaches the chain and she flushes the toilet, leaning back against the bathroom wall.

"You okay?"

142

She nods and rubs her bump in circular motions. "I think we can all agree that avocado and toast with chocolate is disgusting."

I chuckle. "I think so."

It was something about the way she referred to the three of us as all that made me feel all warm and fuzzy inside.

"Thayne?"

I'm broken out of my thoughts and take a seat next to Emberli. "Yeah?"

"Do you think something is wrong with the baby? I don't know if I should still be sick at this point."

My hand reaches out to push back a strand of her hair that falls loosely in front of her eyes. "I think you and the baby just didn't like the chocolate with avocado."

Her shoulders loosen and she chuckles. "Yeah. You're right. That was disgusting."

"But if you're worried about it, I'll take you to the doctors." I didn't want to overstep.

The last thing I found myself wanting to do lately was making Emberli uncomfortable, however I wanted her to know that I was there to support her.

"Hard pass. My midwife was highly judgemental last time."

The protective side of me switches on at her words as she chuckles at them, something I've noticed she does when she's trying not to make a big deal out of something that she actually feels strong about.

"Who was it? Was it Stacey?" Stacey was one of our most qualified here at Shadow Peaks and whilst she was known for such talent, she was also known for running her mouth all around the town.

It breached numerous clients' confidentiality, but of course, she didn't care and no one else seemed to, not until now. I'd get her fired if Emberli clicked her fingers and told me to handle it. But I know she wouldn't. She never asked for help, and even when given it, she was reluctant to accept. I wanted to show her that I could handle all of these things for her, that she didn't have to worry.

"It doesn't matter."

"It matters to me. What happened?"

"Just… is Stacey the only midwife you guys have here?"

"Did she say something to you? What did she say?" I ask, but Emberli seems to find my interest funny, and she laughs.

"It's okay, Superman."

I blink at her nickname as I watch her reach for the side, gripping the edge of the sink to help her stand before she turns on the tap and puts her hands under it. She brushes off our conversation as if she hopes I'll do the same.

"Superman?"

"You're definitely Superman, you're always trying to save the day."

"I'd rather be Iron Man."

"Iron Man is a lot more rebellious than you."

"What's that supposed to mean?" I follow her out, eager to hear her response as she makes her way into her bedroom, turning to me in the doorway.

Fucking hell.

The room even smells just like her.

A sweet scent of vanilla that fights with my own scent around the cabin. Usually I'd be annoyed at the sudden take over. But I'm not.

Not one bit.

I like having Emberli here with me, in my cabin. It felt like she belonged here, like she was the missing piece to a puzzle I couldn't find all these years.

I lean my hand against the top of the doorframe.

"It means, Colton is definitely Iron Man."

I never thought I'd be jealous of my younger brother in front of a woman, until this very moment.

Fucking Colt.

"Why does Colt get to be Iron Man?"

"He's more… I don't know! Why are you asking me this? I need to get ready for work," she cries, waving her hands at me frantically before opening her wardrobe, flicking through the hangers.

I invite myself in and plonk down on her bed, earning a glare from her.

"Why does he get to be Iron Man and I don't?"

"I cannot believe I'm having this conversation." She mumbles. "He's more… defiant! Unruly. Superman sticks to the rules and helps those in need."

I'm taken back to the many times I eavesdropped on Willow and Lynnie's conversations when we were younger. Multiple times they'd claimed that they, and I quote, dig a bad boy.

Did Emberli like that too? Did she like my brother?

I sure as fuck hope not.

"Now out, please. I need to get changed for work."

"Who do you like more, Iron Man or Superman?"

Emberli raises an eyebrow at me before pointing at the door. "Out."

THAYNE: Do you guys prefer Superman or Iron Man?

LYNNIE: Iron Man all the way.

FLINT: Superman.

MACK: What Iron Man are we talking about?

ACA: There's only one Iron Man you simpleton.

MACK: What. The. Fuck.

WILLOW: Definitely Iron Man.

COLTON: Iron Man.

THAYNE: I'm disowning you all except Flint.

FLINT: Oh, I am so honored.

MACK: Was that sarcasm? I can't tell over text.

WILLOW: You're so stupid.

17

Emberli

"What are we doing back at the motel? Are you returning me?"

Thayne snorts at this and shoots me an amused look as he pulls into a parking space outside of the motel.

His truck is the only one here and there's some form of notice on the reception door that I can't read.

I should possibly get my eyes tested.

Okay. I should definitely get my eyes tested.

My passenger door opens and Thayne stands there.

"It's not exactly a rage room, but I spoke to the contractor and they agreed for us to smash up a few rooms."

"You did what?"

I stand there almost speechless as Thayne grabs his toolbox from the truck bed. "They were only going to knock it down to refurbish anyway. I figured we could start ticking off your list."

"Thayne, this is…" So thoughtful. Kind. "I didn't realize it was under refurbishment."

"It wasn't. Until I saw your room. It's not healthy for anyone to stay somewhere like that and it's been neglected for some time. I figured it was worth a letter to the council and some rich guy ended up buying it."

Processing everything Thayne tells me is a challenge, and I've never been good at challenges. But it appears that he did all of this, for me.

Inside, I'm trying my hardest not to scream. On the outside, I manage a tight-lipped smile that must make me look like an idiot.

"But safety first." He appears in front of me and holds out his hand which holds a pair of goggles. I take them hesitantly, still speechless and stand still as Thayne plonks a helmet down on my head, strapping it beneath my chin. I try to ignore the wave of electricity that shoots through me as he does. He turns away for a second and grabs a long sleeved coat that he takes upon himself to put on me, buttoning it up to the very top whilst I stand there in the stance of a penguin.

He steps back, grinning widely. "Hang on."

"Are you making fun of me, Thayne? Is that what this is?"

I hear his laugh as he reaches into the back of his truck, pulling out his camera.

"Absolutely not." I say.

"One photo. Please?"

"Fine. But only if you get in too."

Thayne grunts in displeasure at this, but he doesn't argue. He suits up before setting the camera on a timer a few meters away.

I stand there with a grin and both of my thumbs up awkwardly, which Thayne seems to find hilarious just as the camera does its job.

I zone in on the candidness of the photo and how Thayne laughs at me.

"It's cute." I say, glancing up at Thayne for his opinion. It seems that he hasn't stopped smiling and his index finger points at my frozen stance. "I don't think I've ever met anyone more awkward than you.."

"I'm one of a kind." I wink and set my eyes on the motel in front of me. It has a creepy vibe to it that I don't like and am suddenly grateful for Thayne's company. Maybe I'm traumatised from when Nadia slammed her way through both of our motel rooms.

Maybe I should start seeing a therapist… not about Nadia but about Elijah. Odessa had recommended the idea but I shrugged it off because I thought I was doing okay. Evidently I was in a state of denial because the night terrors I had of Elijah coming to kill me for outing him felt very real.

"Shall we get to work?"

"I thought you'd never ask." I say and he gestures his hand out in front of him. "Ladies first."

Is a twenty-three second stare too extreme if the other party isn't looking?

There's something about the way Thayne slams the hammer into the cupboard and I can't seem to take my eyes off it. Off him.

I watched shamelessly with a great front row view as he continuously smashed at the wood in front of him.

Masculinity and testosterone exuded from him and it was *hot*.

I have no clue where my alter-ego feminist had gone, but I was sure she was condemning me, wherever she was.

He reaches to the hem of his white tee to wipe at his forehead after he removes his goggles, glancing at me like he's been aware I've been staring for so long, and my gaze shoots up to the ceiling like it's the most interesting thing I've seen all day.

"You okay?"

"Huh? Me?"

"No. Noisy Nadia back there." He juts his chin behind me and I jump up, suddenly aware I've been fooled when I hear Thayne's laugh.

"Ha-Ha. You're so funny." I glare before jumping to my feet. "Okay. Subconscious power nap is over and I'm ready to roll."

"Glad to hear it. I thought you gave up."

Whilst Thayne had been working hard at knocking down the walls without a break, I'd been taking several.

Truth be told, Thayne was a lot more skilled in this department than I was, and often saved flying pieces of wood from smacking into my face.

"Pfft. Giving up is *not* in my nature."

He scoffs. "Don't I know it."

Dad was right about rage rooms, or simply just smashing something up. It was relieving, it felt like a weight off of my shoulders, most of which consisted of taking out my anger for Elijah on the poor tiles in the bathroom.

I smash at the mirror, unleashing all my pent up anger as I stare at the cracked reflection of myself. If that wasn't symbolism of an identity crisis, I don't know what was.

An idea for a verse suddenly pops into my head, something about finding out who I am and speaking to my past or younger self.

Can we just act like... no.

Can we just pretend? I don't want to see her again.
A glimpse of the failure. And I don't know what to tell her.

I smash at the glass some more in the hope that I'd be hit with more inspiration, and when I'm not, I dive for my phone on the bed and open my notes app, frantically typing in the ideas as they pass each other in my brain.

Knowing myself, I'll look back in a few days and not have a single clue what I'm talking about. But in the hope that I do, I tap them into my phone.

Being in this town has become my muse. And after so long without one, I'm not sure I'm ready to pack up and leave just yet. Shadow Peaks had become my comfort, which was weird considering the reason I came here. Yet instead of finding that, or more specifically, him. I found peace.

A few weeks pass and Thayne and I have become what I'd consider friends. I no longer just tolerated him, I actually enjoyed his company. I was wrong about him before. Not only was I getting to know Thayne more, but my inspiration for songwriting had hit its peak. I'd written numerous songs. I just didn't know what to do with them. The more I had the time to think about it, I didn't know if songwriting was what I wanted to pursue full-time. I loved it, but I didn't love it enough to do it full time. And I was terrified I'd lose the remaining admiration I had for it if I did.

I flick through the numerous outfits I went out and irrationally bought for Aca's leaving party tonight, sit down on my bed and sigh.

Three options. Just choose one.

It sounds so simple, yet is the complete opposite.

Each and every one of them have new flaws that I didn't pick up on a few days ago when I stumbled into the only dress shop in town and they all have something to do with the way they look on me.

In someone else's eyes, it may not be clear that the navy blue dress rides up my thighs more than I want and that the material makes me want to gauge my eyes out, or that the crimson thin-strapped dress shows too much of my skin and I no longer liked that as I did two days ago. They may not think the black and gold flecked maxi-dress I wear looks hideous on me like I think it does and the entire situation makes my emotions turn on each other and they go to war.

Heat rises to my cheeks and I burst out crying, flinging my dress to the other side of the room in anger before immediately feeling bad for hating it. I bet the dressmaker was so proud of it too.

God. I'm a horrible person.

I'm a blubbering mess as there's a knock on my door and I freeze, I don't even breathe.

"Emberli?" Thayne's voice floods through the closed door.

"Yeah?" Is all I just about manage.

"We've got to leave soon. Just checking if you're okay?"

"I thought I still had two hours?" I panic.

"It's been two hours."

Great.

Maybe I wasn't only losing my mind and my ability to stay in touch with my emotions, but my sense of timing too.

"Are you okay?"

Goddamn it.

"No."

I seemed to break whenever someone asked me if I was okay, when evidently I was not okay and there was nothing I could do to put a stop to it.

The doorknob turns and Thayne appears, a concerned look painting his face and he's over to me in less than three strides, standing in front of me. His thumb hooks under my chin, tilting my face upwards.

"You're crying," he states. "Why? Talk to me."

Talk to me? Oh God. This man.

I let out a strangled sob and the bed dips beside me before I find my head locked in his arm as he holds me against his chest.

There were numerous arguments with Elijah where I'd begged him for basic communication and instead he refused to talk, taking pride in the control he had over me. I didn't realize what I'd gotten myself into, how much I fell for, and how I just didn't know him at all. He knew everything about me and he knew just how to get under my skin. When I inevitably spoke up about it, he turned the tables so fast I didn't get a chance to think that he was the one in the wrong, not me. I realized that he only ever loved me for what I could give him and not as his other half and this past month I tried to take joint responsibility for him leaving me. I knew that I wasn't perfect. Far from it in fact. But I could never understand it. I could never understand him. I guess that's a good thing.

"Emberli." Thayne's voice is low and gruff. Stern as he asks me, "What's wrong?"

"Nothing looks good on me." I blurt out into his chest.

"What makes you think that?"

I pull back and stand to my feet, gesturing to my outfit that he glances over before looking at me.

"You've lost me."

"I look hideous."

A low chuckle leaves his lips as he stands, and his rough-to-feel yet soothing hands place on my shoulders before turning me around to the mirror. He stands behind me as he rubs my shoulders. "You look amazing, trouble."

My breath vanishes from my lungs and I forget how to breathe until I'm forced to, which only makes me sound like a strangled cat.

"But…"

"No. I don't want to hear it." He scowled. "And I'm sure you look just as good in the other choices as well."

I steal another glance at him in the mirror before forcibly looking at myself, but no matter how long I try, I can't see what he sees. I only see my imperfections and there are a whole lot of them.

"I don't know if your way of thinking is because of that asshole you were with. And yes, the dress and all the jewellery you're wearing is beautiful but that's not what completes this look. It's you. And you are fucking stunning, Emberli. You don't need a dress to tell you that. I'll tell you it for free."

"Thayne…" I'm speechless, my heart swells at his words yet I can't say a word, I can't even thank him.

I'm not used to the shower of compliments he's given me of his own accord and yet he gives my shoulders a reassuring squeeze.

"Which one are you going to go with?" I feel his cold fingers tracing over the straps and I give the dress I'm in a once over, though my attention has entirely shifted to the man behind me.

"This one."

"Good choice. Want me to zip you up?"

I nod like I'm some teenager who's just been asked if she wants her first kiss. My own inner teenager practically screams at me as his hand gently moves my hair to the side, his fingers brush against my back that goosebumps immediately invade.

Shit. Shit. Shit.

My heart is about to flatline.

God. How embarrassing would that be?

Please don't faint. Please don't faint.

The warmth of his touch is gone in a matter of seconds. It was only a brief moment, yet it's one I find myself longing for when my dress tightens around me.

It isn't until Thayne leaves my room that I finally let out a breath I feel has been trapped inside of me this entire time.

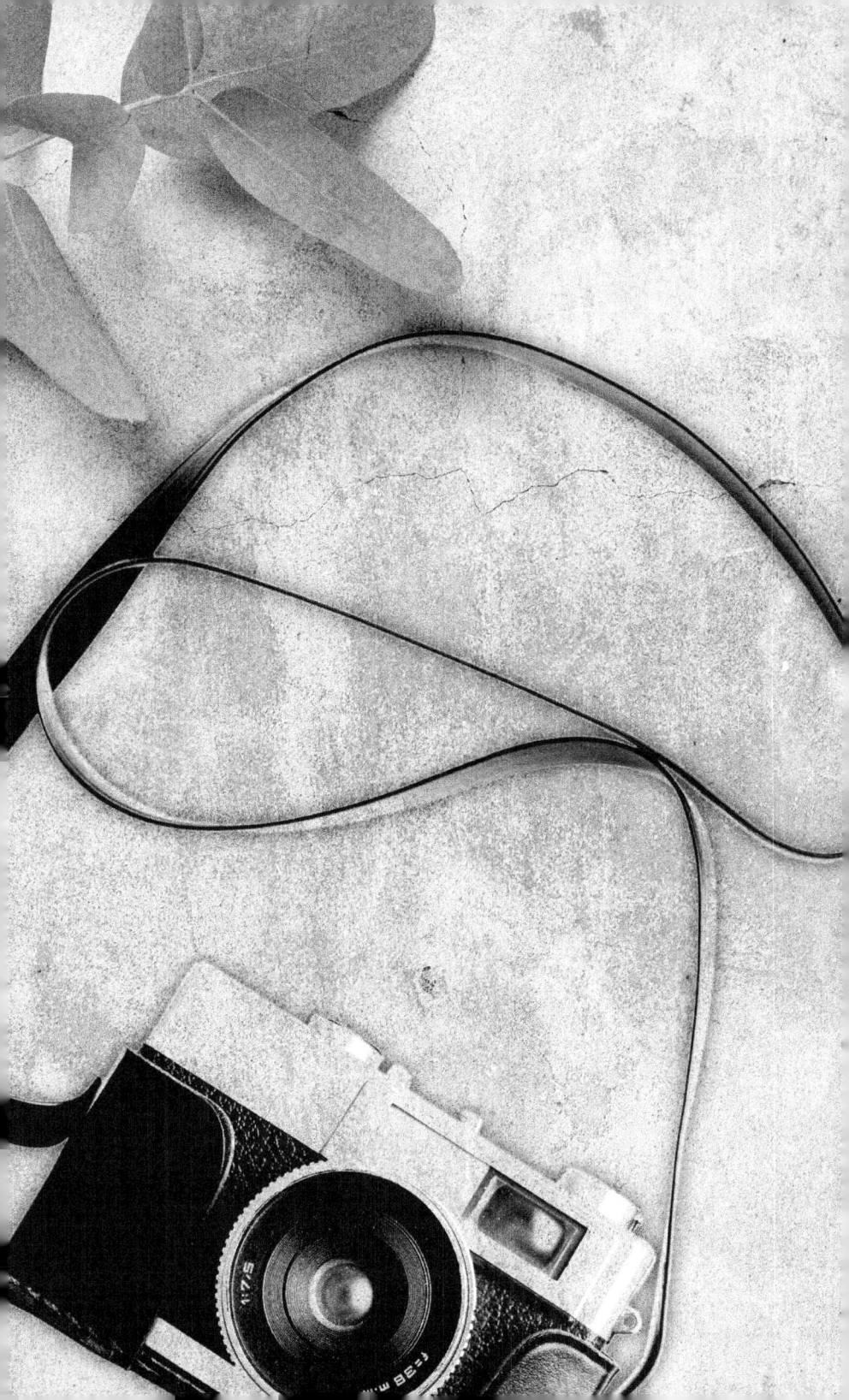

18

Thayne

"So just how long are you going to be on this denial train for?" Aca asks, his arms crossed as he looks at me in amusement. To annoy me further, Colton makes the sound of a train and Mack mimes one with his hands wheeling his sides.

"You're all so immature." I say irritably.

"But we're right." Mack nudges my side. "Aren't we?"

I glance over to where the girls sit huddled together, catching the glimpse of the familiar head of brunette I've gotten used to recently. The one who noticed immediately that I'm staring at her and shoots me an awkward double thumbs up that makes me smile.

"I'm not on a denial train." I most definitely am, but none of these nosy assholes need to know that.

"So you wouldn't mind if I asked her to dance?" Colton asks.

"Fuck. Off."

Aca cracks up at this. "Looks like we're still on, boys."

I turn to him with a smirk. "When do you leave again?"

His arm loops around my head and he tightens his grip around it as I pummel at his back.

"Coming through!" Odessa yells. "Shitheads." She mumbles as she passes through with a tray of drinks, heading straight for the girls' table.

I catch Mack staring at her as she passes, and I shove his shoulder.

Mack and Odessa would be complicated. Not that Mack ever took an interest in my opinion.

"Stop eyeing up my employees."

He scoffs. "So you can but I can't?"

"Face it brother." Colton's hand clamps down on my shoulder. "You're whipped."

Mack mimics the sound of a whip crashing down just as I hear a loud collection of squeals.

Willow's over by the speaker, just as Why'd You Come In Here Lookin' like that by Dolly Parton starts to play, and the girls collectively bunch together, rushing over to Odessa who is the only one sat down at the table.

I made sure that the bar was closed tonight for Aca's leaving party, but this didn't stop locals from going up to Odessa and asking her to make them a drink, which is why she'd been behind the bar for the past few hours.

Emberli's laugh fills my ears as she tips her head back, there's a huge grin on her face as she spins Odessa around. She looks happy. Carefree. Like she belongs here. They're the loudest in the bar, but encourage more of the locals to join the small dance space with them. Emberli's eyes flicker around the room before she finds mine and gestures for me to join in. Mack and Colton are already in the middle of the dance floor, but I don't dance.

Everyone knows that.

I shake my head but clap her encouragingly as she spins. Of course Emberli doesn't give up, she frantically waves her hand at me to join her.

"She doesn't look like she's going to accept defeat any time soon." Aca chuckles next to me.

Fuck it. I guess I'm dancing.

Emberli's smile only grows as I walk towards her, her hand reaches forward for mine and she grabs it, pulling me closer to our tight circle of family and friends.

I've got no clue why she chooses me to dance with me out of all the eligible men here who have made their presence known to Emberli the entire night.

"Having fun?" I ask.

She nods eagerly. "I am. Despite my lack of sleep."

I frown. "You haven't been sleeping well recently?"

Her head shakes at this and suddenly all the noises downstairs at night make sense.

"I didn't know you had moves like this, Superman," she says, changing the subject completely.

I crack a smile at her nickname. "I only bring them out on special occasions."

"And this is a special occasion?"

"You're here aren't you?"

Her head tips back as she laughs. "Smooth."

It was official. I had turned into Colton.

Yuck.

But as I watch her, I realize that the happiness that radiates from her is worth it. It's worth it all.

And if being cringey means I get to hear that laugh of hers, then fuck it. Cringey I am.

Lately all I can think about is her. Everything about her drowns my entire existence, and suddenly I'm obsessed with Emberli Taylor and the baby that she carries inside her. I want to protect her. I want to protect both of them and it's a terrifying feeling because my protected circle only branched out to my immediate family and friends. Emberli, she *feels* like both of those things put together and it's something I've never felt before.

It was selfish of me to drag her into my simple life of work when she deserved so much more. Not to mention that I was an absolute train-wreck. I just hid it a lot better because I had to.

My family relies on me. Being the eldest sibling in my family meant that I was the lead protector of my family, especially since my parents had gone.

However, feeling protective over a woman like Emberli was an entirely new feeling that was almost alien to me.

I swore to myself that I had no time for feelings, only checking in on my family and running my business. But the longer I spend with the woman who looks like she sees straight through me and my walls, the more I find myself asking if I could open up to her, if I could let her in.

"Mind if I cut in?" Popping the small bubble I'm enjoying residing in with Emberli, stands Annie with a fake grin plastered on her face. I feel Emberli's grip loosen on my hands. "Sure."

Her gaze snaps back to me as I hold her firmly in place.

"We're busy, Annie." I tell her, looking straight into the widened eyes of Emberli's.

"One dance can't hurt." Annie persists.

"It's fine. I'll come and find you after." Emberli assures me.

"No. I don't want you to. I want you here, with me."

I hear an annoyed huff before the click of Annie's heels can no longer be heard.

"Who was that? I feel terrible."

"She's not a good person, trouble."

"I still feel terrible."

I chuckle. There weren't many times when Emberli wasn't feeling. A few nights ago I found her in the living room crying over a compilation of lions reuniting with their keepers. I offered to watch The Lion King with her in an attempt to diffuse the situation, but immediately regretted it when I heard the sniffles from the other couch at Mufasa's death scene.

"Would it make you feel a bit better if I told you she broke Colton's heart?"

She stops dancing and nods slowly. "Okay. I feel a bit better."

Her eyes travel over to where Annie stands with a glare and her arms over her chest as she stares at us.

"Don't look at her. Look at me."

Emberli's eyes look up at me once again and a smile curls her lips. "You're not what I expected, Superman."

"Right back at you, trouble."

Willow snatches my dance partner away from me and I laugh, listening to the rain pattering on the roof of the bar that is jam-packed with the locals of the town. Each and every one of them takes turns in saying goodbye to Aca.

Man, I was going to miss him.

But I was proud of him, for getting out of this town. He'd always wanted to and I couldn't blame him, but I couldn't understand him either. Shadow Peaks had always been my home despite all the hideous things that happened to me here. I didn't have it in me to leave this place.

My therapist called it place-associated trauma. I called it survivor's guilt.

"Odessa, can you pour me a pint please?"

"She's not working." My gaze flickers to Mack, who stands in front of Odessa with a pissed off expression on his face. Ryan McMune scoffs at him.

"She's a bartender for a reason."

"She's not working tonight." Mack snaps.

Usually, he's the more level headed brother of us all. It's why he's so good at being sheriff, however tonight, he seemed to be riled up. And my guess was that he'd been watching Odessa being run off of her feet, and stepped in like the hero he is.

Good ol' Mack.

"It won't take a minute." Ryan shrugs.

"Mack, it's fine. I'll just pour him a drink."

"No you won't. She's not pouring you a drink, buddy. It was clear on the invitation to bring your own."

Well, it wouldn't be a Shadow Peaks' party without someone

getting punched. I'm about to step in when Flint's hand stops me. "I got this. You go."

"Go where?"

Flint's head nods to Emberli who beckons me to follow her outside.

"What are you doing?" I ask as the door swings shut behind me, I follow her as she spins and laughs, tilting her head upwards and opening her mouth to let the rainwater in.

"Dancing in the rain!" Her laughter echoes the empty street before her eyes land on me. "Are you going to join me, Superman? Or are you just going to stand under shelter all night?"

"I'm fine watching you." I've found myself liking it quite a lot.

"See this is exactly why you're Superman! Iron Man wouldn't hesitate!"

Fuck it.

I know she's teasing me, but she knows just how to get me riled up. My clothing tightens against my skin as the rain drenches me. Opposite where I stand, Emberli grins as she realizes she's gotten her own way with me, once again. There's not many things I wouldn't do for the woman who reaches for my hand and attempts to spin me around whilst on her tiptoes.

In this moment, she's radiant and exhilarating and I wish she'd see herself the way others around her do. The way I do.

I look away knowing I have to. It would be foolish of me to act upon my new feelings when everything has just settled down, especially for Emberli.

I wouldn't do that to her, not unless she asked.

"Isn't this amazing?" She yells over the harsh sound of the rain that thrashes down on us.

We hadn't had rain like this for months.

"We need a song if we're going to dance, trouble."

"Hold on." Her hand reaches into her bra and she pulls out her phone, the sound of an acoustic guitar plays in the background before she tucks her phone away again. "This is an original. Feel

164

special, okay? Because no one else has heard it."

I listen to every word as we dance to the beat, and her eyes watch me for my reaction when the song ends.

And fuck me. She's just as talented as she is beautiful. Never failing to amaze me.

A part of me wishes it would play again, so I could redo this dance for a second time.

"What do you think?"

"I think you're really talented, Emberli Taylor."

"I'm gonna get that tattooed on me."

"Don't do that. There are so many other things I could say to you."

"Like what?"

"Like…"

The door slams open and there's a huge thud before a groan follows shortly. Ryan McMune is curled up on the pavement meters from my bar with Mack towering over him.

"Get the fuck out of here and don't think about even stepping into this place again. You hear me?"

I dart an eyebrow at Flint as a crowd forms around our brother. "You handled it so well."

"Shut up."

19
Emberli

"Are you screwing my brother?"

"What?" Lynnie and I both ask at the same time, she shoots me an eyebrow just as I shoot one back.

"Not you." Willow waves off Lynnie, who shrugs and gets back to tapping away on her laptop.

It seemed I wasn't the only one who could be a huge introvert at times. Lynnie claimed that she was working on a huge plot twist for her book and needed to get it out and structured on a page. Therefore, my second Woo Woo Wednesday had taken place at their cabin.

Odessa hadn't replied to the newly created group chat for the girls and me about coming tonight, so that just left Lynnie and me, and one skeptical Willow who would not sit down and was instead blocking the TV.

"Please! Sit down! I'm trying to study."

"Study? You can't study a romance movie about football. The rules and everything about it are going to be wildly incorrect." Willow states before turning her attention to me.

"Are you?"

"I'm not studying."

"No. Are you screwing my brother?"

"No." The truth rolls off of my tongue, yet despite it being honest, I can't help but feel a tad guilty.

Nothing had happened between Thayne and I, but that didn't stop me wishing that something had, nor did it stop my delusional imagination when I pictured us kissing in the rain a few nights ago.

But nobody needed to know that. Especially not his sister.

"I won't be mad. I'd prefer it if you were."

"What?" I choke on my drink and pat at my chest.

"What? I'm just saying. I know you'll be in good hands with someone like him."

"Thayne and me… we're not like that." I avoid the flashbacks of our dance in the rain last night as they appear in my brain like a subtle exposure technique.

Willow scoffs in disbelief at this, resting both of her hands on her hips. "And I'm supposed to believe that? I'm just saying, "I like you and I know my brother."

"Do you think that a locker room makeout session would be disgusting?" Lynnie asks. She was zoned out for most of the conversation. The look of determination might as well be tattooed on her face at this point as she practically punched her fingers into the letters of the keyboard at a frantic pace. Her eyes don't leave the screen once.

"I think it would be hot." Willow says, distracted.

"Right. But what about the smell of body odor?"

Willow and I make a face at each other and she wrinkles her nose. "Okay. Now it's no longer hot."

"If I'm reading it, I wouldn't think about the smell of the locker room unless you told me."

Lynnie looks up over the laptop and points her finger at me as if she's just had a lightbulb moment. "Good thinking."

Willow pours herself another drink that she downs in a few gulps, and this doesn't go unnoticed by Lynnie and I.

168

"You okay?"

"Huh? Yeah. Fine."

"I know that look. Something is on your mind, what is it?" Lynnie asks.

Willow looks as if she's debating telling us when there's a huge thud outside.

"What was that? If that's fucking Blaze again. I'm going to flip my shit." I'd heard about Lynnie's run in with the ranch's stud, who was apparently famous for breaking out of his pen and loitering around the town. He had a particular interest in Lynnie and apparently last week was the second time this month that Blaze had made an appearance at Lynnie's window.

Willow peeks out of the blinds before she recoils, her chest heavy with panic.

"I can't see. They have their hood up." She whispers. The three of us stand to our feet awkwardly just before Willow quickly turns the lights off.

Brilliant.

Not only were we being stalked. But now we were being stalked in the dark.

"Go out there! You're the brave one!" Willow gestures at Lynnie, who clutches her laptop to her chest.

"Are you joking? I could die!"

"Do we scream?"

"Are you crazy?" Willow shakes her head. "We don't scream. We're not even here." She places her index finger to her lips before she takes another peek. "They're gone."

What sounds like a flower pot smashes outside behind us just as a low curse leaves the possible intruder's mouth.

Willow begins to act out some form of interpreted dance with various movements that I can't fathom. I only take note of her precise ninja-like movements, as her hands slice the air, and momentarily forget that we're in trouble here.

"The fuck are you doing?" Lynnie whispers and Willow slaps

her hands down at her sides in annoyance.

"You go for the legs. I open the door, jump on their back and Emberli attacks!"

If I survive whatever attack this is, I'll make sure that Willow never takes up charades as a career because what the heck was that?

"What am I supposed to attack with?" I slap my hand to my mouth as a hooded figure appears behind Willow.

The only thing keeping them apart is the back door.

"Anything! Literally anything!"

"It's dark! I can't see shit!" Lynnie hisses as she creeps around the cabin.

My adrenaline is all over the place and I grab the nearest thing I can find.

A pillow. A fucking pillow.

A really nice, feathered and plump pillow.

"Focus!" Willow's sharp whisper attacks me and I hold it to my chest just as Willow flings open the door, jumping on the back of the intruder who, judging by the tall frame and muscles, is a man. Lynnie dives for his feet and holds them firmly in place.

"Do it, Emberli!" I hurl a pillow over at Willow who suffocates the man with it, and I throw two more in the same direction.

"I've run out of pillows!" I yell, searching the couch beneath me for something else. Anything else.

"Not today, bitch!" Willow screeches at the man who flings her over his shoulder like it's light work. She hits the ground with a thud and suddenly I feel like the last man standing in a match of WWE Royal Rumble.

I stumble off the couch and slam my hand around on the kitchen table before my fingers dive into a bowl of fruit, I find myself lobbing pieces at the grunting male like it's a game of in person fruit ninja.

My hand-eye coordination had never been brilliant until this very moment. It was as if I'd been saving up all of my hits for this exact and very real, life or death situation.

"Ow! OW! Stop! Fuck! Is that a banana?" I make out the figure

170

raising his hands to defend himself as I toss the empty fruit bowl at him as a final hit, imagining it in slow motion like one of the final hits of a battle royale game my brother plays.

Damn. I really needed to get a life.

Truth be told, those games were fun and as I hear a clunk and then a groan, followed by a thud, I realize I've won.

"You did it!" Willow sighs happily before she flicks the light on to unmask our intruder, who isn't masked and is in fact her brother.

"Thayne?!" The three of us chorus.

"Let me get this straight." Mack says in between breaths as he holds his chest. He, and numerous other members at the breakfast table, find the telling of last night's event hilarious. The only one who doesn't find this hilarious is Thayne, who sits there with his arms crossed and a scowl across his face. "You knocked him out… with a fruit bowl?"

"Yes. But in my defence, I didn't know it was him." I shoot an apologetic smile over at Thayne who only grunts at this.

Laughter choruses the table as Mack wheezes, slapping Thayne's shoulder as he catches his breath.

"Well, at least you can defend yourself."

"I'd hardly call it defending. What if it was a real intruder? Don't you have kitchen knives?" Flint asks.

"Are you suggesting that I stab my brother? Because you are top on my list at the moment." Willow shoots back.

"No stabbing of siblings, please. As entertaining as this conversation is." Doug chuckles.

"Besides, it wasn't like we had much time to think." Lynnie adds. "You should have seen Willow's attempt at non-verbal communication. I think both Em and I can agree that it is not her strong suit."

"Sorry Willow, Lynnie's right." I grimace. "And I'm sorry again, Thayne."

"It was my fault." Thayne shakes his head and boy, does he look good with a black eye.

Good as in holy shit good. Good as in gorgeous.

I pull myself out of the depths of ogling him just as Willow speaks across from me. "You're right. It is. What if I had a friend round? *A male friend.*" Her hints are clear to most of us, except Mack.

"Why would you? Ew. Gross, Wills."

"Is it so unimaginable to you guys? I'm a grown woman."

"Wills. We're your brothers. We know you're a grown woman, it still doesn't mean we want to imagine it." Colton speaks.

"Against the point." Willow snaps back. "What if I did have someone around and you turned up?" She turns to Thayne, who evidently wishes he could vanish from the current topic of the table.

"Oh come on, Wills. You haven't been in a relationship in years." Mack shakes his head.

"That doesn't mean I don't have sex!"

Forks clatter on the table and numerous sounds of gagging and retching.

"I'm gonna throw up." Colton heaves.

"Can we keep the sex talk to a minimum at the table? Some of us are trying to enjoy breakfast." Ryker speaks from beside him.

"I'm just saying and I will say this once and once only. I do have members of the opposite sex around sometimes. It would be nice if I could please get some privacy at these times."

More groans. More sounds of gagging.

"For fuck's sake, Wills." Thayne mutters into the palms of his hand.

"Can we stop mentioning sex at the breakfast table?" Flint asks.

"You literally just said it." Mack says.

"What were you even going there for, son?" Doug says as he

slaps Ryker's hand away for the last pancake in the tray.

"I hadn't heard anything from them. I wanted to make sure that they were okay." Thayne grumbles.

Sally cooed at this. "See? I think it's sweet how much he cares for you all."

Willow sighs, frustrated, and she stabs at a pancake whilst shaking her head. "You could have at least used the front door."

"Note taken. I'll do that next time." Thayne smirks.

"Okay, now you're just intentionally pissing me off."

20
Emberli

"You barely spoke to me the entire night!" I yell. Elijah launches his guitar at the wall and I watch as it smashes.

Anger.

Guilt.

Sadness.

When did we get to this point?

What about me?

It's one more frequent question I find myself asking of late. The piece of me I pushed so far away to accommodate Elijah instead of myself.

"Just stop!" He shouts. "Stop!"

"No! This isn't fair, Elijah. This…"

"It's not all about you, Emberli."

"You ignored me the entire night."

"I was catching up with friends. Do you realize how fucking stupid you sound?"

"You have to move your body like it has no bones." Alec, our salsa dance instructor, reenacts his entire body relaxing as he body rolls the air.

"Oh my God." Thayne grumbles next to me and I elbow his ribs to keep him quiet.

I'd signed up for salsa lessons which Thayne had refused to come to, something about keeping his reputation around the town. And then I realized that I'd signed up for a couples lesson and when it was too late to refund the money, I mentioned him asking his brothers if one of them would come. And now we're here.

"And you do not want to raise your feet so high off the ground. We like the ground. We stay on the ground." Alec claps his hands at the small group of us who sit on the bleachers in the high school gymnasium. The entire place reeks of old equipment, band aids and a suffocating amount of body odor. It gives me flashbacks to years of physical education and numerous attempts to get out of it at any extent possible. I was, and still am, not an athletic person.

"Now, today we are going to start with some basic moves, such as forward and back and side to side." Alec instructs, demonstrating the movements he wants us to learn before clapping his hands again. "Join me on the dance floor."

"Does he know it's not a dance floor?"

I shush Thayne, who finds this entire set up highly amusing.

"Okay people! Stand in front of your partners and connect with them. Really look them in the eye. Dancing with a partner is intimate."

Thayne perks an eyebrow at me just as he mirrors my stance. I can't hold my grin at how unamused he looks. I feel even better knowing that he only came because I offered to go with one of his brothers instead.

His eyes dart around the room at the other couples just as Alec's hand falls on his shoulder.

"You cannot find what you're looking for anywhere else. Focus on your partner. She is very beautiful."

I swear Thayne's lip curls into a wolf-like snarl before his eyes

176

fixate on me.

"You want to connect with your partner, Mr. Rawlins. Not eat them."

Thayne's fist clench and Alec takes this as a sign to shuffle away.

"You can't threaten the dance instructor." I told him.

"I didn't."

"You just did, without words."

As hot as the man in front of me was, I did not want him to screw this up. Learning how to salsa was something I'd wanted to do for a while, yet never had or made the time to do it.

"Okay. Now I want you to tell your partner one thing you love about them."

"Is he fucking serious?" Thayne barks out, earning a few looks from the other couples who appear willing, unlike Thayne.

"Will you shut up?" I whisper.

"I thought we came to dance. Not have a fucking therapy lesson."

"Yeah well, you could do with one."

Thayne chuckles at this, wrapping his arm around my waist as Alec instructed.

Focus on the class? Vanished.

"I'm sorry. I'll take this more seriously." Genuinity consumes him and I find myself drowning once again in his stare.

He's got to know that one look from him sends more than half of the town thirsting for him. Hasn't he?

I definitely feel more smug than I should about the fact that Thayne is here with me.

It was no secret that Thayne was one of the most eligible bachelors in town, which is why there's a woman down the dance line glaring daggers at me despite dancing with her husband who rigidly throws some questionable moves out in front of her.

"So what do you love about me, Superman?"

Thayne purses his lips together in thought. "I love your voice."

"Awww." An elderly lady coos next to us, obviously eavesdropping on our conversation.

"Sorry. That's just adorable." It really is.

Thayne has absolutely no fucking business looking this good and complimenting the way he does - even though that's part of the exercise. My cheeks warm at his flattery.

"You know what this one said to me?" The lady nods at her husband who only rolls his eyes. "That I cook nice parsnips. That's what he said. Nice parsnips."

"Hell, what do you want me to say, Mary?"

"You should know what to say, Derek. I shouldn't have to tell you!"

Damn straight, you tell him lady!

I'm suddenly hit with a bundle of battle flashbacks with Elijah. He's not here, but he haunts me everywhere, even now. I'm over him. But I don't think I'll ever get over what he put me through and the way he changed my mindset about myself for the worst. It dawns on me that Thayne and I are the only "couple" here who seem relatively sane. Which says a lot.

Mary and Derek continue their squabble over Alec's praises of approval as he makes his way down the line of learners.

"What do you like about me?" Thayne asks, stepping back just as I step forward, copying Alec's movement as he steals Mary to demonstrate how we should be dancing.

Thayne and I are a pair of stiff and awkward beings, who don't dance nearly as well as the others around us.

But that's not why I came here anyway, I came to learn and have fun. And right now, I was having exactly that with Thayne by my side.

"I like how you put all the glasses on the bottom shelf."

"You noticed that, huh?"

"I notice a lot of things about you."

"Yeah? Like what?"

"Like how much you care for your family."

Thayne's cut off just as Alec swoops in, taking my hands in his before he leads us backwards and to the side before swirling me around in a circle. I try not to laugh at the sour expression painted on Thayne's face that he doesn't even attempt to hide.

The death stare he burns into the back of Alec's head is undeniably hot and yet somewhat alarming. Until it's not, and Alec drops my hand, sauntering over to Thayne.

"Your lady has nice moves, Mr. Rawlins. But you should work on releasing all of that tension that is in your shoulders." Alec releases me before capering over to Thayne, kneading his palms into the man who looks as if he's contemplating murder. "I can help you with that if you like."

My eyes widen behind Alec, who is so obvious in flirting with my dance partner.

"No thanks." Thayne grouches. "I'm fine with tension."

"Whatever you say, manimal."

"It is not funny," grunts Thayne from the driver's seat as he drives us back to the ranch.

"Whatever you say, manimal." I wheeze and throw my head back in laughter once again.

"You think you're pretty funny, don't you?"

"The funniest." I sigh. "God. That was the most fun I've had in a long time."

"Well I'm glad that our dance instructor hitting on me is entertainment for you."

"We should do that again." I suggest.

"Fine. But we're changing instructors."

"Agreed. Personally I think your moves are next level. Alec was just intimidated."

"Are you trying to make me feel better?"

"Possibly. Is it working?"

"Weirdly, yeah."

For someone who didn't care much for others' opinions, he'd certainly taken an interest in mine and I didn't mind it one bit. I'd found myself interested in his thoughts too. I would do anything to be in his brain for an hour or two. To see life the way that he does. Maybe see what he thinks of me whilst I'm at it.

Only earlier I had written out some new lyrics and the first thing I wanted to do was show Thayne to see what he thinks of them. I was drawn to him in a way I never thought I could be again, and although it was terrifying, it was also electrifying.

I felt as if Thayne Rawlins was bringing me back to life.

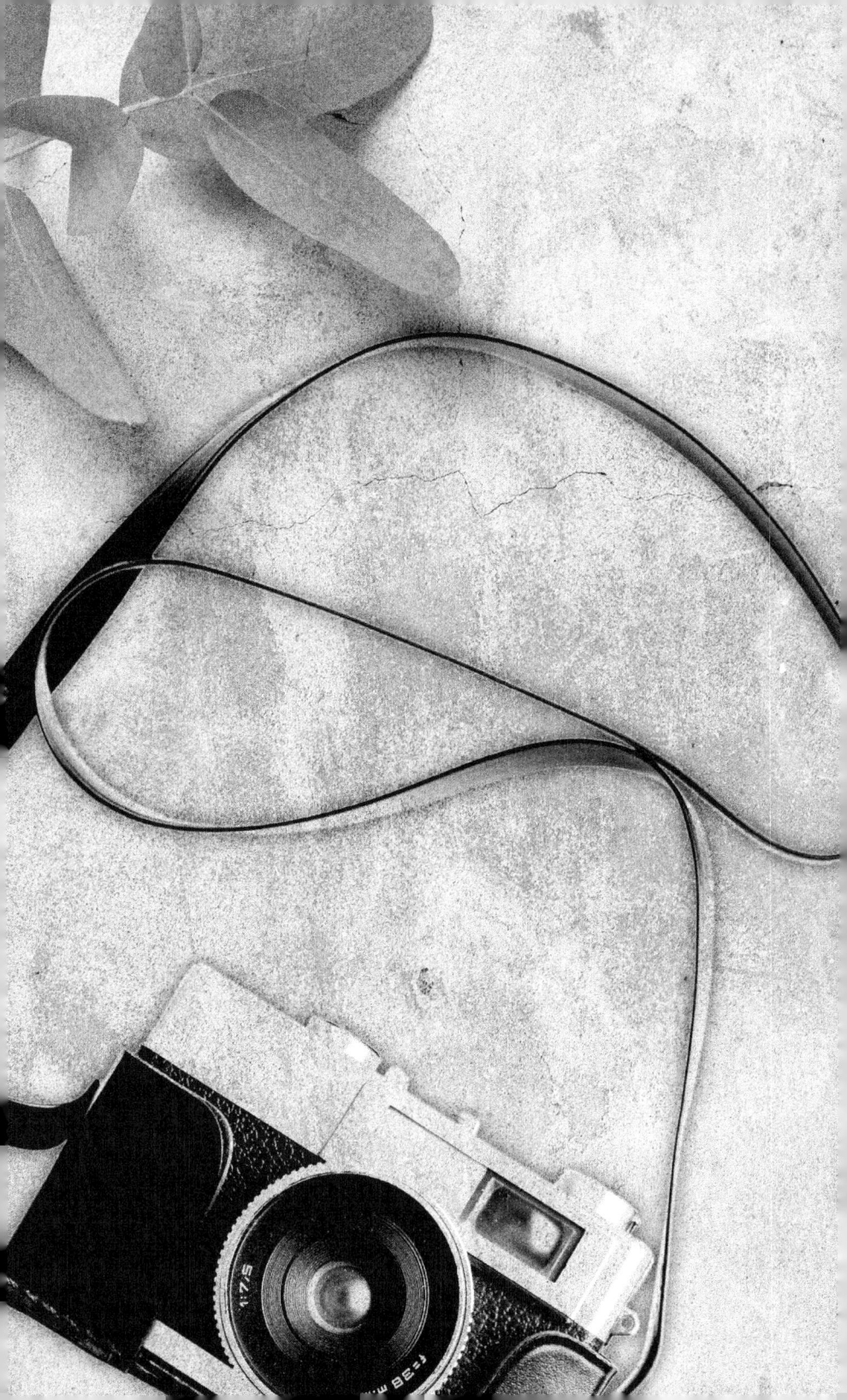

21

Thayne

I was stunned as to how Emberli's surprise baby shower had stayed just that. A surprise. Shadow Peaks wasn't the finest in the secret department but I was glad it had managed to break the curse for today.

The bitter air from outside hit me as Emberli returned from her walk into the town. She claimed that Willow recommended listening to podcasts and they'd proved helpful, which was why every morning at around eleven, Emberli would leave for an hour. It was the perfect time to put in arrangements for the upcoming baby shower and I had put Willow in charge of making sure everything went to plan. As predicted, everything did.

"What's this?" Emberli's hand picks up a book I bought a few days ago about pregnancy. "This isn't one of mine."

"Nah. I bought it a few days ago." I turn just as Emberli leans on her tip-toes, her smooth and cold lips collide with my cheek before she sets down on her heels.

"What was that for?" Not that I minded one fucking bit.

"A thank you."

Note to self: Get more thank yous from Emberli.

"I have a surprise for you."

Her eyes widened. "You do? What is it?"

I gesture for her to follow me into the dining room, where she looks over at me and then the wrapped box on the table. "For me?"

"For you." I confirm and watch her edge towards the box before she begins unwrapping it. A small gasp leaves her mouth before she turns around to me, throwing her arms around my neck.

"Thank you."

"I thought it would help you sleep better." I gesture to the U-shaped pillow I had Odessa help me find.

"This is perfect. I love it."

"I hope you love your next surprise." I wink.

"What is it?"

"Well if I tell you, it will no longer be a surprise. Will it?"

She groans. "When do I get to see this surprise?"

"In approximately three hours."

A smirk crawls onto her lips and she wriggles her eyebrows at me.

"What are you thinking?"

She giggles before running over to the couch, launching herself onto it and setting her feet up on the coffee table in front of her.

I don't even have to ask as she switches the app on the television to *Disney+* to know for sure that we were about to rewatch *The Lion King.*

"I wonder if the baby will recognise the film when they're here."

"With the amount of times you watch it? It's definitely a strong possibility."

"You did this for me?" Emberli asks, her eyes wide in shock as she looks around the town hall I had decorated for her baby shower. "Thayne…"

Balloons fly and party blowers sound around us from every corner.

My eyes find Mack, reminding him to take more photos of her special day.

He raises my camera and sets it on the two of us. He'd helped me make sure this event pulled together just how she deserved, just as the rest of my family had.

Aca even managed to make time to come back for a few nights from his training.

"I can't believe you've done this."

"You deserve it." I tell her, planting a kiss on her forehead as she leans into me, overlooking our friends and family who jump out to surprise her.

"I look horrendous." She looks down at her sundress. *She looks perfect.* But she'll always doubt that because she was her own worst critic.

It was as if she desired to be something else, completely unaware that she was more than enough.

"You look beautiful."

No matter how many times I tell her, she still looks at me the same. Like she isn't sure she believes me, but her widened pupils still stare at me in awe.

"I do?"

"Very beautiful." I correct myself and she laughs, leaning her head into my chest with a whisper. "I love this."

A gasp leaves her throat as Odessa comes over, Emberli's parents and her siblings in tow.

"Mom? Dad?"

Emberli pounces into her parents' arms. "How did you - Ebs! Buck! You're here!"

"Thayne invited us," Georgia grins.

My palms have never sweated harder. Seeing Emberli's family in person was a lot different to speaking to them over the phone. And I knew how much they meant to her.

I could not fuck this up.

Emberli glances over her shoulder at me, a thankful look paints her face before she bites her lip, turning back to her family. "Come on! I want to introduce you to everyone."

"You did good bro." Mack comments as he stands beside me, holding my camera out for me to take. He took a few shots of us when we walked in and I'm staring down at her, grinning like a fool at her shocked expression before she looks up at me with appreciation.

There's a few more photos, one where my lips meet her head, and her eyes close as she smiles, and another where she leans her head into my chest. She's captivating and I could look at her for hours.

I look up to her laughter and grin. She's happy here, with us. With me.

"So when are you going to tell her?"

"Tell her what?"

"That you may or may not like having her around."

"That you love her." Colton sings.

"Don't you dare deny it you idiot." Flint murmurs from the other side of me.

"I want to see you do it before I leave again." Aca says.

"Then you may never leave." Mack snorts and I roll my eyes.

"Will you all quit it? I'll tell her soon."

"Thayne!" Emberli gestures for me to join her. I hand my camera back to Mack and make my way over to her. She holds a balloon out to me, an excited yet nervous look on her face as she does.

"I want you to find out with me."

She shifts closer, holding out a sewing needle for me to take. It's a simple gesture yet it means so much more as I take the needle from her.

"Okay! Ready?" Odessa calls and Emberli looks at me. I look back at her, seeing the complete trust and admiration that she directs towards

186

me.

I don't think I could.

"You ready?" I ask.

Her head bobs. "Are you?"

"For you? I'll be anything."

Her lips thin into a smile just as Odessa counts us down. The two of us admiring the blue confetti that pours from the balloon between us. Once it's dropped, I scoop Emberli in my arms. She squeals excitedly as she buries her head into my chest, her arms locked around my neck. It's as if it's only the two of us here despite the loud cheers and commotion that takes place around us. One thing was for certain, this little boy was going to be very loved.

The rest of the baby shower runs smoothly with the wholesomeness of family being all around. Emberli looks as if she's having an amazing time and that's all that matters to me.

She chats away to Odessa with her mom and sister beside her.

She looks happy. Genuinely happy.

"Thayne." I turn my attention away from my camera as I take a few photos of the women in front of me, and see Des, Emberli's father, standing there. He extends his hand out to me.

"I just wanted to say thank you for looking after my girl."

"Always."

His grip is firm as I shake his hand and he nods before inhaling. "She's not had it easy."

"I know."

Words seem to be at a loss for him and I fill the silence between us. "I'm not going to hurt your daughter, sir."

"Call me Des, please." He pats at my back as he leaves, heading over to Buck who has his face in his phone just as Colton does beside him. They both tap furiously before Buck jumps up from his seat in celebration.

I turn back to Emberli, who I find looking straight back at me with a smile that needs no words.

I know just how she feels because I feel exactly the same.

22

Emberli

"You're getting a tattoo?" My mom's shock is expected when I flip the screen around to show her the tattoo parlor Thayne and I are parked outside of.

I had been in touch with my family since they left, it was bittersweet but mom told me she was happy that I was, and she'd asked me too many questions about Thayne and I. Ones I didn't know the answer to.

It had been a few weeks since the baby shower and I had finally mustered up the courage to book a tattoo appointment. I'd only wanted something small yet meaningful and figured I'd do it before I entered my third trimester.

"Yep." I breathe out. "Slightly nervous."

"I'm so excited for you." I told my parents about the list vaguely a few weeks ago and now, I'm about to tick off a third before-baby endeavor. I was both excited and nervous at the same time. Things felt like they were finally coming together for me. I was doing all these things for me, something I hadn't done in a long time and it felt great.

"You have to send me a picture when it's done." My mom grins before her gaze flicks up to my dad, who appears on the screen.

"Hey Em. You doing okay?"

"I'm doing really well, dad." I say honestly. "How are you guys?"

"We're fine." He chuckles, knowing me too well. "Stop worrying."

"I can't help it. How's Ebs? How's Buck?"

"They're fine too."

"You're not just saying that?"

"No. Everything is great here. Perhaps you and Thayne could visit one time for dinner."

"That sounds great mom."

"So is anyone going with you?" My mom is a smart person, which is why I know that she knows Thayne is sitting beside me. Her suggestive raised eyebrow tells me this.

"Yes." I tell her, keeping my phone close to my face.

She grinds wider. "Hi Thayne!"

I roll my eyes and turn my camera just as Thayne waves. "Hi Mrs Taylor."

"Oh please, call me Georgia!"

"I've got to go guys, it's nearly my time." I say, eager to end the phone call before my mom does something to make this either insanely embarrassing or awkward.

"Have fun Em!"

"But not too much fun!" Dad says desperately before my mom hangs up.

"You ready?" Thayne asks and I let out a deep sigh, one that I feel levitates the heaviness in my body.

"Yep. Let's do this."

"I can't do this." Thayne chuckles, his hand connecting with my lower back as he pushes me forward into the tattoo parlor.

I'm absolutely terrified yet having Thayne here is reassuring.

190

"You can do this." He assures me. "But if you don't want to. We can walk out now."

I nibble at the inside of my lip as I contemplate his offer.

"I'm nervous." I correct myself and he nods.

"That's standard. It's completely up to you what we do next. Okay?"

Nodding, I take a further step into the room where a head pops up from the reception desk.

"Hey Thayne! Hey Emberli!" I have no clue how the smiley female knows my name, but I figure it has something to do with small town talk.

"Hey Astrid. We've got an appointment in five minutes."

Instantly, Astrid's mood puts me at ease and she claps her hands excitedly. "I know! I'm so excited to work with you guys. Don't worry. I'm gonna take care of you."

She's gotta have the most cheerful and western accent I've heard yet as she gestures for us to follow her into the next room where a man is sitting with his shoulders slumped forward and his back turned to us, drawing something up on his iPad.

"This is Brax. Brax!"

Brax turns at the mention of his name before nodding his head at the both of us.

It must be a male thing to greet someone with a nod of the head, because Thayne does exactly the same back to him.

"So are you guys still wanting the same idea as you sent in the email? I've got a few rough sketches if you want to take a look." Astrid suggests.

"Hey. You sure you wanna do this?" I feel Thayne's hand squeeze the back of my neck gently and when I look up, his eyes are softened with nothing but concern behind them.

"Yeah. I'm just… nervous." I blurt out.

"That's perfectly normal, chick. But honestly. This won't take more than five minutes. It won't even hurt. Just a small scratch and burn." Astrid

"Small scratch and burn." I confirm. "Got it."

"I'll go first if it makes you feel better."

I whip my head around to Thayne. "You're getting one too?"

"Yeah. I figured why not." He doesn't say much else, but his words hold more meaning for me than he could ever know. He perches on the tattoo chair where he lets Astrid do her thing, she whizzes around the floor in her chair as she chats away to herself and to Thayne, who seems to have a hard time catching up with her.

"First time?" I glance down to Brax, who's eyes curiously scan any of my visible skin for ink.

"Yeah." I breathe out.

"Where are you getting it done?"

"My shoulder."

"Ah. You'll be fine. Everyone makes a big deal out of it but it's nothing." Says the man who's clothed in them from his neck downwards.

Right. If it hurts as bad as people said, people wouldn't get them done, Right?

"Small scratch and burn!" Astrid chirps and Brax's lips turn into a smile before he looks at me. "Small scratch and burn."

"You want Astrid to do it or I can do it? I've got free time."

"If you don't mind. I'd rather just get it over with."

Brax chuckles at this before nodding his head over to the free tattoo chair.

"Take a seat. I'll be five."

The five minutes Brax takes to get everything ready is excruciatingly long and I feel like it could possibly go on forever until he sits beside me, screwing the cartridge into place.

Oh God. It's happening. It's really happening.

"So how far along are you?" Brax asks, making small talk as he sets up his iPad beside me.

"Just over six months."

Has it really been over a month since I strolled into Shadow Peaks? Wow.

"And you're liking it here so far?"

"Yeah. I love it here. It feels…"

"Like home?"

"Yeah." Brax seems to take the words straight out of my mouth and he nods.

"Yeah I know the feeling."

"You okay?" Thayne asks me from across the room. I let out a deep breath and nod.

"We can stop any time you want to." Brax tells me. "You just let me know, and we'll stop."

"Okay. I'm ready."

The buzzing sound of the machine only gets closer until I feel it vibrating against my skin. I don't know what I was expecting, but it wasn't this.

It was like Astrid had said, a small scratch and burn. It's over within five minutes and I'm sitting admiring the beauty of it in the mirror once it's done.

"Thank you so much." I thank Brax, who snaps a few photos of it on his phone before shrugging. "Ah it's nothing. You took it like a champ."

"That's because she is a champ." Thayne says, hovering over me. "Let's see."

I move my hair off of my shoulder and his eyes harden. I panic for a moment that he absolutely hates it until his fingers brush over the clingfilm, his Adam's apple bobbing in his throat as his lips parted.

"It's the coordinates to this town." I told him.

"I know what it is." He gulps.

I've never felt a moment so tense yet so pure and I want to capture it forever.

"I wanted to remember the place that brought my spark back."

"It's beautiful, Emberli. So beautiful."

"I'm glad you like it." There are pools of emotion in those captivating eyes of his, emotion he doesn't usually show.

Where was the broody, always grumpy Thayne I was so used to?

Not that I missed it. Despite my attraction to the reserved side of him, I was enjoying this side a lot more.

Thayne gets me. And I like to think that I get him too.

"Show me yours." I swallow.

Thayne rolls his sleeve up to reveal three familiar music notes. The exact notes that are in the exact formation of the cover of my notebook.

My heart thrashes in my chest as my fingers trace over his wrist.

It's mesmerising and I can't help but admire it. *Admire him.*

"Thayne, this is perfect." My voice barely surfaces as a whisper and he grins.

"Come on. Let's go home."

Home.

God. Home sounds perfect.

MOM: That was nice of Thayne for coming with you.

ME: It was.

MOM: He's handsome...

ME: Mom. I know what you're doing.

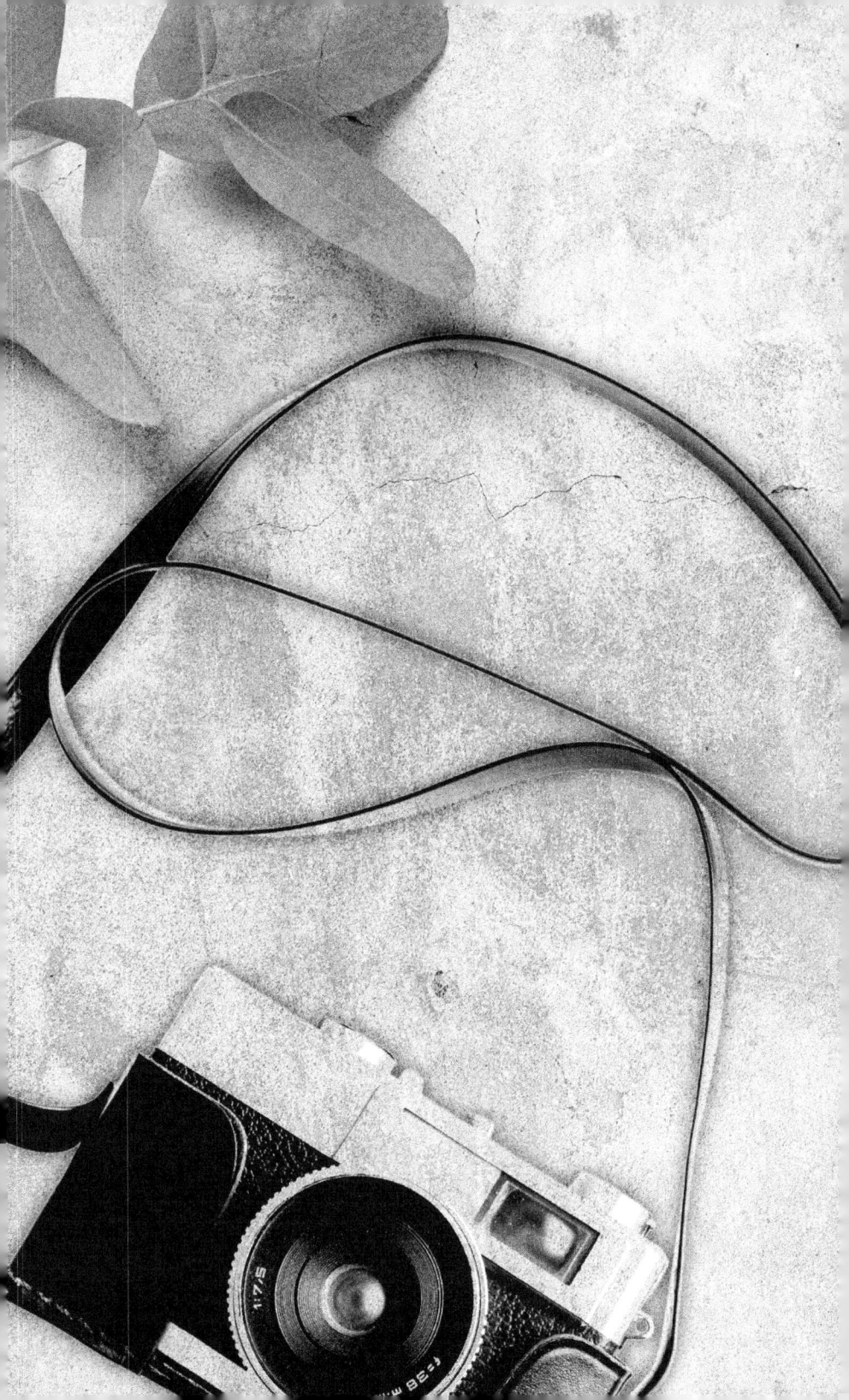

23

Thayne

The drive back to the ranch is relatively quiet. But only because I like hearing Emberli sing Dolly Parton when she comes on the radio.

Her excitement and voice is like no other, and for that reason, I let her fumble around with the radio in my car the way I'd never let anyone else. It's evident the hold she has on me goes beyond my reach.

At first, I wondered if the tattoo was too much. But seeing Emberli's reaction made it worthwhile. I wanted something to remember her by if Willow's plan to get her to stay failed. And I realized when I was looking at her in the tattoo parlor today, I didn't want her to leave.

"Have you thought of any baby names?" She shakes her head at this.

"Have you got any ideas?"

Her curiosity for my ideas is heartening and I shrug. "I've always liked the name Tucker."

"Tucker." She nods. "I like it. Any reason why?"

"No reason." I tell her honestly. "Wanna know what other name I like?"

"Go ahead."

"Emberli."

Her lips stretch into a smile and she looks away as quickly as she can, but not before I

catch her blushing.

"Or we could name it after a character from The Lion King?" I suggest.

She laughs at this. "How about Simba?"

"Perfect." I grin.

"Thank you for today."

I glance over at Emberli, who turns from looking out her window to me.

"You're welcome, trouble."

"I mean it. Thank you." Her eyes are laced with softness and sincerity.

I turned to her. "You don't need to thank me."

"Your argument is void." She tells me. "You literally got a tattoo that resembles me."

I snort a laugh, glancing over to her once again, only this time she squeals, grabbing the wheel and pulling us back onto the road.

"That's a bin!"

I swerve, dodging Miss.Callyman's wheelie bin just in time.

Definitely should focus more on the road and not the beautiful distraction next to me, but it's something I can't help.

"Jesus! I thought I was bad at driving!" She slams her hand to her chest, a movement that takes me back to when Sally was first teaching me how to drive. I must have put that poor woman on the verge of a heart attack several times and not just with my driving.

I was not the most obedient kid growing up, yet Sally and Doug never gave up on me despite all the times I gave them numerous reasons to.

"I highly doubt you can be bad at anything, trouble."

198

Emberli tilts her head to the side. "Thayne Rawlins. Are you flirting with me right now?"

I shoot her another look and she squeals, pushing my face to keep my eyes on the road. "I'm going to die today."

"You're not going to die." This woman had no idea the lengths I'd go to in order to protect her and the unborn baby inside of her. And even if I told her, I'm not sure she'd believe me due to my admittingly horrendous driving.

"I sure hope not." She mumbles. "I'm not ready to die yet."

"Well you're in luck."

"I'm not so sure about that." Her laughter slows when we pull up to the drive. Her face automatically drops and I watch all happiness drain from her face. Suddenly I want to punch whoever made all that pretty light drain from her.

Sitting on the porch,with his guitar, is a man I don't recognise with his guitar. Mack stands over him with a classic Mack stance, both hands on his hips like our grandpa used to do.

I immediately assume the worst from Emberli's reaction, and it isn't until her hand grabs mine that I turn to her, letting go of my door.

"Why did you get the tattoo?"

"What?"

"Why did you get the tattoo, Thayne?"

Her eyes burn into my own with desperation as she waits for my answer, I'm unsure of why we're doing this now. But I give it to her anyway.

"I care about you." There it is. "And I wanted to have something to remember you by in case you left."

Emberli's hand squeezes mine. "I don't want to go."

Her truth has me reeling in my thoughts at just how perfect she is. "Thayne I… I want to stay here."

I swallow down a lump in my throat. "Then stay."

"Okay." She breathes out before her hand retracts. "Hold on to that okay?"

"Hold on to what - Emberli! What are you…" I watch as she jumps out of the truck and rounds the hood of it, quickly stepping towards the guy on the stairs who stands at the sight of her. Which is my cue to get out. Who is this fucker?

I step down from my truck after turning the ignition off and follow behind Emberli.

"What are you doing here, Joel?" Emberli's arms cross over her chest and I stop once I reach my brother.

"Who's this?"

"Joel Peters. Elijah's bandmate. Turned up not long after you left."

"What does he want?" I growl.

"Wanted to hand himself in for a crime and give me intel on Elijah."

"What's the catch?"

Mack nods his head towards Emberli. "He wanted to apologize to her. I've been trying to get hold of you but no answer."

"Sorry. I didn't hear it ring."

"It doesn't matter." He shakes his head. "I have it handled. Honestly, I'm glad to see you're enjoying yourself for once." Mack grumbles, glancing at the interaction in front of us.

"Would it make you feel better if you punched me in the face?" the asshole, Joel, asks sheepishly. Emberli only turns her head away with a scoff before she bites out bitterly. "Yes but I'm not going to do it."

I crack a smile. That's my girl.

"Why are you here, Joel?"

"I heard you were here and I wanted to apologize. I quit the band. Figured I'd hand myself in before Elijah did."

"What do you mean?"

"I stole some shit. Not my finest moment but, Elijah found out. I never wanted to leave you, Em. But I didn't have a choice. Elijah blackmailed me once he heard I wanted to leave the band and I was

200

shit scared."

"It's fine." Emberli says. "There's nothing you can do about it now."

"No. There is something I can do." Joel grabs Emberli's hands in his and in my imagination I'd mauled him for it. "If you take him to court, Em. For everything. I'll be right beside you."

"Court? I can't take him to court, Joel. I'd lose."

I find myself spiraling. Emberli hadn't spoken much about what happened in their relationship and I never pushed her because I knew how it felt to not want to speak about something that had hurt you. But now I find myself reeling at her words, a pit of indignation vibrates throughout my body at not only her mindset, but at Elijah. But he's not here right now, so I take the closest thing to him by the shirt and yank him towards me. "You've got about five seconds to tell me where that dickhead is before I shove your own fist so far down your throat."

"Thayne!" Emberli yelps from behind me.

Joel's hand rises in defence as he shakes his head at me. "Look, I'll tell you anything you want to know."

Damn right you fucking will.

I let go of his shirt and he stumbles back a few meters, keeping a reasonable distance away from me. As far as I was concerned, the dumbass in front of me had also left Emberli stranded and took her car. He had just as much part in this as Elijah did. And I wasn't about to let him forget that.

Emberli appears in front of me, eyes wide and flashing with alert. "Why don't we go inside?" She asks cautiously.

I don't like the idea and only oblige just because Emberli suggests it. The soft spot I have for this woman may as well be a pool of sand at this rate.

Her hand slips into mine like a perfect fit and she gives it a reassuring squeeze, completely unaware that she makes my breath reach a standstill in my lungs.

It turns out Elijah is staying two hours north with a new gig just outside of the city and instead of letting the police up there handle it, Mack was hellbent on going on himself and bringing him back down. I wasn't thrilled with the idea, but Mack had never been one to listen, regardless.

He claimed he needed to leave as soon as possible in case Elijah was on the move and that he wanted peace for our family once and for all, so we all waved him goodbye as he took off in his truck the next morning before breakfast.

"Do you think he'll be okay?" Willow asks.

"He'll be fine, Wills. Mack can handle his own," Ryker assures her.

"It still doesn't mean he should have gone alone. He should have let the local authorities deal with him." Lynnie sighs.

"Who's bike is that?" I ask, once Mack's truck uncovers the pink and black motorcycle that perches on the gravel before the main house.

"Oh that's mine." Willow reveals.

If I had a dollar for every time she tried something new and nearly made me go into cardiac arrest in the process, I'd be rich and living in luxury. It wasn't easy having a younger sister who was set on going against you and your wishes to keep her safe.

I pinch the bridge of my nose in an attempt to compose myself when Flint takes the lead.

"Are you crazy? You've lost your fucking mind."

"My mind is very much in my head. Thank you very much." My sister glares.

"There's no way in hell you're riding a motorcycle around."

"I am because I'm old enough to make my own decisions."

"Obviously not!" The two bicker back and forth before Lynnie steps in, shielding Willow.

"Flint. Shut up. She can do what she wants." Lynnie snaps.

Silence fills the ranch. Only the sounds of birds singing and the distant sounds of horses neighing in the stables surround us.

Lynnie and Flint engage in what appears to be a dangerous stare off. Her hands are balled like she's about to unleash them onto my brother, who glares back at her with the exact same fire that's in her eyes.

The two of them were as headstrong as the bulls we had on the ranch. Neither of them seemed to like the idea of letting the other win, or have the last word. It had been a scene we'd all watched before, numerous times. And, as entertaining as it was, it was also highly annoying and often caused a divide between Willow and Flint.

I love my brother, but he is the walking definition of overbearing. It hurt to see their relationship like it was and I knew it wasn't easy on either of them.

"Okayyy." Colt sings as he steps between them, slinging an arm around both of their shoulders. "What do you say we crack open a few beers and watch the game?"

"Are we seriously just going to ignore the fact that our baby sister has a fucking motorbike? The same baby sister who crashed our tractor four times in a month."

"That was not my fault." Willow objects. "I didn't see the barrels of hay."

Flint looks at me for some help in the situation but Willow looks at me hopeful, like she's asking for me to take her side. I think back to what she said, about being an adult and wanting to be treated like one. And against the internal argument that bickers inside of me, I say, "Colt's right. Let's go inside."

My sister beams happily at this, jumping at me and hugging me tightly. "Thank you, Thayne. I mean it."

Willow was right. She was old enough to make her own decisions and although I might not agree with most of them, she was still my baby sister and I wanted her to be happy.

When everyone else piles inside, Emberli's arm links with my own and pulls us back before her lips press lightly against my cheek.

"That was really sweet of you." She says once we reach the

porch. The two of us stop and the world continues spinning past us.

Her eyes search mine and a smile plays at her lips, like she's about to say something else. I wait patiently in front of her just before Colton slams his hands beside him on the doorframe, interrupting us.

"Hurry up, lovebirds! Or I'm going to eat all the pancakes!"

This captures Emberli's attention as she glares at him. "You dare!"

24

Emberli

Five days have passed since Mack left and they have dragged. What feels like weeks has only been two days, with a short message to Thayne saying that everything will be okay and is under control.

And on the topic of Thayne, he and I had fallen into a pattern of spending more time together than usual. He'd often stay behind at work to drop me home after my gigs and had even accompanied me to my second check-up appointment here in Shadow Peaks, where I was relieved to find a younger and more amiable midwife filling in for the not at all missed space of Stacey.

Her name was Rhea and I was convinced she was a godsend. She'd recently moved into the town from the big city for a more simple and quieter life. Something I too had found myself wanting more and more. And I wouldn't forget the look on Thayne's face as I told her I agreed with her. I think a part of him still doesn't believe I'm here to stay.

Rhea was more than accommodating. She'd even given me her phone number. I'm not sure she knew exactly what she was getting into when she did, but she still answers my texts at midnight saying that I can indeed eat five bananas one after another if I wanted to.

I'd introduced her to the girls and, as expected, she fitted right in. I'd never had an overly-wide circle of friends until I came here. The girls were all amazing. I couldn't ask for any better than them.

After speaking to Odessa, who seemed to have become my unpaid therapist after my gigs, I'd been meaning to work up the courage to ask Thayne about what was going on between us, but I bailed every time I was given the opportunity.

Fear of rejection? Positive.

I'd never missed alcohol more. Liquid courage would have got this sorted out by now. Done and dusted. But instead, I had to be brave for once and not rely on alcohol to give me that extra confidence boost. It was bad enough that I was already lacking in the confidence department.

I spent my time this morning looking around for Thayne, but he's nowhere to be seen.

He wasn't in the cabin and nowhere to be seen on the ranch either.

When I make my way into the main house, it's only Colton who's there, cursing at the video game he plays.

"Have you seen Thayne?" Colton's eyes dart up to me from the television he's taken over as he pauses his game.

"I think he's down at the graveyard. He won't be long. Anything I can help you with?"

I collapse on the couch beside him and run a hand over my bump. "No. Not unless you can pretend to be me."

He chuckles. "I think that might be a bit hard. Wanna talk about it?"

"No, it's okay."

The last thing I wanted to do was burden Colton with my current problems, despite them eating away at me.

His eyes flicker to mine. "Wanna play a game to distract yourself?" He hands me a controller and I don't hesitate to snatch up

208

the opportunity to take my mind off Thayne and I for a little while.

I spent the next hour listening to Colton chat my ear off about a girl he was hung up on, often using it as an excuse for when I won. All five times.

"I just… I don't know. Everything comes back to her. Does that make sense?"

"I mean, yeah." I click the trigger on the controller numerous times as my in game character finds Colton.

"Fuck!" He yells and tosses his controller to the side, falling back into the couch with a groan. "Why are you so good at this?"

"My brother," I say. "Look, if you like this girl you can't be whoring around like you are currently."

"Ouch. But true."

"If she's the one, she needs to know that."

"But the others, they're all just distractions from the way I feel about her. She doesn't get that."

I stare at him, trying to make sure I heard what he'd just said correctly.

"Colt. If you were in her shoes, would you accept what you've just said to me?"

He goes silent for a moment before grunting. "No."

"Exactly. If you want her, you need to show her you do." I shrug.

"You don't understand, I think I've fucked it this time."

"What, so you're just willing to give up?"

"No. Yes. I don't know. Women are complicated."

"Men are complicated." I counter with a sigh.

"It's always been her. But I'm afraid I've fucked it up for real this time. I take every chance she gives me and ruin it just like I do with every other good thing in my life."

"What's her name?"

"Jaycee."

"And does she love you?" Colt nods at this.

"I think so. She always has."

"Then trust me, you can win her back."

"You really think so?"

"I'm a woman. I know these things. Life lesson? Women are always right."

Colt nods firmly. "Got it. Thanks, Emberli. That kid inside of you is going to be so lucky to have you as a mom." A sigh leaves him. "I never really had many memories of mine, but I can imagine she was like you. You're gonna be an amazing mom, Em."

I involuntarily tear up and Colton's eyes widen at this. "Oh God. Are you gonna cry? I didn't mean to upset you, Em."

"I'm fine." I wave him off. I've gotten used to the daily cries lately. Accepting myself not as weak, but as a hormonal, justifiably so, mess.

"I'm not good with females crying. Tell me what to do. Did I upset you?"

I laugh at this but it comes out strained, like a wail.

"No you didn't."

"What did you say to her, shithead?" Thayne's grouchy voice fills the living room and we both turn to him. His eyes bounce between his brother and I before he narrows them. "Are you okay?"

I nod and then sniffle. "Colton was just being sweet. Where have you been? I've been trying to find you." I wipe my eyes.

"I was at the graveyard and then I took a trip to Lacey's for some camping bits."

"We've got a shit ton in the shed out back." Colton says.

"Wanna come help me look?" Thayne asks and I nod, following him in silence into the backyard as I attempt to phrase what I want to say to him in my head.

Hey, so what is this?

Hey! Is there something between us?

This was awful.

Excruciatingly awful and painful.

How does one attempt to bring up numerous situations I need explaining?

I needed to know what this was between us.

Was I even ready? Yes, I definitely was.

Was Thayne?

And if so, would he even want to be with me?

Had I misread everything?

Perhaps he was just helping me out. Perhaps he didn't feel what I was feeling.

"Colt was right," Thayne mumbles. "There's so much stuff in here."

"Did you guys camp much as kids?"

"Yeah all the time. We used to hike into the mountains and set up camp for a few nights."

"I see." I see?

God. How awkward can I get?

Thayne's head dips as he enters the small shed, the man is so broad that he fills up most of the small space as he clatters around.

"Pick up anything you want to take."

"Okay," I say slowly and he turns to me, almost as if he can hear the hesitation in my shaky voice.

I don't know why it was so hard to just come out and ask him if we could talk. I think a part of me was worried that I'd get shut down the way I used to with Elijah.

Thayne was nothing like him, but my fears were all the same.

It appears that being constantly deprived of basic communication would do that to a person.

"You okay?" Nope.

"Yep."

One not-convinced eyebrow raise later, Thayne strides forward to me, his eyes flying up to above my head just as a watering can on the shelf rocks. He grabs it with one hand almost instinctively before it falls, snagging my waist towards him with his freehand.

I try not to gawk at Thayne too much, but it's almost as if it's unachievable. The two of us remain firm in place until he pulls me closer, making this a lot more intimate than it just was. Neither one of us speaks. Our breaths tangled closely and my eyes flicker over his lips as I wonder just for a second what they'd taste like.

Thayne's facial expression remains unreadable. Unaffected. But the heavy intensity of his focus on me is enough to cause every inch of my body to go into dysregulation.

I'd bet money that he doesn't even know the effect he has on me.

I want to capture this moment in a picture that I can remember forever, which sounds awfully cringey and somewhat childish. But that's what Thayne Rawlings has done to me.

"Colt told me I could find…Woah! Sorry! Didn't realize I was interrupting something. Let me just…" Willow startles the both of us and she gracelessly fumbles with the door of the shed as she tries to close it. "Sorry!"

"We're meant to go out riding." Thayne explains as he loosens his grip on me, clearing his throat.

"Right." I awkwardly look anywhere else but at him.

"Look, why don't you take a look in here and see if there's anything you want to take on the camping trip, okay? I'll meet you back home."

"Okay." My throat is as dry as anything, as I wipe the sweat off my hands and onto my dress. "Can we talk soon?"

My words stop him in his tracks and he turns around, his eyebrows knitted together in concern. "Of course we can. Do you want to do it now? I can cancel on Wills, she won't mind."

"No." I shake my head. "No. You go. We'll talk later, yeah?"

"Okay." He smiles, leaning in and pressing a soft kiss against my temple. It's a short and sweet moment that has my heart thumping in its chest even when Thayne leaves.

That man had a habit of making my heart beat in ways it's never beaten before. It becomes apparent to me that Thayne Rawlins owns it. He owns my heart.

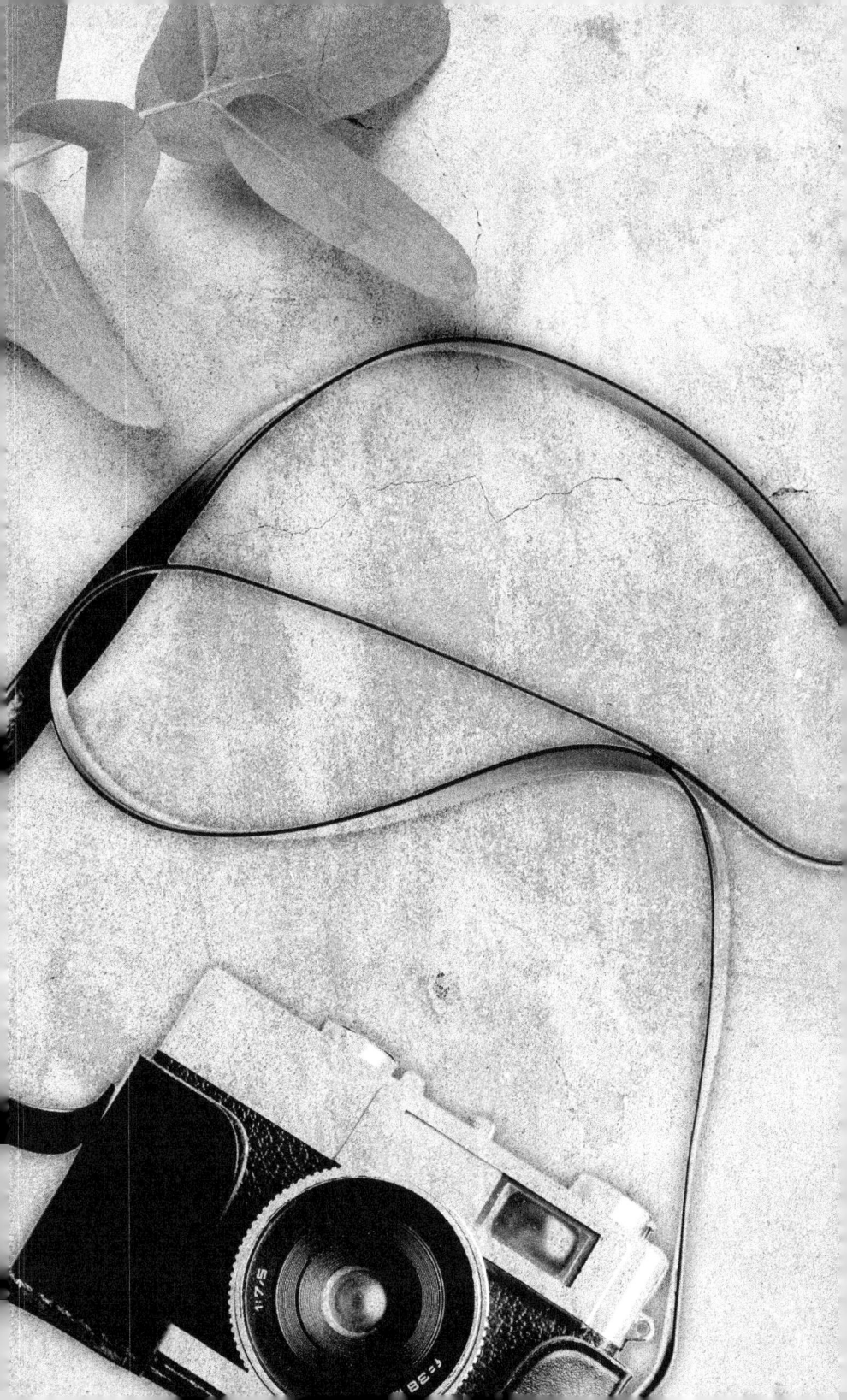

25

Thayne

The blades of grass are overgrown as Willow and I ride through the vast plains, specks of golden and green pasture merge together under the herd of cattle in the distance. The wind is high as it flies over the peaks, whistling past us with a heavy push.

"Are we going to talk about what I stumbled upon fifteen minutes ago?" Willow asks as she rides alongside me.

"Nope."

"Okay. Let me rephrase. We are going to talk about it."

I roll my eyes, I should have known better than to say no to my younger sister, who appeared to never know just when to quit.

Didn't need a DNA test to know she was a Rawlins.

"There's nothing to talk about."

"Nothing?! Thayne you were literally about to snog her face off."

I turn my nose up at her choice of words. "I was not about to snog her face off."

Lucy, beneath me, makes a snorting sound at my words. Like my sister, it's clear my horse doesn't believe me either.

"See? Even Luce thinks you're talking whack."

"Do you like her?" I turn to my sister just as we start to move downhill, she stares at me, waiting for my response.

"Of course I like her."

She nods her head slowly. "And... Do you want to be with her?"

"I'm not having this conversation, Wills."

"Yes we are."

There it is again. That Rawlins' stubbornness I know so well. My sister didn't give up easily, it was one of the best yet worst traits about her.

"It's been a long time since I've let someone in."

"I know." Willow's voice cracks with emotion, I can feel her looking at me even though I look forward. "That's why I don't want you to mess this up and push her away."

"Wills."

"I'm only looking out for you because I love you and I've grown to love Emberli too. You've been through something traumatic, Thayne. And Emberli has only just surfaced out of a really emotionally abusive relationship."

"I know, Wills. You don't have to look out for me."

"You're my brother. Of course I'm going to, dipshit." She sighs. "But I'm serious, okay? If you're all in with her. You have to be all in."

"I am. I just don't want to force her into anything she's not ready for."

216

"She likes you, Thayne. I've seen it."

And whilst I hope what Willow says is true, I can't stand the thought of losing Emberli like I've lost others.

"And I know you'll be good to her. But she wants to give you the world, Thayne. Let her. For once, let someone else take the lead."

"Alright. That's enough about me."

I tend to try to make light of serious situations so they don't seem so serious.

Serious is terrifying and I'm not good at it.

Something I'd need to work on if I wanted whatever this thing was with Emberli to work. Because I do want it to work. I've just never been good at the whole letting people in thing.

Willow shoots me a knowing look, completely aware of the avoidance I'm dancing with.

"What's the deal with the motorcycle?"

"There is no deal."

"Oh come on, Wills. I thought we were honest with each other."

A long and heavy sigh leaves her mouth and I want to fix all the problems she seems to have rushing through her mind. I hate seeing her so overwhelmed. Willow was tested for ADHD as a child, but her results came back and found her not to have it. My family and I didn't agree. Willow had masked her feelings all the way up to the age of twelve and that's when the over excitement and stress went to war on each other. It was as if she was in a constant battle with her emotions and when she'd return home from school, she'd be so exhausted she'd fall asleep immediately. As she got older, her traits changed. Like now, she's obsessed with something new each week, and her determination to do this new thing is always unmatched and excitable. She never falters. But she does get bored, which is why she hasn't had a boyfriend in a very long time.

Willow described to me that she felt her brain never stopped. Even when she woke, she often felt tired like she hadn't slept one bit.

It baffled me how she could continue to stay so positive all day, every day.

She believed that everything in this world happened for a reason, it was one thing we disagreed on most. But apart from that, Willow and I had always been close, which is why she's so worried about my life choices instead of her own.

"You seem like you're spiraling." I tell her. She shoots a glare at me.

"I am not spiraling. I just like the way it feels. I like the control I have. Makes me feel like I'm in control of something in my life." She mutters, a clear dig at Flint who hasn't given her a break as of late.

"Want me to talk to him?"

She shakes her head. "Nah. Don't bother. It won't change anything."

Flint was many things. Strong-headed being one of them.

"Wills. If he's upsetting you this much, I'll talk to him."

"Honestly, it's not him. I've just been feeling more down than usual lately."

"Any reason why?"

"Beats me." Willow shrugs her shoulders as she gives a pat to her horse before jumping off her and stares at the meadows in front of us. "I'm okay. It'll pass."

She was always so hopeful. So positive.

Willow turns to me with a stern look on her face. "However, if I hear you've so much as upset Emberli, there will be hell to pay. Understand?"

I grin at my sister's protectiveness. "Understood."

Her face softens. "When are you going to tell her, Thayne?"

"We're talking tonight."

"You know what I'm talking about, Thayne. When are you going to tell her about Mae?"

Emberli sits so rigid in her chair you'd think she was frozen. Her face is so pale that for a moment I'm unsure if she's unwell.

Seeing her on edge puts me over it. She's even more awkward than usual, blundering around the living room like a spider attempting to flee for its life until I had to forcefully sit her down.

"What's wrong?"

She hesitates.

"Hey. Talk to me."

Her shoulders immediately relax before she inhales a huge breath. "What is this? What is… going on here?"

I'd expected this talk sooner rather than later. Assurance was something I'd noticed Emberli needed and I had no issue giving it to her.

"Like I don't want to get the wrong idea and you're just being nice? Oh God. What if you are just being nice? What if I've…" I'm over by her side in two seconds, sitting beside her and resting my hand on her own as she rambles away.

"You haven't got the wrong idea, Emberli."

"I haven't?" Her eyes flicker to mine curiously.

"No. Look. I like you, a lot. But I don't want to force you into anything you're not ready for."

In the grand scheme of things, it had only been a few months since Elijah and her had ended. The last thing I wanted to do was spring the idea of us onto her when she wasn't ready.

"I like you too." She breathes out.

And fuck, does it feel amazing to hear her say those few words.

"But I'm scared."

"Understandable."

She looks at me nervously. "What does this mean? For us? There's a lot more at stake than just me now. What if you decide you don't want this? What if you change your mind?"

Her worries tear at my heart, knowing that they probably come from a long list of things Elijah has said and done to her.

I grind my teeth together. "I can assure you that nothing is going to change my mind about you."

She nods slowly, taking it in. "I can't promise that I'm going to be perfect."

"I'm not asking you to be perfect, trouble. I'm asking you to be you."

"I can be me." She breathes out.

"Good, because you are all I want."

And even though my words are true, I can see her thinking them over in her head, her brows furrowed as she does.

"Thayne. I'm scared." Her head dips and I catch her chin, tilting it up to face me.

"Hey. We don't have to do anything. We can just see how it goes."

Her face visibly relaxes at this. "See how things go."

"Yeah."

She ponders on this for a second before nodding. "Okay. I like that. I have another question." Her cheeks flush a pink color and I lean back on the sofa.

"By all means, ask away."

"Okay. So this… seeing how things go, does this entail seeing other people?"

Fuck no.

I try not to show any sign of emotion as the words leave her mouth, and clear my throat. "Do you want to see other people?"

"I mean… yeah. I've just… I've spent so long with one person that I just want to be on the dating scene for a while, you know?"

I nod even though I feel I'm in a chokehold. I don't want Emberli to see other people, but if that's what she needs to do before she realizes I'm the one, then so be it.

I'll just have to make all of her dates disappear, perhaps I could take a page out of Flint's book.

Emberli's eyes search my face and I try incredibly hard not to show the jealousy that consumes me whole.

"You're okay with that?" she asks.

I bite out a strangled "Yep." And she bursts out laughing, flying back into the sofa as she shakes her head at me with a huge grin on her face.

"Thayne, I don't want to see other people." She giggles. Thank fuck for that.

I know I wasn't the only one in town who wanted to date Emberli, so I'd have my work cut out for me with all the disappearing acts I'd have to perform. I'd still do it regardless but at least now I didn't have to.

"You should have seen your face." She giggles. "I should have taken a picture."

"Well, how about you picture this… You and I, forever." Her eyes soften at my words and I reach over, squeezing her hand.

"I was trying to be nice. I really don't want you to see other people." That smile I enjoy seeing so much makes another appearance on her lips as she rolls them together.

"So we're seeing how things go, and not seeing other people." She confirms.

"Correct."

"Okay. I'm glad that's out of the way." All seriousness drops from her face as she turns to me with a smirk. "Wanna watch The Lion King?"

I hate that fucking film.

Can you be jealous over a film? I'm definitely envious of how much she pays attention to it.

But I say yes and pop some corn because watching it makes Emberli happy. Most of it anyway.

I grab a box of tissues for when Mufasa's death scene surfaces and plonk myself beside her.

This, right here, is where I want to be forever. By her side.

26
Emberli

Camping was a total and absolute flog.

It turns out that neither of us checked the weather forecast to see that there were thunderstorms and heavy winds due. Dark rain clouds integrated above the truck as we headed back home in an attempt to beat the storm. We made it back fine and had gotten word from Mack that he was also okay. The storm had just missed him. He hadn't managed to locate Elijah and thinks Joel set him up. A part of me couldn't help but feel responsible for it all and for believing Joel would help.

Thayne had apologized repeatedly for us not being able to go camping. I don't think he knew just how much I appreciated spending time with him, no matter what it was.

The storm passed in two days, however it had wreaked havoc. Trees had fallen, gates had broken and cattle had escaped. Not to mention the damage to houses around us, broken pieces of painted wood were scattered throughout the town. It had put Rawlins' Ranch in turmoil to say the least, and Flint was flying off the handle. He had been since three in the morning.

Like the gentleman he is, Thayne told me to get some sleep and rest. But I wanted to help and besides, it was about time I started pulling my weight around here. The Rawlins' family had done everything in their power to help me, it was about time I repaid the favour.

Apparently everyone, their mother and their mother's mother is shopping at Lacey's after the hit we took the past few days, and I'm waiting in line when someone I vaguely recognise waves at me and cuts the queue in order to reach me.

"Hey! Emberli, right?"

I know a fake when I see one, and standing in front of me was Annie. The woman from the night of Aca's leaving party.

Go away, toxic energy! Shoo!

I had no clue what she wanted with me, but I could guarantee it wasn't genuine. People like her never are.

"Annie. Good to see you."

"So good to see you. How's the ranch?"

"We lost a few cattle and a few sheds have blown over but it's nothing that isn't fixable."

"Shame. I can always come and help out?"

"I think we've got it under control, thanks." I put a divider after my items on the conveyor belt and feel her eyes lingering on me.

"It's always just so amazing to see how that family manages to pick themselves up after everything that's happened, you know?"

I nod, taking note of the overly-sympathetic voice she puts on before sighing dramatically and loudly, drawing attention to us. More than I wanted, especially looking the way I do right now.

I have a heavy stained band tee and black comfy yoga pants, and to top it all off… I don't even think I've brushed my hair today.

"I mean, after Mae… just so sad."

"Mae?" I clamp my jaw shut. Aware I've just given the woman beside me something to chew on, she smiles triumphantly but

224

manages to hide it with a pitiful one. "You didn't know?"

I say nothing and move forward in the line.

"I'm surprised Thayne didn't tell you. Considering how close you two are and all."

"Sorry, Annie. I'm kind of in a rush here."

"I'm just shocked. Maybe you and Thayne aren't as close as you seem. I'd understand it considering Elijah killed her."

Suddenly I feel like I've been sucker punched.

What was she talking about?

Who was Mae?

And why hadn't Thayne told me about her?

This is exactly what Annie wanted, and when she sees the shock on my face, I realize I've just handed the trophy to her.

"Oh babe, I'm so sorry."

Murmurs surround us just as a cherry-red head pops up beside us both. "Annie. Outside now."

Annie looks at my savior in disgust, flickering her gaze up and down before turning on her heels and disappearing. Thank fuck.

I can't stand that woman and I've met her twice. God knows how the rest of the town copes.

"Don't let her get to you. Ignore her." Says the woman as she takes off after Annie.

I'm having one of those frequent moments where I forget how to breathe. And when I do it's a shaky inhale that feels like an icicle stabbing at my throat.

I barely even remember paying at the checkout, or walking back to the ranch. I'm in a whirlwind state of confusion by the time I place the bags down on the counter.

I don't know what I'm feeling.

More questionably, I don't know how I should feel.

In the living room, Colton is playing his video game and losing, no surprise there.

Ryker and Flint are talking about what seems to be repairs for the ranch. Doug and Sally hover behind them, listening. Lynnie, Odessa and Willow are talking about Willow's missing motorcycle that had disappeared during the storm, Lynnie blames it on Flint and then she and Flint begin to bicker. Again, no surprise there.

And Thayne was in front of me, both hands on my shoulders as he frowns. "You look pale. Are you okay?"

"Who's Mae?"

If I looked pale, Thayne had just turned into a ghost. His entire face drops. There isn't an ounce of expression on it. None that I can read anyway.

Silence blankets the entire house. It's as if nobody dares to speak, as if I've just brought up something unspeakable.

"When were you going to tell me about her?" When were you going to tell me how my ex-boyfriend killed her?

"Emberli. Listen, I don't want to do this right now."

"Do what right now? I just want to know who she is. Or was I - I don't understand…"

"You don't have to. Okay?" Thayne's tone is harsh and abrupt. "Just leave it."

Mae is obviously someone he doesn't want to speak about. And I should have left it there like I always did, but I couldn't do that anymore.

Something had to change.

I couldn't continuously push away my feelings to benefit others, and whilst I'm sure Thayne doesn't mean to shut me down, he's doing just that.

"I want to know who she is."

"And I don't want to have this conversation."

"Guys. Let's just calm down," Willow suggests and I glance to her, to all the faces behind her.

And then it hits me.

Everyone knew. Everyone except me knew.

Maybe I shouldn't be as upset as I am. Maybe it's the hormones. But the familiar sting of a slap in the face from feeling alone is

226

enough to wake me up.

"You all knew, didn't you?" I'm horrified. Humiliated. My chest is rising and falling rapidly and Thayne doesn't reach out to comfort me when a warm tear slides down my cheek. We stand only centimetres apart, yet we couldn't be further. The irrational side of me takes over and I suddenly have the urge to pack up all my things and leave.

"Oh my God. I don't understand. Why didn't you tell me Elijah killed someone? How did he… What happened?"

"Elijah happened. He hit her with a car. Is that what you want to hear?" Thayne can't even make eye contact with me, or more specifically, he won't.

Did he blame me for what Elijah did?

Is that why he hated me so much when I first arrived?

Oh God.

Everything was piecing together and suddenly there wasn't anything I hated more in this world than the truth. I should have known my short-lived happiness would eventually meet a standstill. And it appeared this was it.

"I want to talk to you about this."

"Enough." Thayne shakes his head. "I'm not doing this. Let's just forget this conversation."

"No." I follow him into the kitchen. "Don't shut me out." I plead.

Everything in my body aches, and it feels like I'm slowly evaporating.

"Nothing you say, nothing I do, can bring Mae back. Okay? Do you understand that? This may come as a shock to you, Emberli. But not everything is about you."

"Thayne!" Someone yells from the doorway and as I turn, as if this situation isn't embarrassing enough, everyone stands there. Willow's eyes flicker between her brother and I.

"Excuse me." Mortification ripples through me and I swear I'm about to be sick any moment now from the revelations that have surfaced.

"Hey." Thayne's hand grabs my wrist, a spark of guilt and need threads through his voice as he spins me to face him. "I'm sorry. I'm sorry, okay?"

I withdraw my hand from his grasp, keeping my head high and begging myself to hold it together until I get outside.

"It's fine. Let's just save the hassle of all of this."

"No. Don't do this. Don't push me away."

"I don't have a choice. I spent years trying to communicate with someone who wouldn't do the same. And it drove me to lose myself. I won't do that again. I deserve more than that, Thayne. I can't do this. Okay? I just can't." I turn, desperately trying to escape and this time, he lets me.

He doesn't follow, and as much as the lover in me wants him too, I know we need our space right now.

And for once, I need to prioritise mine.

27
Emberli

I think your mind sometimes plays tricks on you. I think sometimes when something happens, your mind will erase it, change it or leave it there for you to remember. Or the moment will happen so quickly, you don't know if it even really happened at all.

Elijah's hands tighten on my upper arms, a bit tighter than I'd expected, and my heart sinks in my chest when I realize the intent behind it. He isn't just forcing me out of the doorway, he's hurting me.

I beg him in my head to take it back, to not ruin what we have. Neither of us speak about it, but we both know what had just happened.

It felt like a pinch at first, and I tried to blink to create a mental picture of it. To remember it.

But some sick, fucked up part of me attempts to forget it entirely.

He was only trying to get out of the door. It was my fault I was blocking it because I didn't want him to leave.

Yeah.

It was my fault.

I stand there for a few minutes, not knowing how we ever got to this moment before I move out of the doorway.

I let Elijah leave.

I let him go.

Towards the end of our relationship, Elijah and I would argue daily about the pregnancy, the band and us. We started to never see eye to eye. At least that's what Elijah said.

But I saw it as I finally grew a backbone and told him how I really felt.

And maybe it was my fault, maybe I should have told him sooner. But I was so scared of his reaction that I kept it quiet until the old me was thrashing around inside of me, screaming about how wrong he was treating me and desperate to get out.

I think Elijah realized he didn't have any control over me anymore and from that moment on, things crashed down in a spiral and it was only a matter of time after that before he left me at the motel at junction five.

I never knew him. That was clear to me.

I never knew all the awful things he did to other people, I only knew the awful things he did to me.

WILLOW: Emberli, I'm so sorry.

WILLOW: Are you mad at me?

WILLOW: Who am I kidding, of course you are. I'm sorry I hid this from you.

"Why is it that when something goes wrong, you pack up all your stuff and leave?" My mom asks on the other end of the phone.

"Because." I sob. "I can't stay here. I've embarrassed myself."

"You need to breathe, is what you need to do, Em. You're too irrational. It is not the end of the world. Okay?"

I sniffle. "Then why does it feel like it is?"

"Because that's just how these things feel. It's normal."

"I want to come home." I blurt out.

"No you don't." She chuckles.

She was right. I didn't want to come home.

I didn't want to argue with Thayne either, and I felt like a total bitch for doing so. For pushing him to talk about something when he wasn't ready.

God.

What about how I feel?

How do I feel and why is that not important to me?

"I'm scared that I've fucked this all up."

"Honey. You only wanted to talk. You haven't messed anything up. Have you seen the way that man looks at you?"

I sit down on the bed, overlooking my now packed overnight bag and realize I may have overreacted.

It's a specialty of mine that I'm sure my unborn son will inherit.

The door downstairs closes and I panic, scurrying to shut my bedroom door. "Mom, I have to go."

"Should I expect you at my door within four hours?"

"It's a maybe." I end the call, hearing the heavy footsteps draw closer and closer to my bedroom door before there's a knock.

Do I climb out of the bedroom window?

I toss the bag over my shoulder before sliding it up, feeling as if I'm in high school again, sneaking out after curfew.

Only this time I'm avoiding the man I love. I speedily walk down the drive, hearing footsteps thud after me.

Don't look back. Keep walking.

I adjust the strap on my overnight bag just as it's taken from me.

"Hey! No fucking way." It's Thayne. He holds my overnight bag away from me and shakes his head with a sullen look on his face. "You're not leaving."

I reach to grab my bag from him but he only holds it further away. "I get you're angry with me and we're not entirely good right now, but that doesn't mean I want you to leave. So I'm going to put your bag back in your room and give you space and when you and I are both ready, we're going to solve this. Together."

"Look I …"

"Listen to me. I should have told you. I'm sorry." Behind him, Willow and her brothers stand on the porch a few meters away.

I sigh. "I don't know. I feel humiliated."

"Don't look at them. Look at me." He pleads and his hands reach out to grab mine, his thumbs rubbing circles on mine. "I should have told you. They all told me to and I didn't."

"I just don't know right now." My head was throbbing and for someone who desperately needed communication, I hated it right now. I just needed to be alone.

"I'm not asking you to know. I'm asking you to take the time you need. I'll be here when you get back. Or call me and I'll pick you up."

"Look, I think it's best we cut this off now."

His eyes stare into mine, he sees straight through me. Something no one else does. He sees me. Thayne really sees me.

"No you don't. You're pushing me away."

I fear in the months I've known this man that he seems to know me better than I know myself. And that's why it's so hard for me to not jump into his arms right there and then.

"I need to think. I need to… process."

"I know. It's okay."

I end up forcing myself on a walk around the town and stripping out of my clothes by a noiseless lake.

This looked so much more unsanitary than it did in the movies, but I was going to do it anyway. To complete my list.

234

The water has a harsh coldness to it as I dip my feet in, wiggling my toes around in the damp grass.

Squelch.

Yep. Definitely not the same as the movies.

I don't know why I romanticised them so much, I think it was because everything in them was always so perfect. The guy gets the girl and so forth. It's all every young girl wants. Or at least that was what I wanted.

A prince to my princess.

A knight in shining armor.

The endings of those movies are always the same and as much as I didn't want to say it, unrealistic.

I walk in further, allowing the somewhat slimy yet calm water to pacify me, despite the coolish feeling that invades my skin, before plunging all but my head into the water. An involuntary squeal leaves my lips as goosebumps conquer my body. But I feel safe under the blanket of darker water and moss floating nearby.

It's funny how the weirdest of places can make you feel so secure. Even in the arms of those who've wronged you countless times.

It's eerily silent around the lake until a truck pulls up thirty minutes later. But not just any truck. The sirens blare as the door shuts and Mack stands before me, taking his hat off before he clears his throat. "I got a complaint from Miss Callyman. Something about a nude woman in the lake. You wouldn't happen to know anything about that, would you?"

Fucking Miss Callyman. I should have let Thayne hit her bins when he had the chance. "Nope. But I think she went that way." I point left and he laughs, grabbing a towel out of his truck and averting his eyes.

"Come on. I'll get you a coffee."

The sun beamed through the window and onto the table in the diner where the dreamy scent of Big Al's coffee was enough to level my emotions that had been all over the place this morning. Loud and cheerful chatter surrounds Mack and I in the corner booth where he points a new waitress out to me.

Turns out, she's not that new. She's Big Al's granddaughter and returned home after a year of volunteering at an animal sanctuary in Africa. Her name is Jaycee. And she's the same woman who chased Annie off this morning in Lacey's. She's also the woman Colton is in love with.

It's clear that she's rushed off her feet as she dances around the busy diner with various trays in both hands, barking orders at the other waitresses on the floor who roll their eyes when she isn't looking.

"How come I've never seen Big Al?" I ask.

Mack picks up a chip from the middle of the table before dunking it in a pot of gravy.

"He's often resting at home now he's getting older. Mavis' orders."

"Are they a thing?"

"Who Mavis and Big Al?" Mack chuckles, "since the beginning of time. The real high school sweethearts, them two. Was just a shame Big Al cheated. And then along came Jaycee."

"Did Mavis forgive him?"

"No."

I glance over at Mavis, her stern exterior seems to mask everything else she feels as she pours coffee and talks to the locals.

"But she loves him. So she helps him out."

I continue to stare until she must feel my eyes on her and she looks straight at me. I quickly look away and Mack grabs another chip, tossing it into his mouth before speaking. "You know I once ran away from home with a suitcase that was too big for me and a jam sandwich."

"Yeah?"

"Yeah. Lasted forty minutes before I came back."

"Why did you leave?"

"Wanted to find my mom. Sally said she went to heaven and… I didn't understand at the time. I just thought she left us."

"I'm sorry." I swirl the mug of coffee around in my hands, staring aimlessly into it.

"Don't be. I just wanted to tell you."

"Why?"

"Because I want you to understand why Thayne acts the way he does."

I changed the topic entirely. "When did you get back?"

"An hour ago. Heard the complaint come in about you and figured I'd get you myself."

"Gotcha."

"Thayne has lost a lot of people." Mack says.

I shift in my seat. "Can we not talk about Thayne right now?"

"Okay. Can we talk about Elijah?"

I'm hesitant at first but take a sip of my coffee as I say, "Okay."

"Look. Thayne's story is his and he'll tell you. But Elijah didn't just hurt Thayne. He hurt us all."

Mack tells me everything. He told me how they all grew up together and how Flint offered Elijah a place on the ranch after his parents passed away. How Elijah took the job and took advantage of their hospitality in the process, stealing money at any chance given and turning up to work drunk. That was only the half of it.

It turns out I didn't know Elijah like I thought at all.

"And listen, I know my brother has a habit of pushing people away, but Thayne loves you."

"Then why can't he tell me himself?"

"He's lost a lot of people, Emberli."

"And he never told me. There is no relationship if there is no communication or trust. Believe me, I know that."

"He should have told you."

"Yeah. He should have."

I instantly feel the need to apologize but I shut it down. Change starts now and that means saying how I feel.

"I have Elijah in a holding cell down at the station. Need you to come and profile him, check some CCTV of the night your car was stolen."

His words sucker punch me. He has Elijah.

Was I really ready to face him? I had no clue.

I felt so much resentment. So much anger towards him.

All I can think about is how Elijah is here. After months of hating him, regretting us. Elijah is in the same town as I am.

I hate him but I hate myself even more for allowing him to constantly belittle me and everything I did. I hated myself for wanting his approval, for wearing things he wanted me to wear. I hated myself for allowing him to change me.

Adrenaline seemed to course through my body and Mack settled his hand upon my own that bounced on the table nervously. "Hey. If you don't want to do this…"

I shake my head, cutting him off completely because for months I had pushed the inevitable aside. I had to face him. "I need to do this."

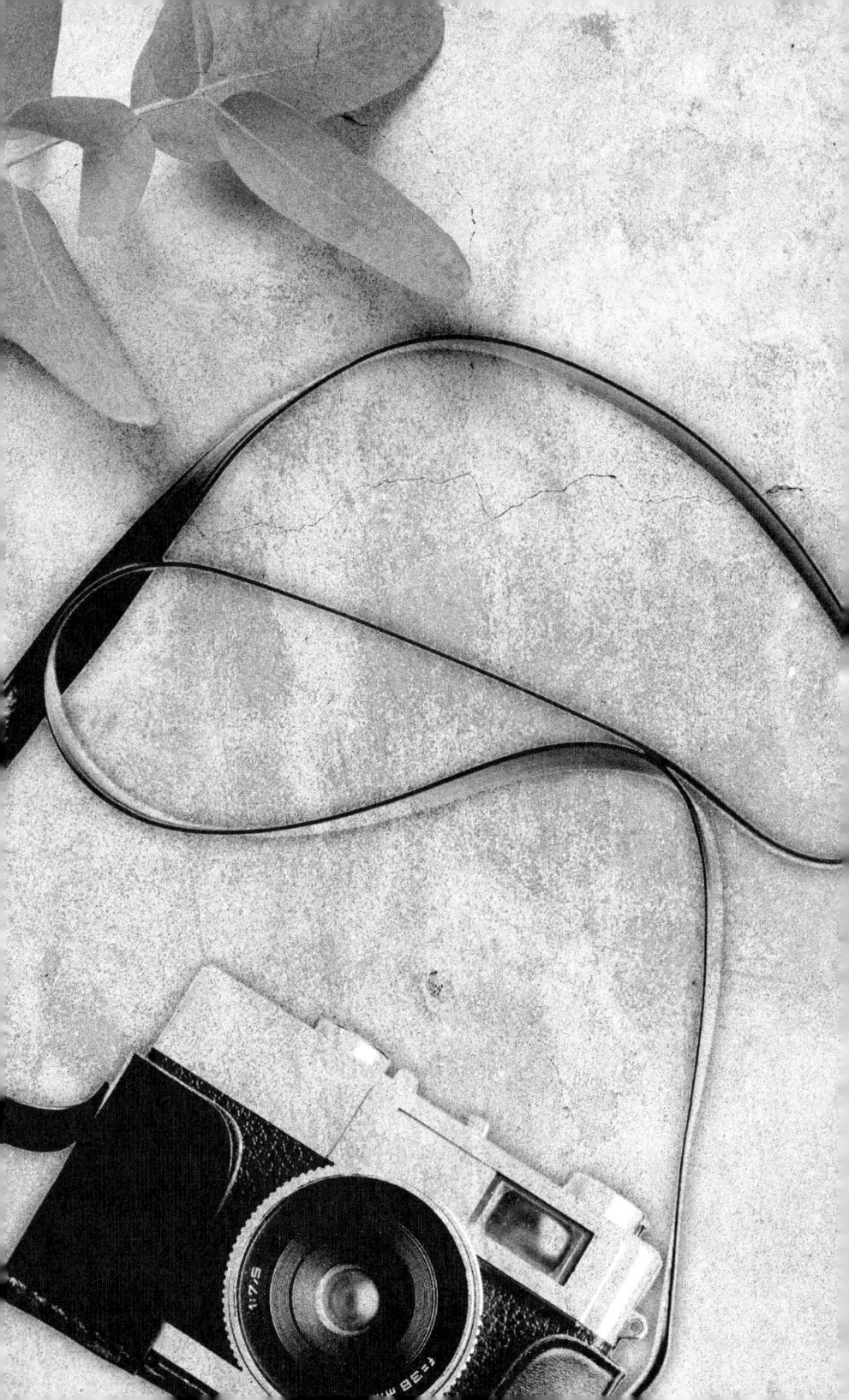

28

Thayne

My foot accelerates on the gas pedal as I drive through the town, attempting to comprehend the last message I got from Mack.

> **MACK:** I found Elijah. Meet me at the station.

I make a ten minute drive in three, my tires screeching at me as I park between two bays, wasting no time in hopping out and barging my way into the sheriff's office.

"Where's my brother?"

"Thayne, now listen. Hey!"

I barge past reception and catch the closing door before me, colliding straight with my brother who holds me firmly at arm's length.

"Relax."

"Don't tell me what to do, Mack." I snap. "Tell me where he is."

"Hey. You can't bulldoze into my place of work like this. It's not a good look Thayne. If we're doing this we have to do this on my terms. Mine."

I grudgingly follow him quietly into the next room. A suffocating aroma of freshly dried paint is all I can process before Mack moves out of my eyeshot.

Through the bars of the cell sits a slouched Elijah, but he hasn't seen me yet. He hums a familiar tune that I recognise as Emberli's stolen song. He doesn't look guilty. He doesn't look at all troubled.

Standing in front of him is Emberli, her arms are folded over her chest and the look of gloominess shadows her.

Her head spins to me and she sighs. "Hey."

"Hey. We should talk." I move over to her and she takes a step back.

"Not now."

I don't follow through on heading towards her, she has every right to be mad at me.

I hear a laugh from Elijah. "Trouble in paradise?"

"Grow up, Elijah." Emberli sighs.

"You're still a bore, I see."

Shooting my hand out, I grasp his shirt in my fist as I pull him against the bars, anger coursing through my veins for all the people he's hurt and gotten away with it.

In him, I see my dad, hurting whoever he wants just because he can and eager to avoid the consequences of his own actions.

"Don't even think about talking to her. You don't deserve to talk to her."

"Maybe I need to remind you since you've both been playing happy families. But that child in there is mine." He says smugly, nodding his head at Emberli's stomach.

"Like hell he is." Emberli replies. "You're going away for a long time, Elijah."

"You're crazy, Emberli."

"No. No. You made me this way. You made me crazy. I second guess peoples' intentions with me every time that they're nice because of you. I can't communicate properly because of you. I am constantly reminded of how you treated me and I don't think that will ever go away. I will not let you do the same to him."

242

"You can't take him from me. There are rules."

"And I'll break every single one of them if it means it keeps you away from them." I spit at him.

"Aw, Daddy Thayne to the rescue. Under that big coat of protection, we all know that you're terrified to lose those you care about. Such a shame about Mae."

He had some nerve bringing up Mae after what he did to her.

"You know she called for you, right?"

"He's lying, Thayne." Mack says from behind me.

"Am I? She was on the pavement and she was screaming your name." Elijah clicks his tongue at me and my heart begins to beat irregularly. Suddenly I can't think straight. I only think of the night Mae died. I could have been there and how I could have saved her like I could have saved my mom and my dad.

"We've got his confession. Let him rot." Mack reminds me.

My knuckles begin to turn white at the grasp I hold on him and I let go, taking pleasure in watching him stumble as far away from me as he can.

Good. He should be scared.

"Rot? Do you know who I am? Emberli! Hey! Don't fucking walk away from me!"

I lunge forward to grab him again, but he only laughs at the bars that protect him. "You can have that slut, Thayne. I don't want her."

"Leave it, Thayne." Emberli's voice rings in my ears and I hesitate, turning around to her. She looks all but amused and she spins on her heels, marching outside.

"Go. I got this." With confirmation from my brother, I track down Emberli before she gets too far.

"Hey! Wait a sec."

"Thayne, I'm tired. Okay?"

"I know. I should have told you the truth about Mae and I'm sorry."

"It's not just about Mae."

"Okay." I nod. "What else? Talk to me."

"Do you honestly think that you're able to love my son?"

I frown. "Where is this coming from?"

"What if he looks like Elijah? What will you do then?"

"Love him. I love…"

"You can't promise that. I saw the hatred in your eyes when you looked at Elijah."

"Emberli, I would never hate the baby."

"You hated me. When I first came into town, you hated me."

"I did not hate you."

Her eyes find me guilty and she shakes her head. "I don't want you to hate him, Thayne."

A tear strolls down her cheek and I hate it. I hate seeing her cry. But she's raised her walls around her again and I can't seem to get through to her. There's no way in.

"I could never hate him. I could never hate you."

"Don't lie to me." Her voice is raised and her emotions heightened as her fists ball beside her.

"I'm not going to tell you what you want to hear because it's not true."

Her lips quiver and she looks away, her voice as cold as ice as she says, "I think I need more time. I think I need to leave."

The next few days are torture.

I'd tried to give Emberli the space she needed but not seeing her, not even being in the same county as her, was driving me insane and I'd been wallowing in my sorrows ever since.

"Willow…"

"Get the fuck out of my way Ryker. Right now."

It's a matter of seconds before my little sister storms into the living room of my cabin. An infuriated expression cloaks her face,

244

her eyes glisten with a mixture of disappointment and fury.

"Why are you still sitting here?"

"Not right now, Wills."

"No. We're doing this right fucking now." She stands in front of the television with her hands on her hips. "Why are you still sitting here?"

After a few seconds of silence, she speaks again. "I'll tell you why you're still sitting here." I hear Ryker murmur her name but she doesn't take any notice of him, her attention remains solely on how pathetic I look as I sit here.

"Because you refused to open yourself up to a woman that was prepared to put up with you and your shit. And she made you feel things that you haven't felt before. Now you're afraid because now she's gone because you didn't tell her about Mae."

My head shoots up. "This isn't about Mae."

"This has everything to do with Mae!" Willow yells. "God I'm so pissed at you right now for fucking this up. You love her, Thayne. We can all see it. I'm more mad that you're sitting here instead of going after her."

"There is nothing I can say or do that is going to make this any better."

"That." She points at me. "That attitude is what lets you down. I love you, Thayne. But you're a fucking idiot if you think that can't do attitude is going to get you anywhere in life, and every minute you sit here, you lose her. Mae is dead, Thayne. You can't live in the past anymore, especially when the future's right in front of you."

Willow was right. Of course she was.

Fuck. I love her.

I love Emberli and that little boy she carries inside of her with every fiber of my being and I'm terrified I've ruined something special.

"What am I going to do?" I mumble.

"Get up off your sorry ass and go and fix this."

Right.

"Do you know where she is?" I grab my jacket and shrug it on. I had to make this right. I couldn't let Emberli go.

I thought that I was beyond repair long ago, yet she somehow managed to change that, and bring me back to life with her smiles and was hellbent on showing me that love wasn't a scary thing that could disappear, it was also beautiful. And that was why I couldn't let her go.

"I'll send you the address." I brush past her until she calls my name. I turn and her hardened eyes meet mine. "Fix this."

She didn't have to tell me again.

I headed straight for my truck, slamming it into reverse.

All the way there I pray that she'll still be there. I've never been a religious person. I've suffered too many unjustifiable losses to believe in it. But I do believe someone up there sent Emberli to me, whether it was my mother or Mae herself. I believed someone knew that I needed Emberli and her little boy who I love so much. And like a remedy for a heartache, Emberli opens the door the next morning, eyes widening when she sees me.

"Thayne?"

Emberli

"Thayne?"

He stands there filling my doorway, clothes drenched with rain and his chest heavy as he tries to catch his breath like he's spent the last hour running.

"What are you doing here?"

"You." He doesn't even hesitate.

"What?"

"Everyone was at breakfast as usual, normal times, normal food and normal… my point is, you were missing, Emberli. And I hated every fucking second of it. You belong with me. You once asked me what got me through the hard days and what got me up in the morning. I'm saying it's you."

I suck in a sharp breath at his revelation just as he closes the distance between us and shakes his head.

"It's always been you."

I let out a breath before glancing behind me, my mom and sister both have shocked expressions on their faces.

I hold up my index finger to them before closing the door behind me and I fold my arms over my chest.

"Thayne, look…"

"Let me finish. Please." He pleads and I nod, letting him step closer to me and under the shelter.

I loved home, but I didn't love its constant rain.

In Shadow Peaks' it rarely rained, it was one small thing I loved so much about that town.

"Mae was my best friend and I was so angry at the world when Elijah took her from me. He was drunk that night when he left the ranch and everyone told him not to drive home. I told him myself I'd drive him, but when I came back from the bathroom, he'd gone. I remember Mack calling me and telling me that Mae had been taken to hospital. Elijah took her there, said it was all his fault, that he hit her. They'd tried to treat her wounds at the hospital but they couldn't save her. She died that night and Elijah took off. I could have seen her. I could have been by her side but I chose to go after Elijah. I will not let my anger for him ruin what I have with you."

I pull Thayne into my chest, wrapping my arms around him as he sobs. I'd never seen him like this.

So open. Vulnerable.

There isn't a side to Thayne I don't love.

I love him and all the baggage that comes with him. There isn't a part of him I'm not truly and undoubtedly infatuated with.

"You couldn't have done anything." I tell him, desperately trying to be the strong one out of the two of us and clinging onto the bravery I needed to have for him. "It's not your fault, Thayne. It's not your fault."

When we eventually pull apart, he stares at me. Puffy red-eyed and pools of sadness within them.

I want to save him from all of his pain.

"I've never been good at opening up to people, Emberli. And I should have opened up to you. I didn't know how and I know that's no excuse and whatever you decide, I understand. But I want you to know that I have never loved anyone the way I love you and that little boy inside of you. You have made me feel things that I never thought I'd feel and now I know what it feels to be loved by you, nothing will ever be the same again. I love you, Emberli Taylor. And I'm sorry if I've done a fucking awful job of showing it. But if you let me, I'll make it up to you. I swear I will and…"

"Thayne."

"And I love you so goddamn much. I love the way you cry every single time Mufasa dies in The Lion King. I love the way that you can't speak to anyone before six in the morning unless you've had three decaf coffees. I love the way you care for my family. I love the way you're so nervous about this baby even though you're going to be an amazing mom. I love your voice. I love your smile. I love you, trouble. Forever."

"I love you too." My mission to not cry failed, and he kisses my tears away frantically as he holds me. He's perfect and I don't think I'd ever deserve him the way he's so sure I do.

But he's as much mine as I am his.

And I can't wait for the rest of our lives together.

"Not to ruin this incredibly cute moment that mom and I have not been eavesdropping on one bit, but would you guys like to come in for lunch?" My sister's head pokes through the front door with a stupidly large grin on her face and I turn to Thayne.

"I'd love lunch."

248

"Have you even slept?" I ask him.

"Nope. Needed to get to you."

"I wasn't going anywhere. I never was. I just needed time."

"I know baby." His lips collide with my own, his hand scoping the back of my neck as he holds it gently, combing his fingers through my hair with his free hand. The kiss is desperate and hungry, but also slow and passionate.

It's everything I knew it would be.

The feeling of his lips on mine linger even when he pulls apart, laughing at the gagging behind him that belongs to my younger siblings.

I stand cleaning the dishes with my mom and Buck after lunch, Thayne and my dad sit in the living room with Ebony. They all laugh about something that floods into the hallway. I'm relieved that my dad and him get on so well.

Up until Thayne, I believed that no one I dated would ever be good enough for me in my dad's eyes. For some reason, he always thought I deserved better. But hearing the two of them laugh in the other room fills me with happiness.

I'm finally happy.

My mom loves Thayne already. I'm pretty sure she decided on that at the baby shower.

"Is dessert ready yet?" Buck sighs.

"Not yet. Go and grab the empty glasses from the table." With a huge huff, my brother reminds me just how fast he's growing up. The unsettling feeling lingers in the pit of my stomach when he returns with them, planting a kiss on mom's cheek as he does.

"Are you going back with Thayne?" Buck asks me as he reaches up on his tip-toes, kissing my cheek as well. I'm hesitant to answer at first.

"Because I like him. A lot more than Elijah."

My mom chuckles as she empties the sink, grabbing another

dishcloth. "God Em, you've never been quick at drying the dishes, have you?"

I roll my eyes before turning back to Buck. "I think I might go back with him. Is that okay?"

"It's perfectly okay." Mom smiles reassuringly.

"Yeah." Buck nods. "We just want you to be happy."

I glance through the door at Thayne and nod. "I am."

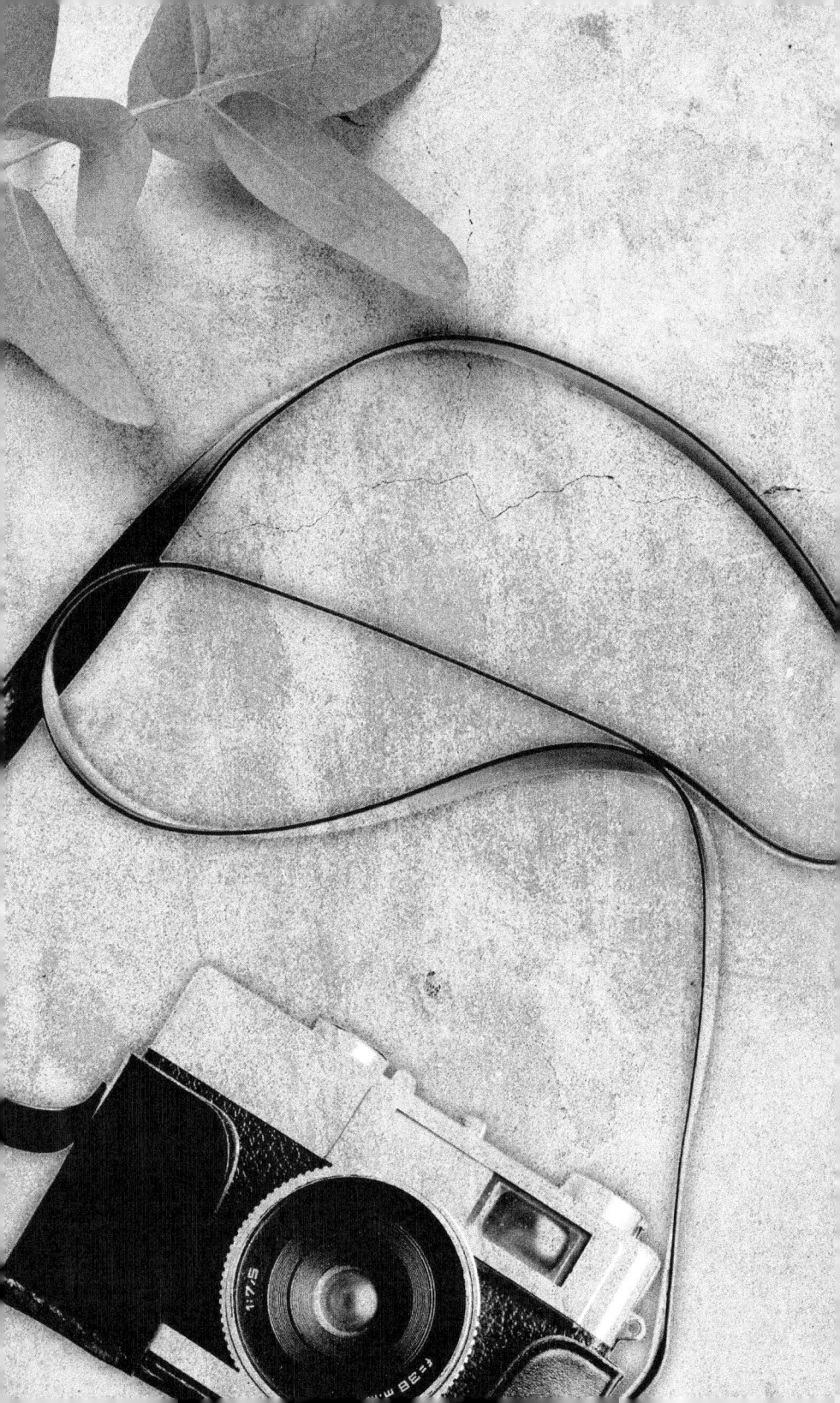

Epilogue – Thayne

FLINT: Anyone seen Blaze?

MACK: Nope.

ODESSA: You lost him again?

FLINT: Correction. Ryker lost him.

LYNNIE: I'm going to need another new glass panel put in. Come and get your bull, Flint. NOW.

COLTON: Oh, she used capitals.

RYKER: It's serious now.

EMBERLI: Are we going to come home to a funeral?

WILLOW: Everything is fine here!

Car horns blare beneath us on the busy road and the people squeezing past each other look like ants from our view on the eighty-eighth floor. Emberli is in the pool peering over the edge as she looks down into the working district beneath us.

Torchbury was known to be the city that never sleeps, I think both Emberli and I had figured out that meant the people who visited too. We barely slept last night. The view of the skyscrapers and buildings swarming us reminds me just how much I love my life back home, especially now Emberli resides there with me.

I stand on the poolside with a towel, waiting for her to get out. She'd inevitably gotten slower this last month and I'd made sure to not leave her side during this time. Odessa gladly took the reins of Spooky Hoots whilst I took time off to spend with my girl.

Emberli wasn't thrilled at the idea of not performing and working around the ranch so she was tasked with looking after the baby animals that were rejected from their mothers' in the main house. Rhea had said that the baby would be due in a few weeks from now, and was against the idea of Emberli flying in a helicopter at thirty-seven weeks so we settled for the next best thing.

A rooftop infinity pool.

Aca had managed to pull some strings which meant that Emberli had completed all of her list, apart from the helicopter ride that I promised to take her on after her son was delivered.

The best part was, Emberli corrected me. *Our son.*

I couldn't wait to meet him. I couldn't wait to give him the world.

"I wonder if people down there think it's raining." Emberli asks, splashing her hand over the edge before she makes her way over to me, steadying herself on the rail and taking the towel I offer her.

"Maybe."

I hear something barely audible and when I look at Emberi, she's frozen before she slowly looks to her thighs where water gushes down.

Shit.

"I think my... I think my waters just broke."

"Fuck." I mumble. "We need to get you to a hospital."

Nine hours later, a gorgeous baby boy had made his mark on the world. Both of our families had arrived hours before and had been waiting patiently in the waiting room.

I place a kiss on Emberli's forehead and stare down at the newest addition to our family.

"Have you thought of a name?" I ask.

Emberli bites out a yawn and then a wince. "Tucker Desmond Rawlins."

Tucker Desmond Rawlins-Taylor

I stare at the incredible woman below me before blinking back tears.

This woman.

"I wanted to have my dad's first name but I wanted him to have your last name."

I zone out completely, glancing up at the ceiling, knowing that my mom would be watching this moment with such pride. I think of my dad, and for the first time in what feels like forever, I'm not angry at him.

"I understand if you don't, but I want him to have your last name, Thayne. Neither of us would be here if it wasn't for you."

I kiss her to quieten her, thanking her before kissing Tucker's head. "I love it. I love you."

Emotion hits her face. "I love you too, Superman."

And suddenly, all the pieces fall into place.

This, right here and now, is where I want to be forever with my favorite people.

Acknowledgements

Wow!

If you would have told me this time last year that I would have finished this book, I would have told you that you were out of your mind. I lost inspiration for quite some time and lost myself in the process. I only discovered her when all of my ideas started becoming words on paper.

I remember talking to my dad last August about the idea of Picture This and to think now it's finally here, I can't quite believe it.
If there was one person I truly doubted more than anyone in this world, it was myself.

A little information about me is that I am a big lover of angel numbers and the one that sticks out to me the most is 111. Intuition. I can't even begin to tell you how many times 111 appeared to me during the writing process for this book. A reminder that I was in the right place, doing the right thing in this new chapter of my life. Here's to me, the one person I never give enough credit to and who is always trying harder to become a better version of herself. I hope one day you look back and realize that you were enough.

To my parents, first and foremost, for picking me up when I couldn't do it myself and for your ongoing help; I would be nowhere without you. I am always so grateful for your support with anything I try to achieve.

To my sister, I hope if I've taught you one thing in life, it's the type of men NOT to date. I am always so proud of you.

To my brother, playing video games with you is an escape from the real world in which I know you will be a gentleman when you're older.

To my nan, who edited and proof-read this book for me. I could not have done this without you and I am so grateful.

To my uncle, for letting me huddle away in his house whilst I tapped away at my laptop, thank you for opening my eyes to a beautiful part of the world. To the rest of my family, thank you for your endless support.

To Georgia, for formatting this book and creating the most beautiful cover I've ever seen. You are honestly a true gem to work with and I could not have done this without you. You have the patience of a saint. I can't wait to work with you more.

To Hannah, Bella, Sabryna and Ellie, who are my guardian angels who shared my excitement all throughout my writing process and helped me shape this book.

And to my alpha readers and beta readers, thank you so much for taking the time to read Picture This. I loved hearing your thoughts throughout and I hope you'll love the upcoming releases I have in store for you.

All my love, Jade x

Printed in Great Britain
by Amazon

62924922R00153